BOOK THREE OF 'THE BLUE WALLS OF HEAVEN'

THE SEVENTH ANGEL

by

Stephen Parr

(Ananda)

Wolf at the Door
Bristol, 2017

Published by Wolf at the Door, Bristol 2017
34 Cornwallis Crescent, Bristol BS8 4PH
Copyright ©Stephen Parr 2017
moon@wolfatthedoor.org

ISBN 978-0-244-03068-6
First edition September 2017

The author has asserted his moral right under the Copyright, Designs and Patents Act 1988, to be identified as the author of this work.

All rights reserved. No part of this publication may be reproduced, copied, stored in a retrieval system, or transmitted in any form or by any means without the prior written consent of the copyright holder, nor be otherwise circulated in any form of binding or cover other than that in which it is published and without a similar condition being imposed on the subsequent purchaser.

A CIP catalogue record for this title is available from the British Library.

Previous volumes in this trilogy available from Lulu.com:

Error Message (2012) ISBN 978-1-908895-29-5
The Egg Man (2014) ISBN 978-1-326-02542-7

Poetry:

An Average Morning in the Galaxy (2013) ISBN 978-1-291-53747-5
The Solitude of Small Doors (2015) ISBN 978-1-326-49940-2

"The new quantum mechanical notion of relationship follows as a direct consequence of the wave/particle dualism and the tendency of a 'matter wave' (or 'probability wave') to behave as though it were smeared out all over space and time. For if all potential 'things' stretch out infinitely in all directions, how does one speak of any distance between them, or conceive of any separateness? All things and all moments touch each other at every point; the oneness of the overall system is paramount. It follows from this that the once ghostly notion of 'action at a distance', where one body can influence another instantaneously, despite there being no apparent exchange of force or energy is, for the quantum physicist, a fact of everyday reality."

– Danah Zohar: *The Quantum Self*, p.18

And I saw an angel coming down out of heaven, having the key to the abyss...

– Revelation 20:1

What you may have missed....

Adam, after his traumatic break with Elaine in the Quantock Hills, sets off on foot to walk south. At dusk he arrives at a brooding walled estate and is met by Joe, who takes him in, in a spirit of good neighborliness. But Joe is not all he seems, and Adam is caught up in his bizarre world of living sculptures and arcane philosophy. While staying with Joe, Adam is forced to face his own long-ignored shadows and demons, with tumultuous consequences.

Eventually after what he believes to be Joe's death, Adam leaves and continues his long-interrupted journey to the south coast. On the way he meets his nemesis Rachel, who he believed he had killed in a fit of sexual rage. Her 'spirit' form tries to help him come to terms with his past actions, and he at last realizes that he himself is wandering in an intermediate world between life and death, where all that appears real are his internal states of mind.

In an effort to end this hopeless death in life, on reaching the coast he leaps from a cliff top, but is saved in his fall by the intervention of his lifelong inspiration, the artist William Blake, who presents him with a vision of divine reconciliation. Thus while one life closes, another opens...

Chapter One

At five o'clock on a bleak January morning I awoke and said to Elaine:

'I know what the problem is. My brain has turned against me. But I'm still using it to think with. Doesn't sound too clever, does it?'

Elaine seemed to be still balancing the pros and cons of waking up. Was my insight worth the effort of becoming conscious, or was it yet another piece of gloop in a long line of gloops? But she opened one eye as a concession to our long friendship. It glared like a cornered animal.

'What the hell are you babbling about?'

We had that kind of relationship where I knew I could wake her at any hour of the night and there would be instant rapport and acceptance. That was worth a lot.

'I'm talking about my brain. Remember those things? Big grey spongy creatures that think they run everything?'

'What about it?'

'It isn't on my side any more. It's decided I'm not a person it wants to be associated with. It would much rather be off with a successful get-up-and-go kind of person. Whatever else I am, I'm not that.'

'Adam, why don't you just go back to sleep and wake up again normally. Then we can talk, ok?'

'I'm not crazy, Elaine. This is really important. I need to stop using my brain to think.'

'And exactly what do you propose to use instead, if I dare ask?' Her voice was full of sleep and I could see I wouldn't get many more complete sentences out of her.

'Well, you know with computers you can get an external drive if you run out of space on your main one—'.

'Oh for God's sake Adam! You aren't a frigging computer! And you surely know you aren't a computer. So why all this faloosh about it? Get a proper job and just try to be normal, why can't you?'

I thought I'd try one last time to communicate rationally, and then just get on with it myself.

'Elaine, what I think's happened, what I think has occurred, is my brain has been subtly altered by the aliens, when they used to talk to me–'.

'No, Adam. Now just listen.' With some effort she propped herself on one elbow and looked at me, both eyes open and smouldering in that intense way she has when she believes she's on to something. 'You've just got to stop this. It's not going anywhere. And you're coming to believe it yourself, which is much, much worse. When these ideas come up, just say no. It's only a little word. It's really easy. Just see that they're only fantasies, and they'll go away. Honestly, they will. They rely for their existence on your believing in them, so if you deprive them of the sustenance of belief they'll wither away, slowly but surely. And I'll have a normal partner again to go shopping with and have wonderful normal conversations about drains and trousers.'

Well, I had tried. No one could say I hadn't. I was beginning to think all women were biologically impervious to mystery. The invisible or irrational was anathema to the female mind-set. I was reluctant to think that of course, because one should distrust huge generalizations. But it is a fact that all the women I'd known were very similar in that respect: all of them (save one, and she was dead, or so she constantly told me) were deeply unsettled by suggestions that there was more to the world than it appeared: that it was in fact a gigantic delusion, created by – ah, but that is not a permitted question. Created by X, where X is a transcendent variable, let's say. Or whatever. Created by mice, for all we knew. Even Les and his hyper-intelligent ilk had no answers on that subject. "Let us modify your minds to eradicate all irrational violence and destruction," was the nearest he ever came to a catechism. God bless him. I often wonder what he's up to now. Has he given up on his great reforming project? Not if I know him (which of course I don't, not even one billion billionth of him.)

I did get back to sleep, but I didn't wake up any more normal. Elaine looked haggard, as though she'd been on a perilous night journey and only just made it back. Watching her put bread in the toaster was like watching an inexperienced knife-thrower at a fairground. It wasn't the image of the girl I'd admired at a distance across many crowded rooms, all green stockings and winning laughter and optimism.

'What you need, Adam, is a job where you interact with real people. Without all those unhealthy books staring you in the face all day long.'

'I do interact with people. And books aren't unhealthy. How can you call Flora Britannica or The Greenways of England unhealthy?'

'They don't challenge you. They don't need anything from you. They don't question you. You get lost in them. If you're not careful you'll end up as a character in one of them one day.'

'Oh give me a break Elaine. I'm very tired. It's a job. It pays the rent.'

'Half the rent.'

'And I do meet people. They buy books. They go on buses. They have lives. I learn a lot from them.'

It was becoming one of those conversations you could never get out of. I stared at the arc of sun on the rim of the water jug, and wondered how many angels were dancing on it right at that moment, and whether they were aware of our small domestic tiff, and whether they cared a toss about the outcome. Perhaps there were no angels at all, on the water jug or anywhere, but only Up quarks and Down quarks and Queer quarks and Diagonal quarks lost in the sheer improbability of it all.

'Why not a hospital?' Elaine was saying.

'An angel hospital? Sounds a great idea. There must be thousands of angels with dislocated shoulders and twisted ankles drifting helplessly around out there, with nowhere to get them treated.'

Elaine sighed and made for the garden, turning at the back door to say: 'Are you carrying on with your therapy?', although what I thought she said was, 'are you carrying on with your therapist?' Either way, I thought silence was, on balance, the best answer.

Since Les had stopped talking to me after the Cube had warped back to its makers there'd been an all-pervasive absence in my life, despite Elaine's intimate presence, and despite my notoriety as a 'Cube whisperer', as one high-profile hack had dubbed me. I didn't mind that.

It gave me the chance to put the case for the aliens' project. But I'd lost something vital that I'd almost come to take for granted: the sense of being part of something so huge it went way beyond the scope of all language or metaphor. It was like – no, it wasn't like anything. It was like a goldfish in an empty bowl suddenly – well anyway it dawned on me that humans were meant to have that golden being-part-of-everything feeling. That's why we'd had that God obsession for so long, after all.

Some people did have it of course. Blake knew the angels were everywhere around him and regularly spoke with them. Thomas Traherne and Henry Vaughan, Walt Whitman and Sam Palmer knew the inches of the earth were sacred measures. Vermeer was the same with colour. They all knew that was how it was meant to be. But Elaine wasn't of that persuasion. She thought we were born, tried to get our needs met, failed mostly; if we were lucky we learned to love in spite of everything, then died, and beyond that was impenetrable dark which wasn't any of our damn business. So all my talk of angels smiling from the compost heap irritated her no end. I learned later she was rebelling against her unworldly and impecunious father who had been part of the generation who'd rediscovered Blake and LSD to the background of Pink Floyd and Tangerine Dream. His love-child had become a career-obsessed pragmatist – which also explained why she was attracted to me as a kind of watered down father figure that she could be in love with or rebel against as the mood took her, which was ok with me provided I knew that's what was happening.

The trouble is I told her a whole lot of rubbish about myself and my background that I came to regret because I kept forgetting the storyline. I told her for instance my father had been an astronomer who had discovered an unknown comet that had been named after him. (Comet Stone? Come off it. Who could believe that?). I told her he had cycled across Africa and discovered a lost tribe of pygmies who could communicate telepathically. And of course I told her about seeing Blake in the middle of a street in Marylebone when I was sixteen, and Blake had told me I was destined to save humanity from destruction. Then when all the seams started coming apart I had to perform some deft footwork to preserve my credibility. But at the root of it all of course was my bottomless need to be loved and admired, particularly by women. Despite the obvious fact that this strategy had always failed miserably and embarrassingly I still went on inventing experience like a headless iguanodon. No wonder Elaine found me uncomfortable to be with: the thing was out of control. It also happened with the smallest everyday details. For instance she sometimes asked me if I'd had an interesting day at the bookshop and I'd immediately concoct some character who'd come into the shop and offered me some fabulously rare travel books for peanuts, and that she'd invited me to her family home in Wiltshire to see the rest of her collection, when the truth was I'd seen nobody the entire afternoon apart from the man who always came in with his dog after collecting his pension to ask if I had any 1950s Beanos. But I considered the truth wasn't glamorous so it had to be constantly reinvented. I suppose I believed deep down if all I had was reality sooner or later Elaine would get bored with me and find someone who 'had a life.'

Of course you've guessed the next step: reality took the hint and started inventing things for me, out of the kindness of its infinite black heart. And the rest is history. I sometimes wonder what recent events would have turned out like had I been scrupulous in truth-telling.

However I do believe Elaine loved me, for all that. There was a chemistry. We looked out for each other in so many little ways: special treats, tea in bed (the right kind of tea, naturellement), the wood-stove cleaned and laid ready. After surviving the crucible of her childhood I thought she deserved a spell of pampering.

Nicola, on the other hand, hardly spoke to me. After the first few months when she couldn't get enough male attention, something changed in her. A deep chill gripped our relationship. If Elaine and I were together, Nicola would instantly vanish. At meals she'd slump over her food, withdraw into some ice-bound world of her own, respond with minimal gestures, avoid eye contact. Naturally I tried talking to her about it, but she wouldn't open up: our conversations remained minimalist and barely polite. Elaine thought it was a phase that would pass, something to do with rejecting the suitor; but I thought it went deeper: at some level she knew I wasn't a normal shopping-type human being; that I wouldn't be around for her when really needed. And of course she was bang on. My heart grieved for her, but what could I do, apart from buy her speciality ice-cream and DVDs of her favourite singers?

And then I went and put the boot in properly by agreeing to do that insane TV interview, which went dead against all my instincts and upset just about everyone who knew me.

Chapter Two

'I want to know what I've done that's so terrible.'

'What makes you think you've done something terrible?'

Clare was pinning me with her steady professional eagle-eye. I'd come to know that gaze well: it was the gaze of insight. But it had taken me years – yes, years! – to realize it, and not fight against it. Yet I did fight. Like a demon. But a demon that knew its days were numbered.

I struggled to articulate what was painfully surfacing.

'There's something very very deep in me that knows something I don't. It knows what I am, at root. And whenever I start getting my life together – like nurturing my relationship with Elaine, for instance – it quietly pulls the rug out from under me, and I'm back in my stinking nest again.'

There then followed an amazing silence in which I actually felt listened to. This was what I'd really signed up with Clare for: that silence. It was like diamond dust, and I didn't get it anywhere else in my life. Not walking alone in the hills. Not with Elaine (though she listened of course: it's just that I felt eternally damned by her virtue, if that makes any sense); not with any of my highly developed friends. Music came near, but of course that was all one way. Literature ditto, but more reflective. No, once I'd got my own resentful ego out of the way, that total listening was worth a thousand pounds a minute (I paid eighty pence a minute, but who's counting?)

'Tell me what happens when you try to communicate.'

'With Elaine you mean?'

'Yes.'

'She has a thing about the truth. It took me a while to see just how important it was to her to know that the person she's with is telling the whole truth. If she gets a whiff of evasion or unwillingness to be completely open she goes ballistic. Well that's my interpretation of course.' I could see Clare's quizzical right eyebrow languidly semaphoring. 'I'm not saying she shouldn't expect the truth; she has every right to, obviously. But with her lying's like kicking a baby: it's so far out of court there's no debate: you simply don't go there. OK. So with me, what happens is, I go into this deep rejection mode. This voice from my brain's underbelly pipes up and and says, "Hey! She's stopped loving you! I knew all along she would. The fact is, you're a piece of shit. And who would love shit?"

Another silence, in which there seemed to be an age between each tick of the wall-clock.

'So that voice becomes the only thing I hear. And everything that's said from there on is suspect. Result: instant ice-walls. Zero communication. Massive reinforcement of prejudices on both sides. Breakdown of trust. Summary abandonment of relationship. And that's how it's always been. Is it surprising I feel hopeless?'

Clare allowed that question to hang in the air between us for a painfully long time – so long that I wondered about sneaking off for a pee in her immaculate pine-scented clients' loo at the end of the hall. But I reckoned she'd probably notice. I'd come to see that such apparently casual hiatuses were in fact strategic: something was happening in them that was crucial to the game's outcome.

Even though I'd been coming to her off and on for going on five years, she could still surprise me, and she did so now. I'd been expecting a bit of prodding to go on with the case of Stone versus Greenwood, but she simply smiled and said:

'You're getting quite good at this game, aren't you?'

I was instantly floundering among my own defences, not knowing what I was being attacked with. Presumably she was implying that I was treating my course of deeply life-changing treatment with an unbecoming flippancy.

'Am I?'

'What I mean is, you've learned all the terminology, and you know how it all fits together. You've given me an excellent essay on why your mind works the way it does. I can't fault it: you've got everything in there, pretty well. The trouble is you've become rather too adept at it. It's so easy to say: 'this is why I'm like this; there are really clear causes for everything that's wrong; but there's no way to change it.'

Of course she'd rumbled me. Adam Stone, the great Alien Intermediarist, author of universally quoted papers on Living in

Harmony with the Aliens – reduced to incoherent babbling and jerking off behind the bushes by his inability to communicate with his beautiful human partner. My life taken apart and exposed for The Sham it Always Has Been by the Great White Therapist who never fails to get to the Pathetic Truth and drag it into the remorseless daylight for the world's gawping amazement.

'Adam?'

'I'm sorry, I was away with the crocodiles. Yes, of course you're right, I know too much. Maybe I should stop the therapy now. Maybe we've taken it as far as is possible. I'm probably wasting your time. I really don't know where to go from here.'

Clare looked Serious. 'Stopping the therapy now would only freeze everything where it is. This is a very common problem. People reach a point where they've learnt their mind's strategies and consequently they feel they can manage the situation fairly well. They're not hurting so much that they have to do something about it, but they're not happy either. So they do a deal with their unconscious: if you don't stick the needle in too much I'll carry on with my life and pretend the problem's gone away. The trouble in your case is you're too intelligent for that to work: you know nothing's really changed: whatever brought you to this process is still there. But you won't deal with it because the pain and disruption to your normal life would be greater than what you're currently tolerating. A classic Mephistophelian pact. You have a hard choice to make Adam. Most men in your position choose sex or drugs as a way out. Frankly I can't see you doing that, somehow.'

I noticed my time was up, but she didn't even glance at the strategically placed clock.

'Well, I might. But yes, I'd notice. As a strategy it would fall flat on its ugly face at the first hurdle.'

Another Pascalian silence, which Clare was sensitive enough not to interrupt. I wriggled and stretched in my seat to restore the circulation. The chest of drawers by the window cracked in the sudden sun.

'I know what I have to do. But it's damned hard when all my life I've longed for a way of helping the world and I haven't found it. And now there is a way, when a path has opened up for me literally out of the blue – and I have to ignore it.'

Still she said nothing, but maintained her total attention on me and the present moment before us. A part of my mind hovering somewhere outside the current dilemma was lost in gratitude to her.

'Being the only human the Visitors have communicated at length with, (I don't count Mark, as he doesn't really take any of it seriously) puts me in a unique position. I'm a species of one, in a sense. To my knowledge no one else on this planet knows at first hand that there is a non-human race of benign hyper-intelligent beings that have powers infinitely beyond anything we can conceive. For me that fundamentally changes everything, at least in theory. We could align ourselves with that race and there would be no stopping us. We could do anything we were capable of imagining, instantly, without limit. Who wouldn't want that? Yet at the same time I'm an asylum of malevolent demons that only want to destroy everything that's positive and hopeful. Imagine opening the Aladdin's cave of limitless knowledge to that Pandora's box of serpents! I hate people who try to make things better, because I know they're full of the same demons – only they don't know it. I want to expose them, bring them crashing down to earth. So what use is a tame super-race if they can't even understand the divided state of human nature?'

'We're straying from the moment, Adam.'

'Yes. I'm sorry. And I'm trespassing on your time too.'

'That's ok. What I'd ask you to think about is your need to play out this role of being humanity's little helper. What's behind that? Not that it's wrong, but what's driving it? You may still choose that path, of course; but it would be good to be clear about the nature of the energy it attracts to it.'

Out in the quiet sycamore-lined street the winter sunshine bathed me in unaccustomed optimism. Even in late January crocus shoots were well above ground, their splashes of purple and yellow like the first tender exploring notes of a Schubert piano sonata. Normal life seemed to be going on in shops and parks and along pavements, as though we were God's chosen people in whom he was well pleased, and we had endless time in which to bask in his infinite pleasure.

But God wasn't pleased. His sadness was greater than anything we could imagine, and in his universe time had no meaning.

Chapter Three

Enrapt in our argument we'd climbed far beyond the stone circle which had become our regular destination and emerged onto a high ridge of limestone outcrop that faced south-west, where the sun smouldered in a nest of gathering rainclouds. It was a stimulating view in all weathers.

For the most part Elaine was the very soul of kindness and empathy. It was the single quality that had made me want her so much in the years when she was my astro-physicist friend Jack's partner, and which had me dreaming of impossible liaisons with her to the exclusion of all other women. But there was another side to her that it had taken me a while to get my head around: she didn't take kindly to criticism. And when you live with someone for more than three hours there inevitably comes a point when you will have critical thoughts demanding a voice. With us it was always the kitchen. I had never made a secret of my complex relationship with hygiene and tidiness. Long story short, I considered them unnecessary evils. Life was too short, I held, to be forever scrubbing and polishing and siding and arranging, and therefore I afforded these rituals the minimum of attention. Thirty years of practicing this shed philosophy didn't seem to have brought any divine retribution crashing down on my head, so I concluded that the great Apportioner of Universal Justice was not offended by a little creative disorder in the food department. Sadly Elaine inclined to the opposite view. Outcome: spasmodic outbreaks of disharmony, followed by silent walks together culminating in muttered apologies (usually on my part) and whispered forgiveness (always on hers). We were well into the silent stage when I fell to ruminating on my one regrettable foray into celebrity status.

It's hard to believe now that I didn't see what might follow from my recklessness. But the fact is when you're tightly focussed on events from day to day, making decisions on the hoof that you think involve only yourself, it's easy to forget to look up and see the huge shapes of the future peering down at you out of the mist. Still, I have to shake my head in disbelief when I recollect some of my decisions.

I'd received a phone call from the BBC asking me if I'd be interested in talking about my experience of the aliens. They'd heard I'd had 'some kind of contact' with them in the days of the Cube, before they got cold feet and high-tailed it back to their hole in the Owl Nebula. Without too much consideration, I said why not?

When I told Elaine, she was gobsmacked.

'You're a dear friend, a caring lover, and pretty intelligent, all things considered. So how can you be so naive as to think it will do no harm?'

'The world needs to know the truth,' I answered pompously. 'The truth will make us free. Didn't God say that, or someone close to him?'

'Adam,' she said in her most patient, definitely-not-scolding voice. 'First off: there are ten million people going to be seeing and hearing you. I'd guess about five percent of them are nutters. Oh, sorry. I mean people with learning difficulties: i.e, nutters. People with a whole colony of bees under their bonnets. People with lifelong convictions that there are aliens out there only waiting their moment to invade and obliterate us from the face of the cosmos. People with paranoid fantasies, who are convinced that everyone they meet has been assimilated into the collective. People who are desperate for some kind of power: they don't much care what kind, so long as it's power. And there'll be thousands of them claiming the aliens have contacted them too, and given them the secret of eternal life, or limitless energy, or telepathic communication. Jesus, it was bad enough with the Christians claiming God had had a chat with one of them and given him the nod to lead the world to salvation! Think how much worse it'll be now there's actually evidence that God exists! Some kind of god anyways.'

'They're not God, Elaine! They're sentient creatures. They just don't use the same biological platform that we use!'

'The people I'm thinking of won't make those fine distinctions. Anyway: secondly, the military. Someone with genuine access to alien technology would be literally priceless to them—'.

'But I don't have access to it! And obviously I would never make those sort of claims.'

'But you do claim to have had sustained conversations with them?'

'Why shouldn't I? It's the truth.'

'And you really expect the military or Middle Eastern militias to believe that in all that time Superman-in-the-sky didn't give you any hint of their technology or working methods?'

'I see where you're going. But I still think you've been reading too many spy thrillers. The problem as I see it – as I've experienced it – has always been precisely the opposite: nobody takes a single thing I say seriously. I'm just one of your regular nobodies whose lives are so empty they have to concoct stories like this to stop themselves dropping dead through sheer boredom! When has anybody so much as listened to me without their eyes glazing over in complete indifference? Oh, hello, it's Adam the Alien! He's worse than the Ancient Mariner! Better make out we have an unmissable appointment with the tax department.'

'There was Joe.'

'Oh yes. I wondered when you'd bring Joe up.'

'He took you seriously.'

'He took me for a gullible acolyte. He only took me seriously as long as I'd play the adoring devotee. As soon as I abandoned that role he transferred his attentions to someone with more need for him.' I amazed myself to hear the spitting resentment in my voice after all this time: Joe seemed to have wounded me more than I cared to admit.

'The point is, the world has an enduring appetite for weird stories. And they don't come much weirder than aliens from a distant star system communicating telepathically and sending us incomprehensible technology to force us to evolve into rational beings.'

'Yet that is precisely what happened. Why shouldn't people be told the truth? Do you realize that after four years there is still a whole crowd of people roaming around who believe it's all a publicity stunt by space tourism companies? They actually think the Cube was a hologram: the biggest 3D billboard ever made! And of course the fact that it vanished a split second before the Iranian missile struck only corroborates their mad ideas.'

'Well, they'll go on believing that whatever you say, because they need to believe it. Anyway you've obviously decided to go ahead with the show. Just don't pretend to be surprised when it all falls down in little white feathery flakes around your head.'

I felt vertiginously lucky to have found Elaine, not only once, but twice: she instinctively seemed to understand my ongoing compulsion to engage with the 'alien problem', as she called it, even though on another level she appeared to imbibe the entire soap opera with several pinches of salt. There must have been times in our relationship that were very hard for her, especially when I descended into gulfs of grim non-communication for days on end for no clear reason. My therapy was helping to throw light on these hiatuses in normal existence, but I could see the pain they were inflicting on her. And what made it all so much more painful for me was that I knew she loved me.

Let me say that again: I knew she loved me. Not suspected, not inferred, not needed to believe: knew. It was something that lived in the air around her, that communicated itself invisibly in micro-reactions of the chemistry between us, in modulations of voice and fleeting prolongations of glances. It was something I'd not experienced before: not loving, but being loved, without having to sing and dance for it. Without having to do sod all for it, actually. It was a fact of existence that I never for an instant doubted. And it had turned my life around. I was a man reborn.

So why did I keep having these regressions into black hopelessness? Was absolute knowledge of absolute love not enough?

Apparently not. Apparently I needed absolute power as well. Otherwise why go through with this ridiculous game of making yourself a sitting target for every monomaniac in the world? What else did I hope to get out of my fifteen minutes of blabbing my secrets?

'If I don't do this,' I said to Elaine as the light failed and we turned back onto the downward track, 'We'll have lost a huge, and maybe unique, opportunity to open ourselves to a new way of thinking, and I'll never forgive myself. We'll have lost the chance to be part of something immeasurably greater than ourselves. And it's not as if they don't know about us. They're not going to forget we're here. You can be certain they're watching everything we do like a hawk. They're paranoid enough for sure. And imagine the danger of denying that the aliens are out there. Infinitely worse.'

We climbed a stile into a cluster of ragged elms and sycamores, and in single file made our way gropingly through them. Elaine was silent until we emerged from the massing shadows. I turned round to check she'd not fallen over a root, and glimpsed her silhouetted figure motionless some twenty feet behind.

'What's up?'

I waited for her to catch up.

'Nothing. Just getting my breath.'

But I knew differently. Her silence was like a scream echoing from the trees. I took hold of her, brought her as close as I could on the treacherous ground.

'Sweetheart. Trust me. It'll be fine. I know what I'm doing. It isn't like I'm going on Celebrity Big Brother you know. This is a late-night political discussion slot. It'll be forgotten in three days.'

Chapter Four

TRANSCRIPT OF VIDEOCAST DISCUSSION BROADCAST
12 MARCH 2012 AT 22.50 GMT

Present: Dr. Andrew Harwood, chair of the UN Liaison Committee for extra-terrestrial affairs.
Philip Gibson, MP, Secretary of State for Science. Adam Stone, writer and First Contact for the Aliens. Moderator: Gavin Edwards

Moderator: Dr. Harwood, let's be honest – this aliens business is frankly all a bit of a fantasy, isn't it?

AH: The truth is, no one knows. Many people think they know, and many people would like others to think they know. But if you stick to the established facts—

Mod: Well you say established facts, but surely the only facts are that a non-human artifact appeared on a farm in Britain one morning and very soon after lots of extremely weird things started happening to the planet – like towns vanishing under the sea, for instance. I take it you accept that those things did happen?

AH: Of course they happened. But there's nothing to directly link those events together, even though people have been trying to do just that for over five years. It's still speculation, no matter how many times you repeat it – egged on by the press and the media desperate to make a story out of it.

Mod: You don't think then that a mysterious object discovered on a farm that defies everything we throw at it is worth a story?

AH: The point is that these stories go way beyond the established facts.

Mod: Alright. Mr. Gibson, the government hasn't a very good track record when it comes to dealing with the unexplainable, has it?

PG: On the contrary, we have put considerable resources into understanding these events: so far we've spent over ten million pounds on research and public security measures to further our knowledge about the so-called aliens—

Mod: So you are also sceptical about the claimed source of the artefact? I presume you still believe it's a student prank?

PG: No, we don't. No one seriously believes that now.

Mod: But you do believe it was not of human origin?

PG: The point of research is to find out as much as we can, without indulging our preconceptions, or taking refuge in myths or sensationalist scare-stories. The people engaged on that research are still doing it, very competently. But you'll appreciate I'm sure that good science takes a long time. Most of it is determined foot-slogging: collecting comprehensive data, collating it, screening out interference, running statistical matching programs – if you take short-cuts you compromise the value of the research.

Mod: But you must have an opinion?

PG: I try not to. I think the research is making good progress—

Mod: But it must be a bit difficult researching something that absconded five years ago and apparently left no trace of its visit?

PG: There was a lot of research and exploration of the Cube done while it was still present.

Mod: But by all accounts you didn't find out very much?

PG: Oh yes, we found out a great deal. For example we found out it could absorb energy at a colossal rate without suffering any disruption of its structure. We found out it was constantly exchanging energy of some kind with something outside it. And we found out that its mass was so great that it affected the rate of the passage of time in its vicinity, just as though it were a star.

Mod: And non of that leads you to conclude that it was the product of a highly-advanced extra-terrestrial civilization? Lots of respected bodies came to that conclusion years ago.

PG: Well they're perfectly at liberty to conclude whatever they like. Whatever we finally conclude will be on the basis of the most rigorous research.

Mod: Mr. Stone, what do you make of that argument?

AS: Well, it's completely predictable, isn't it? They daren't for one moment entertain the idea that we aren't alone in the universe. And not only that, we aren't even the most intelligent life form in the universe either. That's been perfectly obvious to me for two decades.

Mod: But what about the fact that there's no proven scientific link between the Cube and the catastrophic changes we've all seen, unless we've been living on Mars?

AS: Science proceeds on its own railway tracks, and doesn't allow itself to look at the landscape on either side. The trouble with that is most of the relevant information exists in exactly that taboo landscape well away from the railway tracks, which conventional science ignores. It exists in our imagination, which is really just our ability to relate together things that logically don't belong together and create a more meaningful whole. If for example you consider the way people behave towards each other, have you noticed any change in your dreams? Or in the kind of music you listen to? Have any of your habits changed? Have you been feeling more optimistic generally? Have you empathized more with the minds of people that you'd normally feel nothing in common with? All these are areas science takes no notice of: it relegates them to the domain of weird internet sites and SF novels. So there was virtually no research done into any of that. Instead what did science do? It fired huge lasers at the Cube to see if it would melt or explode. It did neither. That alone would suggest to me – even if I had no other source of information – that its material did not originate on earth. But did the scientists consider that possibility? No, because their prevailing mind-set didn't allow intelligent aliens to exist—

PG: They certainly did consider it: there was a high-level convention held three years ago which considered precisely that question, looked at all of the currently available evidence and concluded that it couldn't in fact rule out alien origins—

AS: And retracted it the moment it dawned on them what the effect such a statement might have when the world's press got hold of it. To speak candidly I can't help wondering if your defence minister didn't have his little finger on the scales when that decision was being made.

PG: That's a scandalous accusation with no shred of evidence to support it, if I may say so.

Mod: Could I ask you Mr Harwood what, if anything, is now being done to search for the er, intelligences – let's call them that – behind the artefact we know as the Cube?

AH: Well I'm not privy to everything that goes on, as you know—

Mod: But something is going on?

AH: If you're asking me are we investigating the effects of the artefact on the human mind, then yes, we are.

Mod: I'm asking you what is being done to search for the intelligences who made it, and I note that you seem reluctant to tell me.

AH: I'm certainly not reluctant, I'm just not the person best suited to answer you. There are many facilities that are investigating possible sources of data—.

Mod: I'm getting the sense from both of you that nobody is unduly concerned that we may have been visited by aliens, and that they must now know an awful lot about us. There is absolutely no sense of urgency, and maybe that's because no one besides Adam here has actually spoken with them. [Addressing Adam] That is correct, isn't it?

AS: I've no idea: there may be many others beside myself, but if so they're keeping mum. Understandably.

Mod: Unlike those others, you have decided to talk publicly about your experience. Why?

AS: Because I see openness as the only possibly way to avoid future destruction. The government seems committed to denial, at least officially. But I'm certain that in reality they realize just as much as I do that the Cube was an alien artefact, the product – the gift, if you like – of a race so far ahead of us in technology and social organization that the gap between them and humans is wider than that between humans and bacteria. With a spirit of trust we might have learned an incalculable amount from them, but instead what do we do? Without any evidence whatever we decide it's a threat to civilization and fire a bloody nuclear missile at it! I'd like to ask Mr. Gibson if he thinks that was a rational act?

PG: I must first say the UK had nothing whatever to do with that attack on the Cube—.

AS: So now you're saying any foreign power can attack sites on UK soil with nuclear warheads and your government – our government – will stand back and applaud their initiative?

PG: That's ridiculous! As you know perfectly well the government protested very robustly as soon as the perpetrators were discovered.

Mod: So a rap on the knuckles seemed to you a sufficient response to the killing of three hundred British civilians?

PG: We did everything we possibly could short of initiating a nuclear was against Iran, as you would be aware if you'd been less obsessed with the possible response of the Aliens. And as you also know – because our military surveillance systems captured it at the time – the Cube was not in fact destroyed by the missile: it vanished a quarter of a second before the warhead hit the ground.

Mod: I want to return to this question of communication with the creators of the Cube. Mr. Harwood, if I could address this to you first, it has been verified, has it not, that intelligence of some sort was in fact received over a period of several months before the disappearance of the Cube?

AH: Well, of course that all depends on what you regard as intelligence. It's true that some unusual radiation was detected from the region of the 'Owl' Nebula around that time, which ceased from the moment the Cube vanished. But to my knowledge nothing you could call 'intelligence', in the usual meaning of that term, was extracted. It's a pity that Mr. Stone was so secretive about his, em, conversations with the Aliens, otherwise we might have been able to achieve some useful correlation between these signals.

Mod: Would you like to answer that?

AS: Can you possibly imagine what the press would have made out of that? "Unemployed writer claims Aliens are telepathically dictating plans to redesign humans. Former girlfriend says he's crazy." I'd have been taken apart and not put back together, in very short order.

Mod: But did you have such conversations?

AS: Yes. They told me they'd sent the Cube to cure us of our degenerate tendencies. They said we were a threat to the harmony of the galaxy, and ultimately to the entire inhabited universe, and they needed to analyze the way our minds worked before they could devise a complete cure, and this involved rigorous analysis of thousands of Russian jokes. That was my job: to help them find and analyze the jokes.

Mod: And you sincerely believed all this was being transmitted telepathically to you by a race of intelligent aliens?

AS: Of course. And I still believe it. There's no other possible explanation that stands up to scrutiny.

Mod: Presumably it occurred to you at some point that you could have been suffering from a persistent form of schizophrenia?

AS: Obviously that occurred to me very early on. But the theory quickly fell over when the Aliens told me about the environmental effects of their manipulation of physical constants: I could walk out of my front door and see it happening. In some cases I didn't even have to walk through the door: it was happening underneath the kitchen floor.

Mod: And you didn't think to ask them about the technology that enabled them to do this?

AS: Yes, naturally. But I didn't have enough technical knowledge to understand their reply. It's based on what they called quantum non-location: altering the spin of entangled sub-atomic particles. But frankly that might be scientific hokum for all I know. I mean, it isn't possible to explain advanced technologies between hugely divergent civilizations: we just don't have the concepts to make it meaningful. So I didn't pursue that line. And anyway they were far more interested in changing our 'bad habits' before handing over their technology, as you may imagine; they obviously wanted to be sure we were worthy recipients of their knowledge before opening up the treasures of heaven to us.

Mod: And all the way through these conversations you never doubted for a moment they were originating in the Owl Nebula?

AS: At the beginning obviously I did. But once the landscape started deforming around me, and even the way I communicated began to change, as the alpha constant began to alter chemical reactions exactly as they predicted, it all fell sharply into place.

Mod [turning to Gibson]: It is true, isn't it, that these physical changes have never been adequately explained?

PG: They have been explained, which again if you'd not been distracted by the sensational claims of the Aliens lobby you would be perfectly aware of.

Mod: And the explanation is?

PG: Very soon after the artefact was discovered we detected an intense cloud of charged particles in the region of space the earth was passing through, like a meteor display, except these particles were emitting a type of energy we couldn't classify. The radiation from the cloud was strong enough to modify the electron spin of certain elements —

AS: How can you trot out that kind of pseudo-scientific hogwash year upon year when you must know it doesn't hold up to the slightest scrutiny? No known type of radiation – even gamma radiation – is powerful enough to change the spin of electrons enough to alter chemical reactions. Why don't you just admit what is obvious to anyone who cares to keep their eyes open?

Mod: Gentlemen, I'm afraid we're going to have to leave it there. Thank you all very much indeed.

[End of Transcript]

Chapter Five

There was a blinding full moon leering over the hills in the south when I alighted from the Exeter-bound train and hailed a cab to Elaine's. I thought I'd done a good job and felt connected to humanity again.

It wasn't, unfortunately, how she saw the matter.

'It isn't that you did a bad job: doing it at all was the mistake. Every damned Cubehead on the planet now knows who you are and what you know. You're a marked man.'

'Please stop fretting, Elaine. I can look after myself.'

'I doubt that. Sometimes you seem to think you're playing one of your own computer games. You're not indestructible! There are people out there who quite genuinely believe the creators of the Cube are emissaries of the Devil. There's nothing they wouldn't do to defeat them. If it means taking out a few hundred humans on the way that's the price they have to pay. They won't think twice about putting you out of the way. So please take sensible precautions, will you?'

'If you mean slinking around like a criminal all the time I'm not sure I can do that. I've nothing to be ashamed of. And I do have a lot to offer. Why should I creep in the shadows everywhere I go, afraid to be who I am?'

'I'm not saying you should creep around. Use discretion.'

'Like?'

'Like not answering the door unless you're certain who's there. Like being extra vigilant opening your post. Like knowing who's following you. Like not giving any more interviews. Shall I go on?'

'No. You've made your point.'

She put her head on my shoulder.

'I only want you to be alive a little while longer, that's all. It's taken us long enough to get this far, after all.'

'I know. I do appreciate your concern.'

The sound of the phone shattered our moment's tenuous peace.

'That's it!' Elaine said, turning away. 'That's the end of our beautiful private life. Well, it was good while it lasted.'

'Damn and blast them! It's almost midnight.'
'And Adam? Be careful, OK?'

I picked up the receiver and listened without speaking.
'Adam? Is that you? It's Mark.'
'Mark who?'
'Dobson. The café in Bridgwater, remember?'
It took a while for it to come back to me. But then I recalled the gaunt, nervous, bearded individual who had asked to join me.
'Oh, Mark! Yes.'
'You invited me to meet your friend Joe. Unfortunately I was invited to stay at one of Her Majesty's most expensive hotels for a few weeks. I'm sorry I missed you.'
'How are you?'
'I'm fine, thanks. I saw your interview. I hope it's ok to phone at this late hour?'
'Of course. No problem. It's good to hear from you after all this time.'
'I'll get to the point. You've heard of CubeWatch I take it?'
'Vaguely.'
CubeWatch was in fact very familiar to me: they were the most active of the 'aliens-come-back-all-is-forgiven' activist groups. They were in effect the E.T. wing of Greenpeace, lobbying governments to change their anti-alien policies and generally making life difficult for the little Earthsiders. I supported them in principle, but tried to keep my head down when it came to public pronouncements. Until now.
'Good. I'm director of our Scottish region. More or less set it up in fact. We try to help the government remember the aliens in various little ways: demos, high-profile information campaigns – you know the business I'm sure.'
"I have noticed a few of your events, yes.'
'And what was your impression? Generally?'
'Oh I was impressed. It's important to keep the authorities awake and mindful of their duty.'
'Yes. Exactly my view. Actually Adam, I was wondering if we could meet up? I have a modest proposal I'd like to put to you.'

'Why not? It'd be good to catch up.'

'Are you free tomorrow?'

We arranged a meeting for the afternoon. I was eager to discover what Mark had made of his life since our meeting five years ago. Clearly he'd not been entirely idle: CubeWatch was much more than a bunch of frustrated students searching for a cause; they'd kept up a constant pressure on the western governments not to give in to the Alien paranoia that was percolating through the partially educated sections of society.

'So now he knows your address too,' Elaine said in her best how-naive-can-you-be-and-still-live tone.

'Why shouldn't he? He's an old friend.'

Not exactly true, in the sense of factual, but spiritually true, let's say.

'I'm not sure I want your revolutionary misfits turning up here all the time.'

'Elaine, for heaven's sake! Please trust me. Mark's ok. He runs a high-profile and very effective environmental campaign group. You'll like him, honestly.'

'Whether I like him or not isn't the issue. I'm concerned about him bringing others in his wake. You don't seem to realize what an incendiary issue this Aliens farrago is. I'd rather you kept it at a safe distance.'

'I'll be careful, I promise. We'll hold our bomb-making workshops elsewhere.'

The phone-calls started in earnest the next morning. The Chronicle wanted an interview. A neighbour wanted to argue with me; a sixth-form college wanted me to talk to their 'global harmony' forum; and an obscure film company with the unlikely name of ESPouse wanted to make a documentary about Alien technology and ESP. I said no thanks to all of them and locked myself in the garden shed with a flask of strong Columbian. I needed to think long and hard about which way I wanted my life to go next, and for that I needed to be away from the slightest hint of pressure. There, amidst the spider webs and long broken plant pots I saw I had the classic dilemma: to be or not to be. I could go to ground, speak to no-one, become as invisible as possible, disappear in effect; maybe take up a new identity – in which case nothing would change: humanity would remain locked in its anal world, eternally unable to think outside the cage of its needs and illusions, and unable to take the next step in its evolution; or I could continue the campaign I'd effectively begun with the TV interview: persuade more and more people that the Aliens were not only vastly more intelligent than us, but also entirely benign in their intentions; in fact, much more than benign: they passionately wanted us to overcome our primitive mindset and resolve our age-old differences; to take our place, indeed, in the cosmic community. It's of some interest that, sitting on my Dad's half-rotted tool-chest in my torn jeans sipping hot coffee on that mild, early spring morning, I had not the slightest doubt in my mind that I could achieve that. You may well blanch in embarrassment at the hubris of this, but there it is: my year of being almost constantly in intimate mental contact with the Visitors had made me almost believe I was one of them, and that it would be but a small step to possessing similar powers of world-transformation to those they themselves had.

There were strong arguments on both sides of the to-be-or-not-to-be question. Naturally personal safety was in the forefront, being as I was in my inmost soul an unmitigated coward. Elaine's safety lay not far behind; achieving some kind of belated respect from those in authority likewise figured quite highly; and being taken seriously for once; being considered an asset to my race, instead of a parasitic resource-consuming appendage to it. And then there was the serious money that would undoubtedly accrue from my various unique experiences and connections made during my strange conversations across intergalactic space; it was reasonable to assume that would be enough to buy me all the solitude and comfort I could wish for. And what else could I buy with it? For a fleeting moment I shocked myself with the delicious prospect of torturing all those so-called friends who had humiliated me through the years: no cries for mercy would avail them: I wanted them to taste a little of the misery I'd endured at their hands. Did I say a little? No, let's be truthful: I wanted them to taste many times my misery, even to the fourth generation.

In the end, you won't be surprised to hear that I decided to save the world. In the light of the fact that the world wasn't saved, in the sense the Aliens intended it to be, you might think that decision reckless, risible, insane, megalomanic, hubristic, or just plain daft. But, my Lords, I have to remind you that I had the most powerful hyper-intellects in the known universe on my side, even if they had gone into a temporary hyper-sulk for the duration. I still knew they were out there, and they undoubtedly had one eye cocked in humanity's direction. And when you have God on your side – even if it is only in your dreams – you tend to feel every thought you have is divinely sanctioned.

Mark struck me as a far more substantial figure than I remembered him. He'd retained the beard, but it had filled out in the intervening years and given him the air of a high-level head of a secret service department, the kind nobody ever remembers because they carefully cultivate a completely transparent personality. He wore a charcoal suit of some expensive material, custom tailored I guessed. His almost-black hair was cut short and combed forward so it emphasized his narrow skull, and somehow made him seem more forbidding than he actually was. I was surprised to find that I was glad to see him.

'What did you make of the Newsnight thing?' I asked as I led him between Elaine's boxes full of political and travel magazines into the conservatory.

'I thought you did a good job,' he said, straightening his back and regarding the plethora of plant pots and stacked cartons of honey and soya milk. 'You certainly put that twit of a science minister in his place. 'My God! What a wanker! Who did he sleep with to get that job?'

'It's because I want humanity to survive,' I said.

'Yes, I know. So do we all. That's why I'm here too.'

'I'll get some tea and then we can talk properly.'

Chapter Six

I suppose Mark represented for me the possibility of being part of humanity and its collective life: he was the get-up-and-do-it aspect of me (those expensive therapy sessions were proving their worth now, weren't they?). And what, I wondered while waiting for the water to boil, did I represent for him? The cool voice of reason? Calm, dispassionate appraisal? Passion tempered by experience? Or was it simply that I had some money, and could be articulate on delicate matters of global diplomacy? Whatever the truth, I was glad not to be entirely alone any more in a world where it was impossible to know who was genuinely on your side, and who was positioning himself for a portion of the kill.

'This is a beautiful place,' Mark said, gazing out at the steeply rising woods.

'Yes. It's Elaine's of course. She bought it at the right moment. Probably cost a fortune now.'

'You look like you're fairly well settled here?'

I didn't quite know how to react to this: it looked like an innocent enough observation, but something put me on my guard, as though someone were trying to find out something without actually asking me. So I stalled.

'Sometimes I feel settled: and others I just want to open the door and never stop walking. I get to feeling the company of men is not one of life's sweetest gifts.'

'And the company of women?' His gaze focused on me more compellingly.

'Well, Elaine's company is delightful, of course. The best I could hope for.'

'Do I detect a 'but' buried in there somewhere?'

'I don't think so.' I felt uncomfortable at this pressure to reveal something, and to give myself time made a bit of a song and dance about pouring tea and prising open the recalcitrant biscuit tin.

I said: 'Why don't you tell me what you've been doing since we last met in Bridgwater?'

'Oh, not very much. I had a stab at a love affair, but I think I scared the lady off within two days. Women don't seem to like people who rock the boat too much.'

'No. Rocking boats doesn't tend to go with rocking cradles.'

That elicited a smile, and I relaxed slightly.

'Then I had a go at a college course. Middle East relations. It seemed a worthwhile thing to learn about, given the climate.'

'How was that?'

'I felt it was too unbalanced in favour of US models. I got very irritated at the crude economic agenda behind it, and left after six months. Still I learned something valuable: there's no substitute for hands-on experience. So I took off for three months on a little tour of self-education.'

'Where to?'

'Syria. Jordan. Lebanon. And Gaza.'

I decided not to be impressed. After all, I'd been Chosen.

'Useful?'

'Extremely. I knew what I had to do after that. I knew we weren't going to make it without help. We needed the Visitors back more than anything else.'

'Do they keep in touch with you?'

'The Aliens? No, I'm afraid not. They've gone very quiet since all that fracas with the missile.'

'Well you can't entirely blame them.'

'I wouldn't even entertain such a human concept as blame. They're an entirely different order of mind from us; that's why I'm pursuing this project so doggedly. We have potentially such a fantastic amount to learn. It's the opportunity of our race's lifetime. We simply can't afford to blow it.'

'Any ideas why they stopped talking?'

'Wouldn't you if the person you're trying to help chucked a nuclear warhead at you?'

'Probably.'

'My best guess is they're perfecting another Cube. One that will be more accurately tuned to human consciousness, which won't create all the disruption the last one made. And I don't think it will take them very long. They've acquired a huge quantity of first-hand data about us already. Strictly between ourselves I think Cube Two will arrive within two years. They can't take the risk of leaving us alone much longer than that, knowing what they know about us.'

'If you're right, we've not much time to persuade governments that the Aliens are friendly.'

'I don't think we have a hope of doing that. We'd just create two axes: the pros and the antis. Can you really imagine the West, the Middle East and Asia uniting to welcome them back?'

'Then what?'

'We have to work covertly. Create small groups of people sympathetic to the Aliens' project. Train them properly. Instill vision and self-discipline. Install them in strategic places—'.

'Sounds exactly like a plan for another Al Qaida.'

'No. We have to be better than that. We have to be as disciplined and as effective, but not motivated by hate.'

I sensed a rant coming on. 'You're not asking much are you? You're forgetting we're dealing with human beings here! The people who brought you Treblinka and Srebrenica and Rwanda! The people whose idea of co-operation is selling armaments to power-obsessed tyrants so they can then use them to exterminate their own people! If they're not motivated by hate or avarice what on earth will do it? I mean – Scout badges?'

'Fear of world-wide conflict might do it,' I said.

'Not much evidence for that is there? Tribal hatreds seem to go deeper than anything else. No, only a change of mind-set will do it. And that has to be initiated from outside. So we have no option but to make the world Alien-friendly. And the only way that's going to work is by unremitting education and lobbying. After all it worked with climate change.'

'Yes. until it seriously began to impact on economic output.'

'I sense my role in all this is about to emerge.'

Mark smiled. 'Possibly. But only if you want a role.'

'Well there you have it. Part of me does, and part doesn't. A very large part doesn't, in fact. So which part do you want to talk to?'

There was a sound of a door opening and shutting, followed by a cat meowing its greeting.

'I'll tell Elaine you're here. She'll want to meet you.'

Actually I wasn't too sure she would; but I wanted to demonstrate to her that I wasn't associating with the penurious ragged foul-mouthed bomb-throwing brigade; that in fact my friends could be considered responsible right-thinking members of society just as much as hers; even people you might want to invite into your house without first hiding the spoons.

When I returned Mark was walking up and down among the fruit boxes like a man suddenly shown the shining stone tablets.

'Your role, Adam, if you accept it, will be educator-in-chief.' He stood, hands in trouser pockets, an unremitting half-smile on his face, challenging me to turn it down.

'Oh. I rather fancied something more along the lines of Grand Vizier.'

He ignored my sad little irony. 'Listen Adam. We have to be very intelligent about this. Number one: we must be totally clear about why we're doing it. Number two: we have to trust each other totally. No secrets, right? And number three: we don't make unilateral decisions without both agreeing. The stakes are too high for us to allow petty rivalries and ego-games to deflect us. If you don't sign up to those basic rules, I'm afraid we can't work together. I'd be very sorry about that, but, well, we have to be as sure as possible that we don't have internal rivalries or hidden agendas from the start. Ok?'

I wondered why this all suddenly sounded horribly familiar, until the memory of Joe and his tragically idealistic community swam into my mind.

'To be quite honest, I'm not really a signer-upper to anything. I like to find out how it feels first. I think that's how it has to be. I hate to feel I can't get out of something without perjuring my soul.'

Mark sat down slowly, as though about to make a decision that would change the course of human history.

'I understand that. I'm the same, actually. It's probably why I want us to work together. I don't have a problem with it. But there must be openness. If there are hidden agendas we'll hit the rocks in no time at all. And we can't afford to do that: we need the Aliens on our side.'

'Yes, but which side?'

'I meant humanity's side. As long as there are factions we don't have a hope. We have to heal the collective psyche, to use Jung's language.'

'Oh , right-ho then. Excuse me, I'm just popping out to heal the collective psyche. Shall I pick up a couple of beers on the way?'

'I know it sounds grandiose. But really that's what it comes down to.'

'A global therapy session?'

'Well, it'll be necessary to work in both worlds: intensive education and revolutionary tactics. One without the other will not be strong enough.'

Before I could work out just what revolutionary tactics he had in mind Elaine appeared in the doorway, somewhat under-dressed for the occasion, it has to be said. Not that I minded: Elaine had made understatement into her own personal signature, so much so that she constantly threatened to flip into overstatement. But I did wonder, for a bare fraction of a second, why she had taken such trouble immediately after returning from a shopping trip: if it was to impress me, what had she done wrong that required immediate expiation? And if it was to impress Mark, what had I done wrong that required immediate punishment?

Perhaps it was because I was fully occupied analysing this complex psychological conundrum, or because I was trying hard not to notice the subtle electric charge that ran like St Elmo's fire along an invisible bridge joining their gazes, that I didn't register Elaine's first words at all. What I did hear was Mark saying:

'I'm delighted to meet you too, Elaine.'

'Mark was making me an offer I'm trying my damnedest to refuse,' I said vaguely to Elaine.

For another enduring moment it seemed like my words came to an absolute halt three inches in front of my lips, and hung there, deprived of all power to propagate out into the world. In a spasm of panic I willed them to go on, to reach their intended recipients; but something prevented them; some power was reaching down to render them weightless and meaningless. I didn't seem to be in the world at all: I was in a limbo without life, time, space or memory: a bubble of ultimate stasis; everything was going on normally around me, only inches from my body, but the barrier around that world, although transparent, was absolute.

And then the bubble burst, and I heard Mark say:

'And Adam was giving me a lesson in honesty I'm trying my hardest to learn.'

Elaine replied, looking directly at me with her untranslatable smile:

'Yes, it's one of his many virtues.'

The worm retreated in an instant to its lair on the furthest rim of the universe, and we were simply three friends on the brink of saving the world.

On the third day the letters and emails began. At first a trickle; postcards congratulating me on my outspokenness; some wanting to join my 'organisation'. Some pretty unmitigated abuse: 'alien-fucker' was a phrase used more than once. The vast majority went straight into the bin. As the days went on I had to select what I read: I went mostly by smell.

After a fortnight – on the first of March, to be precise – at 8am, a small postal packet dropped almost soundlessly onto the mat. I carried it furtively into my study and laid it as gently as I could on the desk.

It was extremely light, bore no clue as to the identity of the sender, merely an official printed adhesive label giving no useful information. I phoned down to Elaine.

'Do you think it could be a letter-bomb?'

'Why not open it and see?'

'Right-ho then, thanks.'

'Adam, don't be stupid. Don't do anything with it. Ring the police.'

'The police would probably say what you said. One less nutter to deal with.'

'Adam, this isn't the time for games. Ring the police, now. Ok?'

Something odd had come into our relationship since that wretched interview; an indefinable circumspect quality, not quite a coolness; was it simply that I'd gone against her wishes in doing the interview? It wasn't in her character to take umbrage because I'd followed my own instincts. But had I? Maybe that was it: I'd gone against my own feelings, not hers, and she knew it. And as soon as I'd articulated that thought, I knew it was the truth: I'd done it out of pride – the desire to be recognized and respected. I'd done it in order to be someone. And now the envelopes were coming home to roost.

I drained my coffee and rang the police, who, after buzzing all over the package with their Star Trek probe pronounced it 'safe'. I didn't think to ask them for a definition of safe.

Inside was a single, black metal cube, measuring about two centimetres each side.

Yes, that's right: a cube.

I turned it over and over, shook it, peered into the envelope for instructions, weighed it in my letter scales, tried my metal-file on it, measured it as precisely as I could without a micrometer to hand, decided not to try drilling a hole in it (complete waste of time, clearly), then put it back on the table and waited for it to start growing.

But it didn't. For an hour I tried to stop myself watching it, then gave up my anti-vigil and went out to buy a paper and some stationery supplies. The proprietor of the stationers' was an elderly Polish artist called Bogdan who I'd known for years, and trusted to tell me anything I needed to know.

'What's new?' I asked while he was collecting my various requirements.

'A politician told the truth!' he cackled, revealing a gold tooth that could probably have told an interesting story of its own.

'Well, well. Must be the end of the world. I must cash in my shares.'

'Actually there is something. I found an interesting site last night. Hard to tell if it's genuine, of course.' He handed me my bag of envelopes to ensure he had my complete attention. 'There's a new group emerging that calls itself 'The Front for the Brotherhood of the Faith'. It may of course be quite innocent: it has a lot of words about radical education, liberating our children from western values, opening new doors to God, and so on – all above-board progressive sounding stuff, you agree?'

'Might be. Go on.'

'But after six or so pages there's a link which takes you to something more sinister: a whole page about how the UK still has the Cube, and how the government's cracked its technology, and plans to use it to destroy Islam and enslave Muslims to the West. Of course that sort of thing's been around since nine-eleven, I know. But they seem to be getting more and more organized. For example there are strings of letters and numbers which could very possibly be either dates and locations for proposed attacks, or for secret meetings of supporters to plan attacks. All encrypted, naturally.'

'Ah well, like you say, we've been there many times already. But thanks for letting me know. Do you have the site address?'

He reached inside his jacket and handed me a flimsy till-receipt with a web address scrawled on it in biro.

'You'll need to hurry: it'll be gone by tonight. They'll have scarpered before the security people catch up with them. They're excellent organizers, whoever they are. They plan ahead. Then one day, when nobody's expecting it – poof! An airport's gone, or an express train's blown up.'

I was anxious to find out if my new baby had grown in my absence. I thanked Bogdan for his thoroughness and left with my bag of envelopes.

I measured it again. It hadn't grown: two centimetres precisely. I was almost disappointed at its lack of initiative.

It had to be a joke, of course. Someone thought it funny to send the Cube-Man his very own baby Cube to look after. After all, he's clearly incapable of forming an enduring relationship with another human; maybe he'll manage it with a metal box.

But the following week a second cube arrived. Same day, same district: SW15. Same kind of envelope. Same dimensions exactly.

This gave me some food for thought. One really would expect some variation – at least in the third decimal: very few precision fabricators could turn out chunks of metal accurate to a thousandth of a centimetre every time: maybe nuclear warheads required that, or some critical electronics such as hard-drives. But these must be dirt-cheap alloy trinkets without provenance.

The third week two arrived together. I'd kept the micrometer purely out of laziness; when both of the new cubes measured the same, plus or minus nothing, I was forced to look at them with new respect. Someone somewhere in London was going to considerable trouble to send me a message, and I felt I owed him to take similar pains to find out what was on his mind.

I arranged to meet Mark at a coffee house in the centre of Bridgwater. He arrived half an hour late, full of apologies.

'Traffic was bloody awful. I think a water main had burst.'

'That's ok. I've been enjoying the river view.'

He slung his pack onto the table with dismissive impatience, exactly as he had the first time we'd met.

'How's Elaine?'

'She's well. Thriving, I'd say.'

'She seems a good person to have for a companion.'

'Yes. She can speak her mind about something and then in an instant focus on something quite different. It's a saving grace I don't possess.'

'It must be a blessing living with someone like that. Someone you trust completely. I've never experienced that.'

'She is good for me. I'm not so sure I'm that good for her.'

'You probably are. I could tell she values you very highly.'

'Really? How?' I was suddenly all attention.

'Oh, in small ways. Like her tone of voice. Body language. And particularly the way she listens. In my experience love and listening live very close to each other.'

'That's very perceptive.'

'The fact is, I'm not used to being listened to, so it sometimes goes to my head. I can rant for hours unless I'm stopped.' He smiled.

We sat in silence for a while. People came and went like shadows around us. The clatter of crockery punctuated the ebb and flow of conversations. I knew Mark had his own reason for meeting me, but I wanted to feel our personal agendas were not running the show. If we were to work together, we had to be friends too, and a friend was someone you could sit in silence with and enjoy the way the wind braided the restless surface of the river, or the way the fits of sunlight assayed the trunks of the sycamores and silver birches along the path.

I brought out the latest package I'd received from my mysterious benefactor.

'I'd like to know what you think of these.'

He carefully inspected the little trinkets before setting them between us. Then he picked one up again and his eyes glinted.

'These are special.'

'What do you mean?'

'I mean – I think – that they're not human technology.'

'Not human?'

'For a start, they're practically weightless. 'Here.' He threw the cube to me. It almost failed to register. 'Yet they're not aluminium. Too dark for Titanium. Carbon fibre? I don't know. Could be. They're finely machined, so probably not.' He looked furtively round the room for a moment, then dragged one cube by its corner across the window pane. It left a tiny score mark like a jet's vapour trail. 'Definitely not aluminium! I wonder if it floats.'

He dropped it into a tumbler of water. It barely dipped below the surface.

'How many of these things have you got?'

'Four as we speak. And before you ask, they're identical in every direction: very slightly under two centimetres.'

'As one would expect.' He tossed a cube and let it tick back onto the wooden surface. 'At least it doesn't float in air. Then we'd be in trouble,' he grinned.

'What do you suggest I do with them?'

'Wait and see how many more come. My guess would be quite a few. You could get the metal analysed of course, but that would blow our cover, such as it is. Best keep this as quiet as possible, I'd say. Anyway I suspect we already know the answer.'

'It may yet turn out to be an engineering student in Putney with a weird sense of humour and too much spare time.'

'Yes it may. But why? And if it is he's got access to metals even NASA doesn't know about.'

'Which leaves us with you know who.'

'Indeed it does. Which in turn brings me to what I wanted to ask you.'

Chapter Eight

What he wanted to ask was would I consider doing a small job for him? Hardly anything, really: barely more than a Sunday walk in the park. It was delivering a set of important papers in person to a contact in Edinburgh on a specific day, and bringing a different set of papers back as soon as possible, ideally on the next flight. All expenses paid, naturally. They were too sensitive to be entrusted to any public service: detailed schedules of meetings of high-level government committees, their members and full addresses and contact details; in short – gold dust. He couldn't take the documents himself because he would almost certainly attract attention: he was known to be the Moriarty of the CubeWatch world – the invisible brain directing operations; the worst thing he could do would be to become the public face of the government lobbyists: he was reserving that particular plumlet for me.

Of course, being the ultimate fall guy, I agreed.

The trip itself went routinely – save for one odd detail. I collected the parcel of documents as arranged from my contact at the Crowne Plaza Hotel reception. We had a drink together before I thanked him and walked through the gathering fog of early evening commuters back to Waverley Station to pick up the airport bus. I'd left myself not quite as much time as I should have done to catch the flight, which was the last one of the day, and consequently had to rush across the airport concourse to the departure area. I'd almost reached the escalator when the packet slipped and disgorged its entire contents across the floor, causing havoc for several yards around. Horrified, I got down on my knees to gather them up, helped by a pleasant young man who'd been walking behind me. It was while he was handing me the papers that I happened to glance at one, and noticed something odd about them: they appeared to be photocopies of a printed book. Without pausing to think, I stuffed the papers back into the container, thanked my helper, and raced up the escalator, anxious I'd be too late to board the flight.

Luckily fog had delayed the departure for half an hour, and the plane was still boarding. Once in the air I looked through the papers at leisure: they were indeed copies of a book: *Aboriginal Integration in Western Australia: 1880 to 1960*. Increasingly mystified, I leafed through the sheets – covered in statistics, diagrams and maps – trying to find some connection with aliens, government committees or scientific reports; but the subject of the text could not have been less alien-related: every single page without exception dealt with precisely what it said on the title page.

It was well after midnight and raining steadily when the taxi pulled up in the lane outside our front gate, and I let myself into the darkened house. Elaine was in bed reading, a glass of red wine half empty on the table beside her. She half turned her head.

'Good trip?'

'Exhausting, but no major problems.'

After undressing, I told her about the incident with the papers.

'You read them?' She looked startled.

'Well, of course. I could hardly avoid reading them.'

'But weren't they supposed to be secret?'

'Yes, but when you're on your hands and knees on an airport floor trying to collect hundreds of sheets of paper together you can't help noticing what's on them. And they weren't what they were supposed to be. They were about Australian aborigines.'

'All of them?'

'No, just those in the Western Desert.'

'I meant all of the sheets? Were all the pages on the same subject?'

'Yep. Without exception.'

'How bizarre. You'd better ring Mark, hadn't you?'

'I need to think first. Could it be some kind of cipher? I mean, what if some part of the text has been altered to send a message? And the recipient has a code which tells him what's been altered, and how to decode it. With photocopies it would be impossible to tell which parts have been altered.'

'It's possible of course. But it isn't really your business is it? You're just the courier.'

'I'm not sure I like that. Mark and I are partners. I'm not his factotum. I hope he hasn't given you that idea.'

She seemed to hesitate a fraction of a second before answering, though that could just have been my hyper-sensitivity to any implied slights.

'No. How could he? But the fact remains, they were supposed to be secret documents. And you were entrusted with delivering them, not reading them.'

'Listen Elaine. Mark specifically said there were to be no secrets between us, otherwise we couldn't work together. Honesty and openness were fundamental. So while I accept that the papers were private, I feel I have the right to be let in on their nature. Otherwise it's Mark who's breaking our agreement, not me. Do you understand?'

'I understand that you're trying to wriggle out of a dodgy ethical situation.'

'Well I'm sorry you see it that way. I don't know why you're taking Mark's side anyway. Has he been talking to you about me?'

This was a high-risk strategy of course; but the truth was I felt humiliated by her implication that I was being unethical, and felt I had the right, even the obligation, to question her more closely about her own honesty.

'Adam? For God's sake, I have the right to talk to anyone I choose without consulting you. Or have the rules changed since you moved into my house?'

Her sly dig at my continuing state of impecuniousness did not incline me to answer. In any case I had no answer. I sat instead in stony silence, battling with myself not to descend into personal abuse. When I'd calmed down a little I put on my dressing gown, went down to the kitchen, brewed some tea and sat staring out at the waning moonlight and the dense silhouetted trees on the hillsides.

I knew there was a wrongness about the conversation I'd just had, but precisely what the trouble was eluded me. Elaine had been uneasy and defensive, and her method of dealing with this was to criticize, to make me more concerned with my own failure than with hers; and I equally knew that to ask her what she was feeling would be fruitless: she would interpret it as evasiveness – only confirming that I had some reason to feel guilty. It was the kind of encounter that invariably made me want to walk off into the night with no destination in mind, merely to put as much distance as possible between me and the unfeelable pain.

But I managed not to – if for no other reason than that it was how I'd always dealt with conflict. Instead I reminded myself firstly, that Elaine loved me: this was the primary fact to get clear. Her words, body-language and behaviour ever since our first meeting (and notwithstanding that weird inexplicable hiatus when I was "somewhere else" after I'd finally left Joe's domain) only served to confirm what I knew in my bones; and secondly that I hadn't in fact done anything wrong: the incident of the parcel was an unavoidable accident caused mainly by its not being properly sealed in the first place.

This spacious cogitation did make me feel better, and yet I knew I'd missed something. Over several refillings of my cup I went over every word of Elaine's conversation since I'd got back, trying to locate the spot where I'd felt fear first stir in my guts. But each time I thought I'd lighted on it the phrase seemed entirely innocent.

Whatever happened, I wasn't going to let the past repeat itself like a berserk computer program. Elaine wasn't like any of the others: she wasn't fixated on success, or running away from commitment, or addicted to middle-aged academics with over-inflated egos: she was caring and generous, remarkably free from ambition and at the same time had a huge capacity for love. I knew I was lucky to have found her (if 'found' is quite the right word, considering how long I'd pestered her to live with me) and I didn't intend to fuck up the good fortune at this stage of the game.

Having quieted my demons I crept back to the bedroom. Elaine was apparently sleeping. I rolled back the quilt and twisted myself down beside her. The silence of the night was affirmed by the unearthly screech of a fox prowling nearby in the moonlight. The last thought I remember was asking myself why I hadn't asked Elaine what she'd been doing while I'd been on my wild goose chase across the border.

Chapter Nine

I really didn't believe I'd ever need the shrink-wrap again after five years. But I was wrong.

Things were encroaching on me. Elaine's strangeness. The cube things. The Dwarf dreams. And this continuous feeling I had that a boundless void was opening directly beneath my feet. So one morning I made an appointment with Clare. She seemed pleased. But then at forty pounds a hit why wouldn't she?

'So how've things been for you?' She smiled brightly, as if to say, there's still hope, despite appearances. She had a new extra-comfy chair and a bright new potted plant by the window. Key indicators.

'A bit bumpy of late,' I said.

Pawn to knight one.

'In what way?'

'I – feel things are closing in on me again. Like before. I get this terror that things are just repeating themselves out of control.'

'Can you be more specific?' The notebook. The pen. But not yet the box of tissues.

'Well, you know I used to get this feeling that I was being constantly laughed at? Well, not literally. I mean I was not regarded as a serious proposition. People just saw me as an opportunity. A kind of scapegoat...' I was running out of ideas, but Clare made no move to intervene. Just the ever-reliable impartial gaze. 'I'm sorry. I don't know what I want to say. I just have this feeling of terror that creeps over me—'.

'Where? Can you point to where you feel it?'

I indicated the general area of my long-suffering guts.

'Do you feel it now?'

'No. Well, yes. Slightly. Momentarily. It's difficult to—'.

'Take your time. There's no hurry at all. What I'd like you to do is remember a particular situation when you felt that terror, and try to stay in it. Don't let your mind get distracted by ideas about it.' She did something with her left hand and the light dimmed. I prepared myself for the swinging pendulum business, but she didn't try that.

'Don't try to remember: it's not about making an effort. Just relax and go back into the experience. Let the experience flow around you and into your mind.'

Relaxed was far from how I was feeling just then, but I still managed to let myself flow a little, and then all at once I was with Mark and Elaine in her conservatory, and herself was saying, 'Nice to meet you Mark,' and himself was smiling and making some ingratiating remark, and I was paralysed in my bubble of fear, and nothing could get in or out, no matter how hard I tried, and there was a deep bellow of pain welling up from some forbidden basement I didn't dare visualize—.

'Don't force it, Adam,' a soothing voice from outside found its way to my fear. 'Let it come in its own way, when it's ready.'

But it never came. Something I couldn't control came and battered it down again, and tethered it in its black basement.

'I don't know what's happening,' I said after a long interval. 'There's something I can't handle that keeps getting called up whenever I get close to someone. I keep hoping and hoping it's gone for good, but then something happens and it's back, ready to tear everything apart again.'

'It's just the past, Adam. We repeat situations over and over, because we need to heal ourselves, and we can only do that by experiencing the hurt and fully accepting it, and what caused it. Blame and denial stop that happening, because it's easier to do that than feel what wounded us. So we keep on going round the same boring old circle. But I think you've made progress. You're still in a relationship, which suggests you're ready to deal with the thing you need to deal with.'

'Elaine means everything to me,' I said. 'She's the first woman I've felt unconditionally loved and accepted by. She doesn't judge me.'

'That's good, Adam. But a word of advice: don't make her into a goddess. She's human, and bound to have failings, just as you have. And she'll need your acceptance and forgiveness, just as much as you need hers.'

'Sure. I recognize that nobody's perfect. I'm the very last person to expect perfection from anyone.'

'I'm glad you've finally found someone who accepts you. That should make you free to become who you are. To let go of some of your masks.'

'Yes. But there's still this terror in me of losing her love. Even though I know she completely accepts me. That's a weird contradiction.'

'Not really. It's just that real change – whole being change – always lags far behind conscious-mind change. Sometimes several lifetimes behind.'

'Oh. That sounds like bad news.'

'Only if you give up trying. Try anything long enough and your unconscious will eventually get the message and let go of its fear. Anyway, I'm afraid that's our time up for today.'

'What if I pay you another twenty pounds for some more time?'

An almost coy smile, as if to say, I know this game. 'I'm sorry Adam. Another client. Make another appointment.'

'Thirty then?'

The sphinx smile fades, finally unamused. A bell spews its contempt over me.

Chapter Ten

Meanwhile the krazy-kube deliveries kept on appearing, dead on schedule. By the fourteenth week I'd amassed almost four hundred of the little bleeders, and my specially purchased safe was no longer adequate for their welfare. I clearly had to do something quickly, ie, before the following Monday.

In more innocent times my instinct would have been to seek expert advice; but since paranoia had generally driven out innocence that seemed a dangerous route to take, and the more 'expert' the more dangerous, since nearer to the eye of government. So I had to tread with care. After considering the possible outcomes I rang Magnus, my old university tutor from Sheffield. (For a long time our once mutually fruitful friendship had been in a parlous state on account of two things: one, I had severe doubts about his ontological status, and two: I'd discovered him in the act of fucking my one-time almost girlfriend Rachel in his aptly-named alchemical library, which had resulted in my putative strangling her to death in a fit of extreme jealous rage – which, I again emphasize, my Lords, I do not for one moment seek to justify. In fact I still feel rather bad about it – or at least I did until by chance I found her over a year later wandering around in the woods south of Taunton, dressed in a weird kind of full-length grey shawl, to all intents and purposes alive and conscious – though her complete lack of interest in food or drink did give me pause for thought, I'll admit.

Magnus had helped me a lot during the days of what I used to call my education: he'd been the main instrument of my awakening from the dream of believing that those self-appointed arbiters of knowledge known variously as scientists, doctors, professors, lawyers and psychologists actually knew what they were talking about: life seemed to be a case of the blind and deaf leading the lame and dumb. What Magnus did was instill into me an intimation of what it might be like to be an autonomous thinking and feeling entity, rather than a passive consumer of received opinion – which of course is the true role of education.

'Adam! Great to hear you.' The voice sounded strained, as though his efforts to speak at all cost him considerable pain.

'You too. How are you both?'

'Alas, Myra is no longer with me.'

'Oh. I'm so sorry.'

'No, she's fine. Just not with me. She felt she was having too cosy a life here, and went back to the Middle East to find some suffering. I told her it wasn't necessary to go that far to find it, but she'd made up her mind apparently. She's the kind of person who needs to plunge her hands into gore to feel her life is real. Well she has my blessing, but I have to confess I struggle to maintain the standards I was accustomed to under her meticulous attentions.'

I could imagine it: the place had been chaotic enough even with the long-suffering Myra there. Things must be bad for him now: he was used to having the unquestioning support of his acolytes.

'Magnus, I hate to bother you. But I have something I urgently need your advice on. I don't know anyone else I can ask.'

'Ask away.'

'Someone's sending me hundreds of tiny identical metal boxes. More and more each week. And I've no idea who, or why, or what the hell to do with them.'

'I see,' said Magnus. 'Could you send me a few?'

'If it's all the same to you I'd rather bring them. I don't trust the post.'

'By all means. It'd be great to see you after all this time. I could show you my unique collection of invisible Tibetan pigs.'

'Pardon?'

'Only joking. Come whenever you like. As you know, the door's always open.'

I arranged to visit him the following week, equipped with a lunch-box and a rucksack bulging with the metal beasties – which I barely noticed because they weighed virtually nothing. Elaine drove me to Bridgwater at an ungodly hour of the morning with surprisingly good grace. Her valediction was to the point:

'Try not to embarrass yourself with confused young women looking for a father figure this time, alright?' I actually think this was offered in a spirit of genuine friendship.

It was early afternoon when I alighted from the train at Dunkeld station and caught the post-bus that ran through the glen to Castletown. The journey took over two hours, in which time the clouds lowered and the rain came on, dressing the landscape in weaving scarves of mist and trailing curtains that played tricks with distance. Around five o'clock the bus pulled to a halt opposite the grocery store where I'd asked directions to Magnus' house on my first visit. I felt grateful it was still there, even though I no longer needed its questionable help.

Walking up the generously potholed lane I began to experience the old anxieties all over again. Was this another stupid mistake? Was Elaine just a bit too enthusiastic about my leaving? Would Magnus prove an even worse companion than on the first occasion? Would I in fact embarrass myself yet again through misconstruing the situation? Should I turn round and catch the first train back south in the morning?

In the event Magnus was delighted to see me, and my doubts about coming at once melted to nothing. He led the way into his back kitchen, where I had my first intimation of the true condition of his life: the place was an unmitigated midden. The table in the centre of the floor was sagging under the weight of domestic detritus: books lay in tottering towers on every surface; unwashed dishes rose from the sink like derelict wrecks. The stone floor clearly hadn't been swept since Myra's departure; a sickly odour of general decay pervaded the place.

Magnus hunted round for the kettle.

'I'm really sorry about all this,' he said. 'The truth is I haven't the energy to deal with it. It just gets more and more out of hand.' He found some mugs and made a pretence of washing them with cold water.

'Can't you get someone in to help you?'

'Tried it. They take one look inside and you can't see them for dust. No, I've made my bed and now I must lie in it.' I hesitated to imagine what his bed must look like.

He lowered himself into his decrepit gone-to-seed armchair by the stove, which gave me my first chance to study him. He looked much older than when I'd last visited. His hair had absconded entirely from the crown of his head, but still clung on to the sides in anarchic white cataracts. He wore a plain beige shirt beneath a stained and threadbare navy-blue waistcoat. His fleshy hands were swarthy and mottled; when he spoke they repeatedly tried to get airborne, but invariably crashed back to earth in a gesture of disgust, as though signaling to any observer: "beware: this is what philosophy has brought us to."

'Does Myra keep in touch?'

'She wrote once. A good letter. She's in Ramallah, of all God-forsaken places.'

'What's she doing?'

'Beats me. Feeding the five thousand I should imagine. She's attracted to suffering like a bear to bees: she has to do something about it. Personally it mystifies me why people can't be satisfied with doing something about themselves. The Middle-east will never be solved: age-old hatreds never run out of fuel. Speaking of fuel, do you want some brandy?' He offered me a half-full bottle of Napoleon.

'No thanks. Tea's fine.'

'I always take a tod with my tea in this weather. It sets me up.'

'And your health?'

'Best not ask, if you don't want a litany of contemporary human ills. I have prostate cancer. I have bad circulation. I have bad digestion. Bad heart. Bad eyesight. And – you'll be especially glad to hear – no sex-life whatever. Not even an imaginary one. But apart from all that I couldn't be better.'

'Sounds like you should be in a more manageable place than this then?'

'So they tell me. But can you imagine me without all this space? Without my library? They're where my imagination lives.'

'To be truthful, no. But you really do need help.'

'Adam, it has to be faced: I'm dying. I should be dead already. It's only my infinite ego that's keeping me alive. What's the point in being comfortable if my demons desert me?'

'Well, it might not be a question of comfort. It might mean you stay alive a bit longer and pass on your wisdom to people like me who need it.'

'Wisdom do you call it?' He gave the stove a savage poke with something that might once have passed for a Queen Anne chair leg. 'I've given up using those kinds of words Adam. Along with knowledge, truth, peace, values, altruism. We survive as long as we can. Then – the Great Silence.'

'What about your group: Don and Harry and the rest? Do you still meet up?'

'We haven't met in four years. Don travelled to the East – Thailand I think – and went native, as far as I heard. I think it was the child sex that got him. So much for his philosophy. Still I suppose in a way it was good that something turned him on. I can't even get off on pornography any more. Divine retribution, no doubt. Oh, and by the way, while we're in that neck of the woods so to speak, I owe you a very big apology.'

'Oh, don't even think of it. Rachel wasn't even my girlfriend. I'd only met her a couple of days before. I was just a jealous possessive prig in those days. All you did was bring me up against reality rather sooner than I wanted. I can't hold that against you, can I?'

I was shocked to the core by Magnus's physical deterioration; it pushed any past misdeeds of his well into the domain of irrelevance. If I was honest, I was seeing myself a few years down the line: bitter, penurious, friendless, disorientated, with good health and optimism little but a receding memory, and frankly it scared the shit out of me. I wanted away: I wanted my secure and sunny past back – except it had never really existed outside my inventive imagination. What had happened to my optimism? My enthusiasm for new experiences? My eagerness for knowledge? I wasn't yet a physical wreck, but my life seemed to be strewn with the emotional equivalent. And it seemed only logical that in time one would lead inexorably to the other.

'You're too forgiving. The truth is, my friend, it was the last gasp of a desperate animal who had to prove to itself it was still in the race. Now I know I'm not, and frankly, it's a relief. Who needs all that huffing and puffing and blowing other people's houses down? And if that's all a lifetime of studying philosophy gets you, well too bad for philosophy. The fact is, I was wrong: I have one of the best philosophical libraries in Europe upstairs, and it's all worthless to me now. It let me down exactly when I relied on it for a way out. It's all just so much dead and decaying paper. Better to have left it as trees: at least they're alive, and give something useful to the world.'

'I'd like to remind you of something you said to me once. You said alchemy is a code, or a set of codes. All it does is tell you how to order your life to activate your higher energies. But it can't actually do it for you. You have to get up and do the work yourself. I'm sure you remember that.'

'Oh yes, I remember. And thank you for so gently bringing that back to me. But I think I no longer have the will to do the work. It has all gone too far. I didn't see it coming, and nobody told me. Now I've blown it. I'm a wreck of good ideas. And they were good ideas. I haven't forgotten the long nights of soul searching that went into their making. I don't want to ditch the entire engine because one of it's mechanisms is flawed. Trouble is I've ignored my friends for too long; treated them like children. All the time they were probably telling me what I needed to hear, had I only been able to listen. Ah well, better luck next time eh? Shall we find another bottle? There's still some good stuff stashed away somewhere under the archeological debris.'

Somehow he managed to raise all the parts of himself out of his chair at the same time and faded into the gloomy reaches of the lobby in search of his precious elixir. At that moment I saw something that had to be done. It wasn't a question of duty, much less of guilt; nor was it compassion or disgust: it was a simple, quite logical progression: here was a man reduced to dire extremity and suffering as a consequence of neglect of the proprieties: here was I, able-bodied, in receipt of much hospitality, at liberty to direct my own life, in possession of most of my faculties, the most relevant in the present circumstances being empathy; ergo – I do the washing up.

I threw down my coat, rolled my shirt-sleeves, and set about dismantling the leprous edifices of pots, knives, spoons, cups and shoals of crockery. When Magnus returned with his treasure I was well launched into the process of purgatorial renovation.

'Good God!' said Magnus, almost falling over a column of books on the floor, 'We can't have an honoured guest doing the housemaid's work!'

'It needs to be done, and you're not well enough to do it.'

He collapsed into his chair with the sound of a major rockfall. 'Adam, you've proved me wrong: there is still altruism in the world. All is not quite fallen.'

He poured two generous measures of brandy into tumblers. 'Not quite the way one is meant to drink this, but what the hell, who's watching?'

He savoured the fiery demon in his glass for maybe thirty seconds. 'Did I tell you I used to be a bit of a mariner?'

I turned to him, surprised.

'Merchant Navy. In the days when they had proper ships: brass, oak and mahogany and no skimping. And no GPS positioning gadgets to make you go soft in the head. Well, anyway, in such circumstances you get to know the men you're working with pretty well: some of those trips lasted for months. And you got a feeling for the people you could trust in an emergency – even without an emergency. Often they were the people with an off-putting manner or an unsociable way about them.

On these trips I always kept myself to myself, socialized as little as possible. I took refuge from boredom in philosophy. I thought it would do the business you see, so I wouldn't have to encounter my shortcomings. It took a particularly hairy incident to bring me to my senses.

We were on the return leg of a South American run, about twenty degrees south of the equator. The ship was an ancient tramp steamer with a full cargo of timber. About three days out we hit a force ten storm and dropped anchor to sit it out. The forecast seemed to indicate it wouldn't last more than twelve hours, so we weren't too worried; but instead of blowing itself out it crept up to force eleven, and somehow we'd swung round in the night so we were taking the full force of it amidships. Very soon we had a twenty degree list. It turned out part of the cargo had broken free. That was bad news, because it's well-nigh impossible to stow it again without getting a crane down there. So the following morning the storm was still throwing everything at us and the list had increased. Three of us were sent on deck to do some emergency repairs to the radio aerial. I was trying to grab hold of one of the antenna stays when I lost my footing and got hit by a thirty footer and went over the side.

Now we had a young signals officer called Flynn or Finn or something like that, who I'd hardly spoken a word to since we'd left Rio. In fact I had the distinct impression that he avoided me whenever he could. I never once saw him smile or greet anyone or do any of those grooming things that humans do to lubricate their interactions with each other. He was a minimalist in every sense: size, speech, gesture, drink – he even seemed to eat as little as he could get by on. Off duty he would sit motionless in a corner for hours on end reading or just staring. I remember he had this strange behavioural tic where he'd simply freeze for maybe five seconds in the middle of whatever he was doing – exactly like a toy that had suddenly had its power disconnected. Then he'd carry on exactly as before, ignoring the bemused stares or comments that were inevitably made. But the really odd thing was most people seemed to respect him: he wasn't harassed or ribbed for his behaviour. It was as if we all sensed he had some inner strength that made him impervious to the attitudes of others. Or it may have been simply a very effective mask he'd learned to wear to disguise his vulnerability. I don't know. All I know is on that terrible morning when I was convinced my time was up he was in the water within five seconds of my falling, and his spontaneous action unquestionably saved me from being dragged under the ship.'

Magnus paused, while the silence of the night thickened in all the room's corners.

'When I'd recovered enough to speak I went to thank Finn for saving my life. He merely nodded, paused for maybe two seconds before turning away to continue with whatever he'd been doing. Fortunately soon after that incident the storm did abate, and we continued northwards with no more trouble. Finn never spoke to me once, or even met my eyes, for the rest of the journey.'

'Did you ever try to get in touch with him?'

'No, I didn't. The truth is, I felt ashamed. I owed my life to him, I knew. But I had to admit, if our roles have been reversed, I doubt I'd have been so ready to do the same. My instincts were always not to get involved, to wait for others to take the initiative, in case I got it wrong. And I invariably had to undergo a mental battle to overcome those instincts – even when it was obvious what was required. I never learnt the knack of acting immediately from my feelings.'

'But you stuck with your philosophy?'

'Yes. I had some conviction that, despite my own total inability to live up to it it still held important truths – particularly the idea of transforming my own mind and body. Alchemy is sympathetic magic: it follows the principle that whatever happens in the physical world with atoms and molecules must have a direct counterpart in the mind. And on the whole I still believe that. This world is nothing but a web of subtle connections through time and space. Wisdom consists in being able to apply them to real life, to the here and now. And you're looking at a man who has failed miserably in that department.'

'But you're still alive,' I said, manoeuvring through the beached debris to get nearer the stove.

'Yes, I still hang on to a form of consciousness, if that's what you mean by 'alive'. But that's merely an unavoidable instinct. An injured rat will close down everything but its vital functions in order that a seed of rat consciousness may be preserved. I am an injured rat.' A further long pause, while the gashed logs collapsed one by one into the flames. 'And what's so great about consciousness, when nothing else works any more? It's a joke: we'll give you this stupendous world to enjoy: inspired music, glorious paintings, spectacular sunsets and monumental mountains, scintillating snow peaks, stimulating friends, heart-gladdening birdsong, mind-stretching starlight, divinely proportioned women, oh-my-god orgasms – oh, and by the way, we'll also make you deaf, give you cataracts, a stomach ulcer, a touch of sciatica, lame you, introduce a few chronic shooting pains in your neck, shoulders, back, abdomen, pelvis and calves, make you impotent and incontinent, and just in case you take refuge from all this in philosophy and literature, we'll make your brain rot slowly until you no longer know who you are, or even care'. Still gazing at the noisily burning logs, he said, 'Oh Adam! Was it for this the clay grew tall?'

I didn't feel like engaging him in counter-argument; he needed to get this bitterness out of his system and start with a clean slate. So I suggested I cooked a meal and then we could talk free from the distractions of hunger.

'Ah yes, food. You'll find some green things in the freeze-box. They might still be food. And there's sausages too, if my memory serves me right.' He hobbled over to the refrigerator and rummaged among the festering plant life that had claimed its shelves. 'Some of this goes back a bit, but no doubt it will serve.'

I cooked up some rice and thawed out the sausages; all the while Magnus was telling me what a fake he was and what a mess he'd made of his life.

When he finally paused, I said: 'But your teaching changed my life! Without you I'd still be a software writer for Oracle, slowly going out of my mind with boredom. Your lectures woke me up to the possibilities in being human, nothing less. You introduced me to all the major thinkers of the century: Camus, Beckett, Joyce, Jung, Feynman, Powers, Bohr, Sartre. Dammit Magnus, you taught me to think! I'd no idea what my brain was for before I heard you speak!'

'Those people you mention inspired me because they were grappling with their own demons. That's what made them great artists. They wouldn't settle for a comfortable life, they valued truth too much. It's that quality above everything else that makes them human. And that's why they matter to us: they're a hundred per cent alive and human. Encountering their minds stops us falling into the sleep of indifference.'

'So how can you say your life has been wasted when you've brought that kind of experience into people's lives?'

'Maybe you're right Adam. Maybe I've not totally fucked up. But look at what the world's become, despite all those great awake minds. Despite art and philosophy and beauty being all around us. There isn't a moment when there isn't some obscenity disfiguring the beauty we inherited. It's as though there's a cancer in the heart of every living cell that's just waiting for its moment to destroy everything that's been achieved. You blink one moment and it seizes its chance.'

We ate our supper in relative silence, punctuated by gasps and groans from Magnus and thunderous cracks from the stove. An east wind had arisen again which intermittently shook the window casements and howled like something demented through the ample cracks around the door. After the meal a bottle of port appeared and we sat in the subdued glow of the fire and felt the world was maybe not such an inhospitable place after all.

'A shelter in the storm only affirms the wrath of the storm', Magnus quoted. 'But it's no less welcome for all that.'

'Who said that?'

"I made it up,' he chuckled. 'Now. You said you'd brought something for me to look at.'

I cleared as large a space on the table as I could and tipped the contents of my rucksack onto it, feeling like a first-time salesman hoping to divest himself of a consignment of worthless trinkets and maybe make a quick fortune. Then I stepped back as though they might immediately turn white-hot and precipitate a conflagration. But they simply lay in a normal kind of heap reflecting the sullen firelight. Magnus whistled.

'Ye gods! What have you brought?' He picked one up, held it beneath one of the desk lamps, examined it closely. 'You say these came in the post?'

'Yes. Every Monday, regular as Rennies. Though the parcels got bigger each week.'

'How bigger?' His eyes in the light of the stove had suddenly acquired a gleam of his old intensity.

'Well, quite a lot bigger. The last few had to be left on the drive.'

'No. What I meant was, exactly how much bigger? I presume you counted them?'

'No, I'm afraid I didn't. It didn't occur to me.'

He froze in disbelief.

'Are you really telling me it didn't occur to you that numbers might be the key?'

'No, it didn't. I just assumed it was some sort of joke or advertising stunt. You know, someone had found my address after seeing the TV thing, and thought I'd be an easy target.'

He threw me a look of mock-despair. 'It seems I taught you to think but not to count! How could you make such a bloody silly mistake, Adam? Do you remember how many came the first week?'

'Just one.'

'And the second?'

'Another one.'

'And then?'

'I think the third week two arrived together. Then three the next. After that I can't remember. Maybe four.'

Magnus began to pace up and down the kitchen.

'I put it to you, sir, that you received five.'

'Could be. I honestly don't remember. I just kept adding them to the pile in the safe.'

'Ok Adam. This is what I think is happening. You'd better sit down. You are being sent a kit. Something to build. What you have here is the start of a Fibonacci sequence. I presume you know what that is?'

'Something to do with the golden number, as I recall. Isn't it the basis of a lot of natural forms, like the spacing between leaves and petals?'

'Well done! It is indeed. And more to the point it's a universal indicator of order: it binds together mathematics, geometry, music, architecture as well as nature itself. So understanding it is an indicator of a reasonably well developed intelligence. These little boxes are not human artefacts; I'd guess they were made by the same entity that made the original Cube that caused such havoc six years ago. And I'd further guess you'll receive a few more deliveries before they stop. So you'd better be there. Did you bother to count the number of weeks they've been coming, or did that seem irrelevant as well?'

'Eight, up to last Monday.'

'Well you might have some more. It depends on what you're supposed to make with them of course. I'd guess there would be some clue to that somewhere in the cubes themselves.' He picked one up again and shook it. It failed to sprout antennae or sing a jingle, or do anything at all except perfectly reflect the firelight. Then he cleared a space and placed one of the cubes in the centre. It seemed to be calling to us to put another one alongside it. Magnus did so. Nothing happened, but I had the feeling we were on the right track. The two cubes seemed to send out what I can only describe as a silent 'congratulations, you've made it to level one!' kind of signal.

He made no further move for a long while, but stood absorbed by the scene on the table, as if contemplating a crucial chess move. Magnus said:

'The next stage has clearly got to be adding two more cubes. The question is, how? How many ways can you add two to two?'

'That depends what the rules are,' I said. 'Can't we make them up? No one's sent us a rule book, after all.'

'How do you know? How would you recognize an alien rule-book?'

'I've no idea.'

'Well think, man! What media are available to it?'

'What do you mean, media?'

Magnus began his exasperated shuffling again.

'Adam, they're not going to send a manual printed in English, are they? Neither would they bother with such clumsy ephemera as magnetic tape, vinyl disks, digital disks, videos, flash memory, or any similar crude human technology. Yet they need to communicate with humans. How did they first communicate with you, when the original cube arrived?'

'Voices in my head.'

'Ok. So they're probably refined their system a bit now, I imagine. What have we left?'

'Lights? The original cube had lights inside.'

'It's possible. But we haven't seen any lights yet, have we?'

'No, but they may take a while to start working. Harry's cube was completely black for the first few weeks.'

'Alright. But think back to what you felt when I put the first two cubes together.'

'I felt a kind of – rightness. Happiness almost.'

'Exactly. So did I. My guess is that came from the cubes. That's how their instruction manual works.'

'So the next logical step, if we're talking cube-language', I said, warming to this game at last, 'would be to make a two-unit cube, wouldn't you say?'

'Try it.'

Feeling like a toddler making his first leap of spatial intuition, I tentatively placed four more cubes on top of the first layer. It felt like the proverbial giant leap for mankind.

'How does it feel?' Magnus asked.

'Fantastic.' I stood back to survey my work. 'I know this sounds ridiculous, but I feel as though I've just created something living.'

'Well let's hope it doesn't call you Dr. Frankenstein,' Magnus muttered.

It was only slowly sinking in. The aliens were talking again; coming out of their long state of mystical contemplation or whatever it was they'd been doing for the past six years, and saying, 'Hi guys! We're still here, and ready to do business!' And these unassuming tin boxes were both the medium and the message. If only we could learn to put them together in the one way that would show them we'd at last risen beyond solving a problem by hurling a nuclear missile at it.

Chapter Eleven

The bedroom phone rang while Elaine was still swimming through sinuous chasms of sleep. Her first thought was that nuclear war had begun and she must contact her mother and tell her to lock all the windows, get bottles of water and go down to the basement immediately. Then she was reaching for the receiver and glimpsing the burgeoning glow of sunrise on the opposite wall.

'Hi Elaine. It's Mark.'

She adjusted her pillows to conversation position.

'Oh Mark. How are you?'

'Well, thanks. I wondered if Adam was around?'

'No. He's gone to Scotland.'

'Again?'

'Yes. He needed to visit a friend. You could call his mobile.'

'Actually Elaine, it was you I wanted to talk to.'

'Well that's easy then, isn't it?' She smiled at his transparent subterfuge.

'No. What I mean is, I'd like – I need – to ask you a big favour.'

'Ok.'

'I need to ask it in person. If you wouldn't mind.'

Something in her baulked at this, for no clear reason. Maybe it was simply the fact that he'd rung her at such an unsocial hour, disrupting her essential journeying.

'I'm not sure, Mark. Can't you give me some idea what it is now?'

'Well, very briefly – I urgently need help with CubeWatch. I can't do everything that needs to be done, and since the firebombing everyone seems suddenly busy looking after aged relatives.'

'What sort of help do you need?'

Mark seemed to hunt around for his answer. 'PR mainly. Briefing media. Lobbying agencies. Answering letters. Generally giving us a friendly and competent image. And most importantly pressuring the government to change its paranoid policy towards the aliens.'

'I see. So not that much really? Mark, you don't need my help: you need the biggest, most professional and most expensive public relations firm on the planet.'

'Yes, probably. But we have to start somewhere: we can't just say this problem's too big for us. The stakes are too high for that.'

'Actually I've just thought of someone who may help you. An old friend. Janet Morrison. She lives just over the hill from here. She's eighty-three and has done everything. She was one of the most influential early advisors to the government on climate change, when it was regarded as a bit of a loony-leftie obsession. She's virtually a hermit these days.'

'I'd love to meet her. When shall I come?'

'Could you make this afternoon?' She didn't want to ask him to lunch in case he treated it as an opportunity to return the favour. What had he done, she wondered afterwards, to make her so distrustful?

She caught herself choosing a pale blue off the shoulder summer dress that praised her figure better than a Keats sonnet could have done; then she put it back with a fleeting twinge of regret. What was going on here, she wondered? Was she feeling abandoned merely because Adam had taken a break to see an old friend? Was she paying him back in advance for his inevitable, but as yet unacted infidelities? Or was it displaced guilt for her desertion of Jack in a moment of – what? What was it a moment of? Strength? Clarity? Independence? – Betrayal? How could she ever know what it was when so many supplicants clamoured in her brain, all claiming kinship? And she'd talked it all through with Jack so many times, before they'd actually separated. There had been no trace of deception or abandonment; in fact it was the very last thing she'd wanted. Jack had already been married to his sisters in the sky, his celestial soulmates, and had no space in his life for any earthly wife. She'd tried as hard as any human being could be expected to do to convince herself she was in love, and he was in love, and they were perfectly matched, perfectly satisfied and stimulated; that the connubial equation was as perfectly balanced as it could be, given human fallibility. But it had all collapsed into ash at the first intrusion of reality: she'd been living in a make-believe marriage;

Jack was actually incapable of empathy or reciprocating her feelings, and in fact always had been: it was she who had manufactured the partner she needed and had tried to bolt the mask onto the man she actually lived with. So it was in fact her fault, not Jack's at all; all he'd been guilty of was not noticing what she'd done.

Mark had arrived out of breath and encumbered with a vast unmanageable bunch of pink prima- donna lilies which he offered to Elaine with both hands, as though they were fabulously rare specimens he'd brought back with immense difficulty from the only place they grew in the heart of the Amazon rainforest.

She laughed out loud when she saw them.

'They're gorgeous! You must want that help pretty hard.'

'How about we go for a walk somewhere? I've been cooped up for days in that foul rabbit-hutch they gave us. I'm starting to get cabin fever. Literally.'

'Poor you!' said Elaine, retrieving a vase from the top of a wall-cabinet. The flowers had ruffled her equanimity: they were undoubtedly designed to make it harder to deny Mark's favour. She decided that the bull had to be grasped by the horns, even before it had come into sight.

'I take it these are a bribe?'

'Oh that was mean! What do you take me for?'

She immediately felt full of remorse. 'I'm sorry. I didn't mean to be unappreciative.' Already she felt on unsafe ground, unable to decide what approach to take with Mark. He was charming and attractive in a boyish way, but she was certain he wasn't about to proposition her or suggest anything inappropriate. She changed into jeans and an oversize mauve jersey, and retrieved her faded green wind-cheater from the conservatory, wanting to cover up her body as much as possible, even though the day wasn't at all cold.

She struggled with the zip of the ancient jacket. 'Shall we get going then?'

Once away from the road she began to relax as she realized that Mark simply wanted someone to talk to, a sympathetic mind in a world close-seeded with enemies. Nature always had this effect: opening her to the wonderful web of life that teemed in every microscopic cranny and burgeoned in every direction she looked.

'I'm sorry for being paranoid back there,' she said. 'I bought that house to get away from demons, but of course they sniffed me out.'

'Tell me about them.'

'What? My demons? I don't know. It feels a bit – premature. And demons are difficult to talk about.'

'Have you ever told anyone about them?'

'I don't think so. I seem to always end up with people who are far more interested in their own demons than mine.'

They followed the path over a stile and into a small wood of evergreens which flanked the hillside and sent long straggling outriders out westwards along the ridge. Elaine suddenly knew she desperately wanted to be alone with the trees and the wind, free from the endless unassuageable needs of the world. She began walking again, clutching abstractedly at the new bracken on either hand, feeling the coolness of the small leaves in her palm, as if to confirm her connection with something ancient and simple.

She kept wondering why she felt so resistant to Mark's request. Maybe it was his salesman's technique that irritated her: he was convinced he had a superior product and that she needed it, if only she would admit it. Well she didn't need anyone's damned product just now; she just needed to be left alone with the slender silver birches and the glorious songs of the blackbirds.

'Look,' Mark said, catching her up with difficulty. 'Humanity won't survive without the help of the Visitors; we've all but ruined our planet and eliminated ninety per cent of its species. There's no evidence that we're learning from any of our mistakes, so it's a safe bet that within three or four generations we'll reach the end of the road. However, you and I and maybe a handful of others know the aliens have a method of transforming our destructive instincts: we've already seen it beginning to work—.'

'Hang on a minute. We've seen it chew up the landscape and destroy a few small towns. As far as I know, that's all they've achieved. The rest is speculation, plus a few weird stories going viral on the internet.'

'That's true. But personally I'm convinced they can directly alter emotional states. And if those paranoid Iranians hadn't tried to nuke the Cube I'm certain we'd have seen some powerful positive effects within a year. That's why we have to get it back and make it work for us.'

She stopped short and faced him. 'But that's exactly your problem, isn't it? The Cube was seen as an instrument of invaders – an alien race who wanted to take over our minds and destroy all of human culture. You're going to have a massive job changing that perception: it simply flies in the face of almost every science fiction film or novel there's ever been!'

'Yes. I'm well aware we have an image problem. But that's precisely why CubeWatch exists: to transform the aliens' image. It can be done. It has to be done. And we need you on board!'

'If we could persuade the aliens to send the Cube back to Earth covertly we wouldn't need any PR. It would do its own.'

'But they won't because they don't trust us not to try to destroy it again.'

'They might. But we need to be able to communicate with them. And without the Cube we've no link. So we're back at square one: we've got to educate people.'

Mark suddenly stopped and peered ahead at the series of hilltops that had come into view. Elaine realized she knew next to nothing about him, except that he'd lost his mother to cancer while very young, and had never quite managed to throw off the image of an orphan trying to put on a brave face. Maybe, she wondered, that was the reason he'd become close to Adam?

With uncanny timing he turned to look directly at Elaine.

'How do you find Adam these days?'

'To live with, do you mean?'

'Yes. Would you say he's changed significantly?'

She was silent, torn between wanting to give an honest answer and – for some inaccessible reason – not wanting to think about Adam at all.

'Yes... yes I think he has. He's less angry at the world. He's stopped blaming it for its ugliness and chaos. But—,' she stopped walking again, perplexed by her visceral reluctance to think it through.

'Go on.'

'He's very... self-obsessed. He's mesmerized by these metal boxes that someone's constantly sending him.'

'Wouldn't you be?'

'Absolutely. I'm not blaming him. I just wish he'd be less secretive. Open up to people. I feel I'm living with some kind of mad scientist. He's a lovely man, I owe him a lot, but I'm afraid I'm just repeating what happened with Jack: I'm living with another unreachable person: I always seem to choose people who are emotionally unavailable, and I hate it. I need intimacy, not paranoid obsessives.'

'Well, this is a chance to change that.'

'Meaning what?'

'Change the kind of people you choose to be with.'

'But I've already chosen, haven't I? You can't go through life changing partners the moment they exhibit some strange behaviour.' She felt unaccountably angry at his implication, as though Mark had personally ensnared her into making those choices.

'No,' he said. 'That's true.' He smiled at her vehemence. 'But you can learn about your motives for making those choices in the first place.'

They were out on the ridge now, following the path's anarchic impulses as it leapt onto summits or dived into the cover of an isolated stand of birches or aspens. She straddled a stile, and suddenly took heart as the wind found her and forcefully buffeted her face.

'I'm not leaving Adam, you know. I've been through all that. It's alright when you're twenty, but not at forty. I've made my bed and I have to lie in it.'

'That's nonsense! What's that all about? Thaa's nobbut a sprog! It's awful to hear you talk like that, as though you're closing down your life. You're just on the brink!'

'Maybe. But there are still rules.'

'Rules are made for people who're afraid to live. I want you to live! A relationship should help us to be more alive, shouldn't it?

'In any case, suppose I did leave Adam. What would I do? Most likely fall for the next emotionally unavailable man that came along. No, Mark. The buck stops here. It's the only way.'

They left the ridge path after a while and began to descend through patches of scrubby birches into rough pasture. Most of the trees were in young leaf and their intermittent small shadows on the ground lent Elaine a sense of protection, as if she were processing through a sacred grove. A pair of buzzards wheeled overhead, no doubt peeved at the intrusion of humans on their hunting ground.

'Janet's cottage is just the other side of that farm. Ten minutes walk.'

'Tell me about her. How long have you known each other?'

'About two years. I wrote to her when I was studying the Middle-east conflicts. She put me in touch with some good people. After that I made a habit of calling on her, and we made a strong connection. She's a bit of a role-model for me I must admit: she's done all the things I'd have liked to have done myself if I'd been clearer about my life.'

'She must have a strong personality to live alone out here.'

'I think she chose it deliberately to cut out all distractions. She's had such a full-on life she felt it was time to try the full-off life while still in possession of her marbles.'

'Good for her. Has she any family still around?'

'I think she has a younger brother. He's something to do with medical research. I don't think they see much of each other. She had a son, who she doesn't get on with either. I don't know what happened. She tends to be dismissive of her family's values. Hence her retreat to this place.'

They walked gingerly through the flooded farm precincts to the accompaniment of suspicious barking dogs. Elaine unlatched the gate across the lane and they climbed until they came in sight of Janet's cottage at a bend in the road. It was one of those old dwellings that seemed to have risen organically out of the earth around it, rather than being constructed by human agents. Its square windows were tiny, and it had a thatch roof in a bad state of repair. A pair of iron horse-shoes flanked the stone entrance.

They felt like truant children as they processed down a narrow corridor whose walls were almost invisible behind cheek-by-jowl framed pictures: smiling family groups, grim-jawed men in uniform, portraits of young girls in hats laughing among roses, and silver-framed postcards from long-ago seaside resorts – all the standard rituals and excursions of a human life. Mark noticed that a thin layer of grey dust resided along all the tops of their frames. Elaine called out before going on, her fingertips lightly brushing each wall, into a dim room pervaded by the optimistic scent of fresh wildflowers.

A woman in her late sixties, with shoulder-length grey hair and wire-rimmed spectacles, hung on a cord was sitting at a table close by one of the deep window embrasures. On the table were a number of tumblers full of cut flowers, and a large chess board with pieces laid out as though interrupted in the middle of a game.

For a moment the woman seemed not to notice that she had visitors. She was reading a long handwritten letter and at intervals emitting a high, staccato cackle which didn't seem to bear much relation to amusement. Elaine said:

'Hello Janet.'

Janet lowered the letter and glared first at Elaine and then Mark.

'He's an utter fool!' She took off her glasses and looked more closely at us. 'Met another woman and decided she's the one he was born to spend the rest of his life with. Idiot! It'll last six months and then he'll be down in the depths of despair again! Hopeless. Utterly hopeless. How do people get into such a state?' She threw the letter onto the floor in disgust. 'Well what are you both standing there for like a pair of stupid tourists?'

'Janet, this is Mark.'

'Yes, I can see that for myself,' she replied. 'Has he got a name?'

'Mark.'

'You call that a name? Why don't you sit down and let some light into the room?'

They did so.

'The trouble is I'm losing my patience. I have no patience with anyone any more. It's not a good sign is it, at my age?'

'I don't know, Janet.'

'Of course you do! It means I'm on my way out! Patience is absolutely essential if one is to live in this world with other human beings. Why are people so stupid? Why don't they think? Has it always been like this?'

'I think it probably has,' Elaine said.

'Then God help us.' She reached painfully down to retrieve her letter. 'This is from my son in America. He's an expert on gene therapy. Can you believe he knows more than anyone else in the world about it? Corporations pay him millions of dollars just for his advice. Or it might be cancer. I'm not sure. It's something very cutting-edge anyway. But when it comes to women he just hasn't a clue. Hasn't the faintest idea. They smell his money and that's it: his brains instantly turn to boiled cabbage. Do you have brains or boiled cabbage?' She returned her glare to Mark who had moved to a tiny raffia chair in front of a window that had a view onto the garden.

'Well, I've been a vegetarian for ten years,' Mark said, 'So I suppose—'.

'And of course you're in love with Elaine.'

Mark stared blankly at the unfinished chess game. Elaine stared at Janet, not believing what she'd heard. Neither answered. There was no possible answer.

Janet said: 'Yes. I see it's true. And you can't do anything about it, that's the worst of it. Words don't count. Rational argument doesn't count. People will just do what they want. Or what their chemistry demands. Never mind. We'll all be dead in a little while, and thank the Lord for that. Imagine if we all lived forever! Can you imagine it? It would be hell. Unmitigated hell. Jealousies and feuds and wars and passions going on forever! Thank God we don't have that, at least. A few years and it's all done with. Do you want ginger beer? Or vodka?'

Mark said: 'Ginger beer please,' but she gave Elaine the ginger beer and Mark the vodka, then subsided into silence, while a thrush launched into his piercing praise-song outside the window. Elaine said:

'Mark isn't my partner, you know. I already have one: he's called Adam.'

'And where is he?'

'Scotland.'

'Why is he in Scotland?' The question was almost an admonishment.

'He had to see an old friend.'

'No, I meant, why is he not here?'

Elaine thought Janet hadn't heard properly.

'He's gone to get some advice from his old tutor, about something technical. He'll be fine.'

'Did he discuss it with you first?'

'No, not really. He's free to go where he likes.'

'Of course. Of course he is. Does he know you're here with Mark?'

'No. We didn't exactly plan that. Mark rang me after Adam had left.'

The old woman looked gravely at each of them in turn. Elaine felt her soul was being taken apart and scrutinized in minutest detail.

Janet said, 'Now you both listen to me. We rarely find completely good people in this world. You have to create goodness in yourself first. Be the change you want to see in the world. Gandhi said that. One of the wisest things that has ever been said. Don't expect anything from others. Least of all those you think you love.'

She poured herself a generous measure of vodka, then added soda before pushing the bottle across the table to Mark as if it were a shining transparent chess piece. Then her face broke into a redeeming smile.

'You are both good people – though not too good, I'm sure. But good people can weaken, just as easily as not so good people. There are moments when we are all tested, usually when we think things are going swimmingly and we're off our guard. Believe me: I know what I'm talking about. The world is full of traps. We are our own traps as well. We must love one another or die. Auden said that. Great poet. Nobody seems to read him any more. Do you like rice pudding?'

'Yes, but there's no need—.' Elaine started up from the table, but the old woman waved her down again.

'I always have rice pudding at tea-time. It's an immemorial custom of this house. You can talk to each other while I'm getting it ready. I'm fairly deaf so you can say exactly what you like.' She rose, slowly negotiating past the labyrinth of chairs before merging into the shadows of her kitchen.

Elaine found her voice first.

'I'm sorry Mark. I hope you're not offended.'
'No. Not in the least. She's right.'
'About what?'
'Everything.'

Elaine found herself unable to bear the silence, and followed Janet into the kitchen. It was unbelievably cramped.

'Did I say too much?' Janet asked. 'I usually do.'

'No, but—'.

'Life is too short for prevarication. There is a time for reticence, of course; but I thought that was not such a time. People need to have the courage to own their feelings, before their feelings own them. That does happen, you know: feelings can take over the domain of judgement. Then you get chaos. As I know only too well. Have you read Tristan?'

'No.'

'Read it. And while you're at it read Iphigenia. And while you're about that read Phaedra. Those should give you something to think about.' She handed Elaine a stack of bowls.

'Are you saying don't fall in love with anyone, ever?'

'No, dear. I'm saying don't disengage your mind while you're doing it. Will you take those through for me, please? There are spoons in the dresser.'

They sat round the elegant walnut table spooning Ambrosia rice pudding and strawberry jam down their throats like three kids on the first morning of their summer holiday. Janet gave a running commentary on the ills of human society and how wonderful was mother Nature's wisdom.

'We've forgotten how to listen. We've forgotten the knack of being alone with ourselves and listening to the great living tides of the Earth. Spring. Summer. Autumn. And then everything sinks into rest and replenishment. You think it's blind chance that the planet circles the sun at twenty-two and a half degrees rather that straight up and down? Well it isn't. It's the cosmic mind. That's what I've learned in my exile here. Though really it's everyone in the cities who are the exiles. Have some more. There's a whole cupboard-full out there. It takes me a long time to get through it. Just help yourselves.'

She sat back and watched intently like a stern housemistress while they refilled their bowls. At one point Elaine looked up and caught Mark looking at her with a gaze of such kindliness and softness that she felt as though an ocean was about to break into her body from some world she'd almost forgotten existed, and felt her face flushing beyond her control. Then Janet's claggy voice saved her.

'Look! Butterflies! Watch a butterfly for five minutes and the butterfly soul inside you begins to wake up, unless you happen to be made of concrete that is. Or worms, moles, spiders, beetles. Almost anything in fact. We have the equivalent of everything within us. That's what this place has taught me. Do you think I'd have learned any of that in London? Not a bit. I'd have learned to compete and make money and succeed at the expense of others. That's what I did for years, in my ignorance.'

'What did you do?' Mark asked, striving to concentrate while accomplishing his assignment of pudding-eating.

'Marketing and public relations, for my sins. Which means image-selling. Re-engineering the truth in accordance with clients' bizarre requirements. And we certainly had some interesting clients. You'd be amazed. All wanting their soiled images reinvented, and their mistakes rewritten as acts of genius. A grubby business I can tell you.'

'I can see how you'd want to get out of that.'

'Oh I actually enjoyed it for a while. When you're young you're only interested in moving up the trough to the deep-end. Of course you kid yourself you're there to change things, to help people; but you soon begin to see you're becoming just like everyone else. I worked for several big-wigs in various government departments, and company heads wanting to paint themselves green, and to a man they were all pleasant, intelligent, socially aware, generous and even kind. But the system always got them. I could see it happening before my eyes. Ideals were quietly abandoned once they'd acquired a secure perch. Promises were either forgotten or redrafted to fit their needs. Compromises were made. Dodgy deals were struck. And I'm sure they never realized that all this was turning them into different people. In the end they were trapped in the prison of who they'd become. And I saw that happening to me, so I jumped just in time. I'm not proud of any of it. It has damaged my faith in people. But I still have my secret soul.'

'I can see that.' Mark smiled in recognition. 'What about your love life?'

'Ah! So you have some curiosity after all! That's good. For a moment I thought you were a Silent Disdainer.' She leant forwards and steepled her hands like someone explaining a difficult scientific concept. 'My love life was very painful and intense. The trouble was I knew exactly what I wanted in a man – and of course it didn't exist. It couldn't.' She gazed wistfully at the fruit trees outside.

'Actually the great love of my life was an artist. I met him in Italy on a long summer holiday between jobs. His name was Giorgio. He was a Venetian, and had lived all his life in Venice. He was becoming quite well known for his painting, and always had at least one exhibition going in one of the main cities – usually Florence or Venice itself. He was tall, wiry, self-possessed, emotionally open, loved eating of course, always had time to listen to my problems and ideas. I started going to all his exhibitions and being me I barraged him with endless questions. What motivates you to work? Do you care about criticism? What are you trying to achieve? How did you get started? Do you have lots of women? Does having sex help to you paint? We started going for long walks and boat rides together so I could continue asking him questions, as I had the idea of writing an article on him for one of the glossy art magazines back in England. We began going out for meals together in Venice, taking rides out to the islands and having picnics, lying in fields listening to the bells, and having endless arguments about art and changing the world. Of course through all of this I was slowly falling in love with him. It became an overriding passion: my every waking moment was filled with delightful images of him and plans for our future.'

Mark asked: 'Did you like his work?'

'Oh but of course! I was in love with him! How could I not like it? He did these increasingly vast canvasses, all abstract planes of colour, and mysterious things happened where they met – or failed to meet, a bit reminiscent of Rothko. But often in the middle of these colour fields he'd drop intricate images of familiar things: a baby, a tree, a computer, a clock, or some mechanical contraption, but invariably immensely detailed and in hyper-real colours. So you got this sense of the familiar enclosed within an alien immensity. A bit like human life, don't you think? Anyway, as he got more confident his canvasses got bigger and bigger – we're talking six by thirty feet now – he said once that he wanted you to lose the sense of a frame altogether – and the details he put in got smaller and smaller and more and more detailed, like whole miniature worlds. You felt you could almost climb right into the picture and explore them like cities. It got difficult to find galleries big enough. He once thought of building his own gallery – but you can't realistically do that in Venice or Florence.'

She took a sip of vodka and sat upright in silence for a time, her glass held loosely in one hand and the other planing over the table surface in odd swirling motions, as though trying to uncover some hidden image buried in its varnish. Then her eyes became very glittery and Mark realized she was remembering something painful.

'Then it all changed. It was towards the end of April. Venice was overflowing with tourists as usual, all desperate to see the same things. Well some of them were worth the bother, I suppose. But by no means all. Anyway Giorgio was spending most nights in his studio finishing off what he thought was his greatest work yet in readiness for the Biennale that summer. We'd moved in together the previous July into a tiny two-room flat in Dorsoduro, right behind a gondola-building factory. It was incredibly cramped, but we were in love and I was thrilled to bits with it. There was a local bakery on the corner that produced the most incredible aromas around five o'clock each morning. And it was ten minutes' walk to the Academmia art gallery, with all the luscious Tintorettos and Titians and Bellinis. What could ever be more romantic?'

'So what went wrong?'

'I'll tell you. Giorgio had left some fresh coffee behind one night that I thought he'd need at the studio. He always gave me strict instructions never to disturb him at his work because he needed total concentration. Which sounded perfectly reasonable. But I suppose there must have been some part of my mind that had suspicions, and I broke the rule and took the coffee. I let myself in with a spare key and climbed up to the studio floor. Giorgio wasn't in the studio, although there were signs he'd recently been working at his new painting: the lights were on, a plate of ham sandwiches lay half-consumed nearby, his pots of paint were all opened on a trolley to one side of the canvas. I called out, feeling suddenly very uneasy.

There was a door off to the right which led, I think, to a small store-room. Suddenly this door burst open and Giorgio stood there dressed only in his underpants. Behind him, on the floor, among the saw-dust and paint stains and used wine bottles lay an attractive and well-developed young woman, completely naked. She didn't bother to get up or even cover herself as I stumbled through the paint-cans and brushes towards her, my eyes brimming with tears and my heart panicking like an injured beast. Giorgio screamed like a madman: 'I told you! I told you never come here at night! Didn't I? Now you've ruined everything!'

'I tried to think of some outraged remark but there really was nothing to say. I turned away and flew from the room. When I was safely in the street again I leant against a lamppost and took a deep breath before breaking down completely. I spent the rest of that night walking, quite oblivious of where I was going. I just needed to get as far away from that studio as possible. Unfortunately you can't get very far from anywhere in Venice: it has the strange tendency to bring you back to where you started from. At last I felt too exhausted to go on and sat on a bench in one of the squares feeling utterly hopeless. I'd been so totally convinced that he was in love with me that I never for one moment entertained the possibility he was seeing someone else regularly. I was consumed first with jealousy, then rage and despair in quick succession. As the sky was lightening about six o'clock I went into one of the early morning cafes to get warm, and it was there that I began to plot my revenge.

'All along I knew it was a disastrous plan of action, but something in me refused to listen. I was incandescent with fury, and set for handing out justice. What particularly galled me was that Giorgio seemed to feel he was in the right, that it was I who had the problem, because I'd broken his no-visiting rule. I felt completely humiliated, trashed, abused, insulted, and all I could think of was to hurt him as much as possible. But not just physically: I wanted to injure his pride, curb his arrogance, expose his hubris. I wanted to wound him in his soft invisible underbelly – which was his idea of himself as a great and celebrated artist. It had to be the painting. It was his crowning glory, and was to be the centre-piece of the Italian pavilion at the Biennale, the biggest piece he'd ever worked on. He'd been developing the design and then the canvas itself for over a year: I knew what it meant to him. It had to be destroyed.

'The problem was, how to achieve the destruction quickly and get far enough away before the hunt was on? Fire would be the most effective method, although of course the most dangerous. It had to be done in the early morning when he always slept. I could get hold of petrol easily enough, and getting into the studio was no problem; but getting away was going to be the challenge: moving anywhere quickly in Venice is difficult at the best of times; but on a spring morning simply moving at all was problematic. I had to have some kind of time-delay device that would give me a couple of hours start. Of course I moved out of our cosy menage immediately, and rented a room under a different name in a passage off Campo Santa Margherita, and spent several weeks planning my escape in precise detail. The delay would only heighten the satisfaction of wreaking vengeance on the nearly completed work when the day came.

Well, the day did come, at the beginning of June – only a week before his exhibition opened. I'd booked a flight to London and planned to be at the airport by the time the thing went up. By the time he'd found out I'd be well airborne.

'I gathered up everything I needed in my rucksack, trudged through the already teeming lanes to his studio, and let myself in. I crept up the stairs to the third floor, when some tiny sound stopped me. It was a brief noise of something creaking, possibly a stool or an easel. I inched towards the studio door, and saw Giorgio working at his masterpiece. My heart froze. My plan was already unraveling, without my having the satisfaction of inflicting a single scratch. This was the moment, and I had to seize it, or be a victim the rest of my life.

'I had the can of petrol ready to throw over the painting, and made sure the matches were to hand, then peered cautiously through the small window. At that exact moment Giorgio got to his feet, picked up something from the paint trolley, and strolled across to the fire escape at the far corner of the room, lighting a cigarette as he went. At the last moment, the gods had delivered him into my hands – almost as though they were egging me on to do the deed of darkness, whether from malice, boredom, or mere curiosity I don't know.

Giorgio had gone out onto the fire escape, allowing the door to close behind him, which meant he wouldn't hear or see me by glancing back into the room. I wondered if he had accidentally locked himself out, which would have been a nicely ironic touch by the watching gods. In any case I thought I could count on maybe two minutes of grace. I crept towards the huge canvas edifice, my heart going like a steam hammer, unscrewed the cap of the can and threw its contents as high as I could manage all along the length of the painting. It seemed to take an eternity. It's actually quite difficult to get a liquid out of a canister onto a vertical surface that is higher than your own head without most of it missing its target and ending up on the floor, but in the end I thought I'd got enough onto it to make a satisfying dramatic finale to Giorgio's career, and to our relationship. I stood back for a moment, fumbling for the matches; but it was at that instant that Giorgio came back into the room. If I'd lit the match the whole place would have become an inferno in seconds. I couldn't do it. I still don't know why. Some other part of my mind took over and prevented me; or maybe the gods had tired of their spectacle and had directed their savage curiosity elsewhere. Instead I turned and ran for all I was worth, back into the street, into the already warm and bright morning.

Somehow – I don't quite know how I did it – I caught my flight back to England, and went to recuperate at a friend's house in Winchester. I calmed down within a few days, and began the long process of becoming sane again – because I do believe to this day that love had unhinged me. I never found out what happened to Giorgio. I presume his precious painting survived, though I don't know what effect its liberal drenching in petrol might have had. It may well have made it a lot more interesting. But I am infinitely grateful to the gods for staying my hand at that crucial moment, and saving my fragile soul from eternal damnation.'

Chapter Twelve

It was early evening and they were well along the ridge path before either of them spoke. Neither was able to put out of their mind Janet's prescient observation regarding Mark; it hung in the air between them in the glow of the sunset, like a living creature that had followed them hopefully for a long time, but which had now taken its place in their lives and could not be avoided. For Elaine it gave rise to such turmoil that she had to distract herself by dwelling forcibly, yet gratefully, on the terrible image of Janet throwing petrol over Giorgio's putative masterpiece.

'I've just realized,' said Mark, 'that we never got around to asking Janet about helping us.'

'Don't you think she helped us then?' Elaine asked, her mind still conjuring the lethal inferno.

Instead of answering, Mark put out his hand until it found Elaine's, and caressed it. To her it felt like a young bird trying to find protection in the camouflage of her fingers. Tears brimmed in her eyes, but despite her shock, she held onto him, and almost involuntarily brought him closer.

'Elaine, don't say anything. You know what I feel, don't you?'

She nodded, exploring his palm and knuckles and fingertips, as if they were a wholly unsuspected continent. They walked on, silently, into the motionless shadows of the wood.

Over supper Elaine steeled herself to hold to her decision.

'Mark. This absolutely has to stop. It's pointless. It can't go anywhere at all. I'm sorry. There's no way we can do this.' She stared miserably into the calm darkness outside the window, as though it might miraculously offer a way of doing it if asked correctly.

'I understand, of course,' Mark said. 'But it in no way alters the situation, does it? We've fallen in love.'

'You may have, possibly. I haven't.'

'I don't believe you.'

A desperate edge came into her voice. 'You have to believe me.'

'I don't. The only thing I have to believe is the truth.'

'Mark, listen to me. I left Jack because I believed my relationship with him was ignoring both our needs: I needed intimacy and he needed his work. He already had what he needed, I thought. Then I chose Adam because I believed both our needs coincided: we both needed intimacy. I thought care and openness would do the trick, turn things around. But he seems to be just the same as Jack, withdrawing into his obsession with these aliens. I feel stranded again.'

She stopped, her voice breaking under the emotion.

'I can't just go on breaking up people's lives because my needs aren't being met. I like you enormously. But who's to say the same thing won't happen with us, four, five years down the line? I've done enough damage. And anyway you have your work, which is important. I have to find my own way through this. I don't want to become dependent on you. Maybe I should just go away and live alone, like Janet. She seems to have found some peace.'

Mark took her hand lightly. She could not withdraw it.

'So you're not going to ask me to stay?'

'Adam will be back.'

He spoke very quietly, so she was obliged to look at him directly to hear his words.

'That isn't an answer, is it? No, don't say anything. What I see, what I think you're doing, is saving Adam from himself. You justified leaving Jack by convincing yourself Adam needed you more than Jack did. That you could bring him round, make him happy. But you can't, of course: he has to discover his own path. And there's another thing you seem to have ignored: in all this time I haven't heard you once say you love him.'

Elaine looked utterly miserable.

'I just don't know anymore. I've no right to talk about love to anybody. I've no right to even say the word. I feel a complete fake.'

'Maybe we're all fakes.'

'No, we're not. We're all hurt, warped, or damaged, but not fakes. At least not most of the time. In any case, I'm not going to hurt Adam like I hurt Jack. I've learn't that lesson at least.'

'In trying not to hurt him you may end up hurting him more.'

'Mark, what are you trying to do? Prove that whatever I do I'll inflict more pain? Well I know that already, and I can't bear it.'

She stumbled across to the window, hiding her face in her hands, while her body surrendered at last to a storm of weeping.

He came up to her and held her lightly. After a while she calmed, blew her nose, and returned to the table.

'I think it would be best if you went now, Mark. I'm really sorry.'

He knew what she was saying, and felt a quiet tide of happiness pass through him.

'Yes, alright.' He gathered his things and moved towards the lobby. 'Can I call you sometime?'

'Yes,' she whispered, unable to trust her voice to obey her. Then finding courage, repeated more loudly, 'Yes, of course you can.'

She stood listening to his steps fading down the deserted lane, until they were quite gone. Then she went to the bedroom and sat with her head propped against the pillows, feeling more alone than she could ever remember.

Chapter Thirteen

I lay awake for two hours in the bare room at the top of the house before abandoning my attempt to sleep and returning to the still-warm kitchen. The stove gave out an unvarying furtive glow from deep in the pit of its iron crucible. Our little cube-construction still stood in its clearing on the table like a house that had been reprieved from demolition amidst the rubble of spare cubes and the encroaching domestic debris. I lit a small lamp in a corner and contemplated the scene.

It was beautiful in a way that entirely transcended its physical form; somehow it communicated the living body of beauty, or harmony; it had a wholeness – a health – about it; and as I watched, the idea came into my head that it wanted to grow. I went over and quickly added another layer, making it a four-unit cube, but I knew it still wasn't happy, or I wasn't quite happy, and I immediately made it into a five-unit cube. This seemed at once to satisfy its need for growth, and I returned to my seat by the stove feeling I'd done a good night's work in thirty seconds.

The wind that had sounded like the voices of a hundred howling demons earlier in the evening had finally dropped to a dead calm, so that every crack of the fire and every shift of a roosting bird seemed magnified against the huge absence. I wondered what I should do with the next two days: explore the hills, read some of Magnus's rare books, or see what else I could build with my alien construction outfit? All the options seemed attractive, yet when I thought of Magnus and his physical state it seemed obvious what was needed: immediate and practical help with the house cleaning. I could spend these next days cleaning the place and making it, at the very least, somewhere where an old friend in his last years might find some peace.

Even as I was weighing up the pros and cons of this radical course of action I was finding a mop, bucket, broom, bin-liners, dust pan, cleaners and disinfectant, and making a start on clearing several years of grime and rubbish from the flagged floor. By four o'clock I was still doing it. By four thirty my initial energy was starting to flag, and I took a break. The stove was almost cold, and I decided to feed it with dry wood before it went out entirely. It was while I was engrossed in this pleasant diversion that I heard a small noise like the accelerating slide of a soft garment to the floor behind me. Naturally I assumed it was Magnus, come down to investigate the unaccustomed nocturnal activity. Without turning I called out:

'Hi Magnus. I'm sorry if I disturbed you.'

There was no response. I finished feeding some larger blocks into the firebox and clanged the door shut to generate a draught, before turning to satisfy my torpid curiosity. I don't think I will ever forget the sight that met my eyes in the gloom beyond the table: it was the figure of an attractive young woman of about thirty, of slight build, with greyish matted hair reaching well below her shoulders, and dark, liquid blue-grey eyes: it was Rachel.

Without any conscious decision I rose to my feet and stared across at her, as the wedding guest might well have stared, slack-jawed and speechless, at the demented face of the ancient mariner on the windswept cliff-path. She gazed back at me, with an expression I could not read – not hostile, but not quite friendly either; not unhappy, yet entirely free of anything that could be construed as gladness. And then I remembered the time I'd last seen her, in the disaster-zone that, before the Visitors started mucking around with the universal constants, had been a pleasant market town near the Dorset coast: the same dispassionate, and at the same time oddly compassionate, unwavering intimacy.

In shock I cried out, 'Rachel! It's impossible!'

'How are you, Adam?' Still no trace of the mobility that might have become, given propitious conditions, a smile.

'I thought... you were dead!'

'Yes. That's right.'

'But you're talking to me!' She moved round the table towards the lamplight, and I saw she was dressed in the same full-length grey, almost featureless woolen dress I'd last seen her in five years ago: shapeless yet uncannily feminine.

'Try to let go of all these labels, Adam. They're just no use. You've conjured my form up, and here I am. I can be both alive and dead. I can do all the things I did when I was what you call 'alive', plus a few more, except stay forever, because my form is still dependent on energy.'

'It's very good to see you, anyway.' And it really was: I felt unaccountably grateful for her coming, in spite of the fact that I'd known her in life for such a short time. 'Are you cold? Come and warm yourself.'

'I'm not cold, thank you. I've come because there's a bond between us, and you needed me.'

'Did I? How did you know?'

'I'm part of your mind.'

'Oh Jesus! That's way too metaphysical. Do you mean telepathy?'

'If you like. Though distance in the physical sense is meaningless.'

I suddenly had the feeling that she was like a guardian angel, watching every corner of my life – even the corners I couldn't see into myself – from some perch slightly to one side of time and space, and without my saying this out loud, she immediately responded:

'Angel isn't a bad image. Though it doesn't imply I'm any kind of special being. I'm just a human: not particularly good or wise.'

'You know, I find that oddly comforting. I hate good people. They make me feel I have to be especially bad, just to balance things up.'

Still no smile. But I knew she understood me.

'I'd offer you tea, but I seem to remember—.'

'That's ok. I don't need to drink.'

'Rachel, if you're really my guardian angel, I'd appreciate your advice.'

'Of course.'

Maybe, I thought, the smile was in her voice.

'I've made so many bloody stupid mistakes in my life, I can't afford to make any more. I want to set things straight. Get it right at last, before I pop my clogs for good. But there's something that always stops me. I've no idea what, but I've got to root it out and get rid of it. It's literally driving me insane. It's sabotaging all my attempts to be close to people.'

'You've already given yourself the answer.'

'What do you mean?'

'Helping Magnus. That's making you close to him.'

'But it was just obviously the only thing to do.'

'And you did it. That's what's different.'

'It seems easier with men. Women – forgive me saying this – seem to drive me up the wall very very quickly.'

'Women are people.'

Was that a dead-person joke, I wondered? Maybe there was hope.

'I suppose so. But they have a knack of conjuring up my worst demons. The ones I prefer to keep well chained up in the deepest basement.'

'Oh yes. I know that.'

In retrospect it wasn't the most appropriate thing to say, given that I'd attacked, raped and strangled her to death a very few years ago. But Rachel genuinely didn't seem to harbour any trace of a grudge: she simply acknowledged I'd lost the plot with her in a rather serious way, and was now trying to redress things. Perhaps that was one of the little skills that angels – sorry, that is to say, not particularly good people with angel status – happened to have: helping people to change their lives by virtue of being both in and out of life at the same time.

'Everything you do,' she went on, 'makes a difference. How much of a difference generally depends on how hard it is. Some things are impossible for us at one time in our lives, and relatively easy later on, when we're a bit more distant from the pain. For instance what caused all the bother between you and me was nothing to do with Magnus having sex with me, but what had happened to you many years before. Your behaviour was simply the gradual working out of all that pain and shame when you were young that was never resolved.'

'Yes, that kind of makes sense. Though it doesn't justify what I did.'

'Justice has very little meaning in eternity, Adam. What we generally want isn't justice but vengeance. An eye for an eye.'

'But we can make amends though, can't we?'

'We can try to change our habits. If we're sufficiently motivated.'

'I really want to make it work with Elaine. She's the best woman I've met in this life.'

'Then you must be completely open with her. Don't run away when your demons get stirred up.'

'Do I?'

'Why did you come here?'

'To see Magnus. I needed his help. And he needed mine.'

'Maybe Elaine needs you more than Magnus just now?'

'You think so? She's very self-sufficient. She needs a lot of space.'

'But she also needs intimacy.'

'So do I.'

'But you avoid it when certain things are challenged. You blame others who are not the cause of your pain.'

'Rachel, how the hell do you know all this?'

'You keep forgetting: I'm dead. There are far fewer barriers.'

'Between you and living people?'

'Yes. And between past and future. And between worlds.'

'Can you move about in this world? I mean, could you be with me when I'm with Elaine?'

'If necessary. Although it does take a lot of concentration for my consciousness to be in one place for a long time. I'm beginning to drift away from here already, for instance. I won't be able to stay much longer.'

'Will you come to Elaine's? It would be infinitely helpful having your advice and perspective when things get difficult. I mean do you have much else to do?'

'I go where I can be of some use. But it takes a certain energy to maintain my human consciousness, memories, remembering how to walk and all that. But I will visit you.'

'Thanks. I've got so many questions.'

'Yes. Everyone has. But not everyone gets the answers they want. Just remember, if you value Elaine, it's vital that you trust her.'

'But how do you trust someone who—.'

I glanced towards the window for a second to see the first quickening of the dawn sky, and when I looked back she'd gone – or at least her grey-clad figure had become indistinguishable from the shadows. I called her name, and fancied I heard a faint voice, like embers dropping, from the still-dark corner, but it was almost certainly only my weary brain losing the plot again.

Chapter Fourteen

I slept deeply and dreamlessly until almost midday. When I at last emerged into the kitchen Magnus was deep in his chair clasping his huge rainbow-coloured mug, and sunlight was nestling among the washed dishes, wineglasses and stray books stacked on the table. The little cube-house was still in the place I'd left it when I'd had my unexpected night visitor.

Magnus said through a mouthful of something:

'Adam, I want to say how much I appreciate your efforts. They are heroic! I don't deserve it, that's for sure. But I'm grateful.'

'The pleasure's entirely mine,' I said rather self-importantly. 'But I can't stay much longer, and you're going to need some long-term help. We must fix something up for you before I go.'

'Oh I really don't know about that, Adam.' He squirmed around, trying to get comfortable. I could smell the brandy he'd jazzed his tea with, and it made me feel slightly nauseous. 'The old body is finally rebelling against the garbage I've shoveled into it over the years. Absolutely everything aches.' Another protracted attempt to relieve his discomfort. 'Adam, my advice to you as a dear friend: don't get old.'

I debated whether to tell him about Rachel, and decided against it. In the calm morning light my bizarre conversation had begun to seem more and more unreal, almost dangerous, as if my mind were tipping over the edge, and part of me wanted to banish the memory to the realm of a guilt-created fantasy.

I cooked up some porridge for both of us, then positioned myself at the table so I could see the outside world coming into new and normal life. After we'd eaten Magnus said:

'I want to show you something, Adam. If you wouldn't mind helping me up to the library. A small discovery I made which may interest you.'

The climb must have taken us twenty minutes, every moment of which was an effort of will for Magnus. The tottering stacks of books at every turn which had been such a hazard in the gloom five years ago had evolved into cobwebbed libraries in their own right. The prints on the wall had gone though, and not even a dust-free shadow remained to betray their existence. The stranger thing though was the light: it got decidedly dimmer as we ascended, even though there were prominent windows at each landing.

'I've been thinking for some time,' Magnus wheezed as he negotiated the staircase, 'of moving everything down a floor, so I'm spared this odyssey every time I need to consult a book. But I don't suppose I'll get round to it now, especially without Myra.'

'I could do it for you.'

I immediately saw what a vast task it would be, and half regretted making the offer.

'That's kind, but you couldn't possibly do it alone. There are nearly two thousand books up there. It would probably kill you.'

We'd got half-way up the first flight, and Magnus had to rest against the panelling. 'The alternative of course, would be to sell it to a suitable university. As a going concern, so to speak.' He chuckled.

We managed a further four steps before Magnus launched into a tirade on the decline of the universities.

'Dammit Adam, they've no right to call themselves universities any more. They're just machines for serving the needs of industry. What has learning got to do with that? They're nothing but pimps. It's bloody sickening. They ought to be creating the values of society, revivifying the roots of our culture, but instead they just trim their sails to the current breeze – which is, whether it will make money – which of course we all know means attracting foreign students who pay huge fees – then it gets into the curriculum. What hope for alchemy? Let alone what used to be called the liberal arts? Oh Adam, I've become an exile in a profane world! I don't think I want to live in it any more.'

I was about to say that many great philosophers and artists have found themselves exiles and still enriched the world, but the truth was that I found this lament so distressing that I wanted to abandon myself to a fit of sympathetic wailing for the lost glories of once noble humanity; but I was the helper now, and I had to somehow get Magnus at least to the first floor and out of danger of falling headlong over his own disowned learning.

'Five more steps, Magnus. Can you do that?' I got his arm around my shoulders and heaved upright until his huge figure responded.

'Blasted Labour government –,' he was almost shouting up at the indifferent landing window – 'that's when the rot began. Pretending they were making higher education available to everyone when in reality they were abolishing it altogether! How dare they? They all deserve fucking shooting!'

'Forgive me Magnus, but as I recall, in the days when you were my tutor you were railing against the academic boards for insisting on the classical syllabus! Or am I misremembering?'

He stared at me as though I'd pulled a gun on him.

'Et tu Brute?' Then he broke into a deafening thunderclap of laughter. 'Yes Adam, it's true! You're right.' And the laughter uncoiled, rattled the window and resounded high in the unvisited recesses of the house. 'But what I was really set against was dead teaching, not the classics themselves. Teachers who taught because they had to, without conviction, and the students just learnt it mechanically, without any love or understanding. That's what brought out the rebel in me, and got me into such trouble. Still, I reckon they benefitted from my presence, all the same. Every school needs its maverick. I got that streak from my Dad. He was far worse than me.'

'Can you make another three steps?'

'Of course, dear boy. Just for you. Just need to get my breath first. Wouldn't it be great if we had a gravity switch at the foot of the stairs, like we have a light switch? Could you get your little cubic friends to fix it for me?' He laughed again, then erupted into a hacking cough. 'Just switch off gravity and float up like a balloon. What d'you think?'

What I was thinking about was the curious coincidence of Rachel appearing just after I'd completed rebuilding the cube. Was that co-incidence? Or could my arrangement of little cubes have somehow conjured her from my unconscious? After all, I'd spent more time in her company in that house that anywhere else; maybe the cubes were using the energy of my association with her to recreate her for my pleasure and edification?

I told him what had happened in the night.

'Do you think that's possible? That that cube-thing could have something to do with it? Or am I just being weird again?'

'I think it's entirely possible, given what tricks the original one got up to. The human mind is still ninety-nine percent a mystery to us. Actually, make that ninety-nine point nine percent. So who's to say it can't interact with alien technology?'

'After I'd added that extra layer to it I felt elated, you know? As though I'd just created an original work of art, or fallen in love. And then out of nowhere Rachel appeared, as real as rain. And what's just occurred to me now is, what would happen if we added yet another layer? After all, we've a lot of the blighters left over. Maybe the effect is proportional to its volume?'

In this way we at last made it to the top floor, where Magnus was forced to rest. A large gilt-framed mirror was leant against the wall facing the window, as though it had been put there temporarily the day it arrived, and no one had got around to hanging it. Because of its position and size it felt like an open doorway into another part of the house. I imagined the world transformed into a place of doorways opening onto more landings and galleries and unsuspected vistas.

'Yes, he was a right bloody bastard,' Magnus muttered from the grey wicker armchair he'd fallen into, his hands splayed out over the wide arms of the chair like things which might set off on a journey of their own at any moment. 'Overbrimming with inexplicable hatreds and prejudices. How I managed not to murder him all those years I'll never know.'

'What did he do for a living?'

'He was into cement. He built up a substantial fortune by doing lucrative deals with various local authorities. But there was something dodgy about everything he did: he seemed compelled to add something to the simplest business deal that benefitted himself and exploited someone else. I don't know how he kept out of prison to be honest. He was a genius at covering his tracks. I think I've inherited some of that. Dammit, why can't we just shut the door on our past and have done with it? Why do we have to drag it all with us to foul up the beauty of the present?' He was in genuine distress now, as though the accumulated failings of his life had at that exact moment achieved critical mass and crystallized into a physical form before him. He fumbled for a handkerchief and blew his nose noisily several times. 'Let's make another attempt on this wretched mountain, shall we?'

We managed to make it to the next landing in a single assay, before Magnus had another excruciating fit of remembering.

'You know, Adam, what I really hated was the way he'd cheat on my mother. It was despicable. He'd no consideration at all for her feelings. In fact I think he genuinely believed she didn't have any: he used her to get his own needs met and then he'd just ignore her until he needed her again. Why she stuck it I'll never know. He was wealthy and provided a kind of security I suppose. He'd invite tarts to the house right in her presence without a word to her. Some nights he'd have two at the same time. He made no attempt at all to be discreet about it. I could sometimes hear him fucking them in the bedroom while my mother was downstairs trying to drown out the sound with the radio. I felt so angry on her behalf because she never once stood up to him. I still feel bloody angry actually. Time doesn't seem to dim that particular memory, even if it devastates everything else.'

I couldn't help thinking that his own behaviour with Rachel betrayed more than a hint of like father like son, but I refrained from saying so.

We lurched like a couple of oxygen-starved climbers up five more steps before Magnus veered sideways and grabbed the bannister, his voice cracking and his eyes streaming.

'It's insufferable! Insufferable! That poor woman went through hell! Ye gods, why? She could have walked out and been free; she was still good-looking. She could have started her life again. She pitied him, I suppose. She imagined she could save him. God in heaven! Why do so many women try to save savage irredeemable men? Answer me that, will you?'

Again I had no answer. How could I? I'd been savage and irredeemable myself. I'd been a monster too. That night with Rachel I'd thought of nothing but my own monstrous needs. I hadn't cared a fig what might happen to her: I'd become less than human; I'd turned into my own demon. And worse, I'd got away with it. For some unaccountable reason I was still living while Rachel was dead – even though I'd just met her and held a long sensible conversation with her. I wished I'd talked to her about that. Was my being alive a mistake? Should I have turned myself in as soon as I'd seen what I'd done? But then I'd watched her walk out of my flat smiling and thanking me for a lovely evening. Didn't she realize I'd just raped and murdered her, only a few hours before?

'Magnus,' I said, trying to manhandle his whale of a body onto the next step, 'I'm entirely as savage as your father was; I can't condemn him. But I certainly pity him. Let's hope he learned something from it.'

'I can't pity him, Adam. I've still got too much hate for him. Those images won't simply dissolve. And now he's probably one of those wailing souls up to his neck in the boiling tar of Dante's inferno, screaming throughout eternity, stabbed and skewered continually by the red-hot blades of those ghastly demons, with no hope of an end to it. And still I can't pity him! I still want him to suffer agony for what he did. There's the real tragedy. For God's sake let's get to that damned library, if it still exists. I have a bottle of very good Jamesons up there that might mitigate our woes. Onward and upward!'

Somehow we reached the library and staggered inside. It was just as I remembered it, though far dustier, and had a derelict air about it. Magnus sank into yet another decayed armchair, raising a thick cloud of evil-smelling dust, before giving directions for finding the whiskey he'd secreted against just such a time of need.

'To hell with the whole sorry heap anyway!' he shouted as he gave me a glassful of the pale golden liquid. 'Long live life!'

The table where I'd found him in copulatory bliss with Rachel was still loaded with his prized alchemical and philosophical tomes; her prone slender half-naked figure bedded like a sea-nymph between the reefs of books was still imprinted on my memory like a nuclear shadow-image. I wondered if he recalled that moment now with pride, shame or indifference? But of course it was one of those questions I couldn't ask.

At the base of each ceiling-high stack of shelves was a shallow drawer which he now directed me towards.

'In one of those drawers you'll find a blue box. Could you bring it to me please?'

I gave him the box. Inside was an irregular black lump of something like coal, about two inches long.

'You remember this?' He handed me the piece of rock. It took me a while to recognize the fragment that he and Rachel had found lodged in a recess of the hermit's cell out on the moor. It felt astonishingly light.

'I had it analyzed. It's not terrestrial. They thought it must be a fragment of meteorite until they discovered they were completely unable to get it to interact with anything at all. But I'll bet you anything you like its composition is identical to your little tin boxes downstairs.'

I was beginning to put two and two together at an alarming rate. 'Has this been up here ever since you found it?'

"Pretty well, yes. Except for its brief visit to the analyst.'

'This may strike you as bizarre, but it might just account for that weird experience I had with an illustration in one of these books.'

I told him how one of the figures had changed position and then reverted back again. 'I couldn't believe what I'd seen at the time. I put it down to lack of sleep and general disorientation. But if this is cube-material, I'd rule nothing out.'

'You could be right,' Magnus went on. 'The alien technology is clearly capable of interacting with our minds directly. The question is, how much more of this stuff is scattered around the world? Maybe it's the remains of a previous attempt to renovate our primitive mental wiring? Maybe they've been observing us for thousands of years, and there've been many attempts to make us into cosmic citizens? They must really be serious about it.'

'Oh, they are.' The truth was I couldn't imagine them giving up until we were rendered safe – in which case it was arguable that we would no longer be human.

'In that case we have to take them seriously. You have to crack the code of those bloody tin cans downstairs. How about, for a start, ringing Elaine and finding out how many more you have? Then we'd have some figures to go on.'

I hesitated, although I knew it was a good suggestion. 'I'm reluctant to talk to Elaine just now, Magnus. I don't know why.'

'What do you fear might happen?'

'I've really no idea. I just feel she needs more space. I don't want her to think I'm keeping tabs on her.'

'Are you?'

'Possibly. I don't want to go back to that state of constant paranoia I was in with Cora. I think that's what finally did for our relationship.'

'You know Adam, trust is a strange thing. It steers a very narrow course between dependence and indifference. And it so easily slips from the one to the other without anyone noticing.'

'You think that's what is happening?'

'I don't know. But with Cora and Rachel you were undoubtedly emotionally entangled, if you'll excuse my saying so, in a neurotic dependence. I think the danger with Elaine is you'll shift to indifference, merely out of the fear of its opposite.'

'Does it have to be one or the other?'

'No, but it's a present danger, I would say. The ghost of your past relationship with Cora lies so heavy upon you that you steer directly towards indifference – an assumed indifference, that is – to avoid it. Scylla and Charybdis, my friend. It requires a very experienced pilot indeed to navigate those waters.'

'Rachel was warning me about that, I think, just before she disappeared.'

'Then you must take it seriously. Phone Elaine.'

But the day went by and I put it to the back of my mind, and it was early evening before I got it together to phone her, and then I got her answerphone. If I'm honest I have to admit it was a relief not to have to speak to her.

I'd spent the whole afternoon cleaning the other rooms of the house, while Magnus remained engrossed in his library, looking for a particular text dealing with the variously hued serpents of attachment and indifference. He eventually staggered downstairs with the book, and presented me with it as if it were the original Dead Sea Scrolls.

'I want you to have this Adam. A small token of my gratitude.'

It was a book of alchemical texts and commentaries, printed in the early eighteenth century. It must have been worth a fortune.

'Priceless,' Magnus agreed. 'But there's no one on earth I'd rather give it to. It contains the true life-story of the heart.'

From its weight I could well believe it. It had thick dark-red boards with various symbols gold-stamped on the front, back and spine. The title was only on the spine, and read: 'The Golden Art'. There was no author mentioned. When I opened it, the pages felt stiff and crisp, and their surface slightly rough, and were untrimmed on the fore-edge. There was no doubt that this was indeed a very early, if not original, edition from the great age of printing, and I was stunned that Magnus had made me a present of it. I stared at him, bereft of words.

'I'm more than happy for you to have it. I know you'll make good use of it. And I'm not likely to read it again. One needs a certain kind of energy to engage with that kind of work, and I no longer have it, I fear. But a word of caution: it's only a book: it can't do the work for you.' He poured himself a drink and lowered himself by degrees into his chair. 'Which reminds me, did you speak to Elaine?'

'I left her a message.'

'Ah.'

'I really don't want to pester her, you know? She's probably working. She switches her phone off for days at a time if she's deeply into a project.'

'Well you know her best.'

After Magnus had retired for the night I stoked up the fire and sunk myself in the book, half wondering if Rachel would appear a second time. The bizarre thing was, for all that she was clearly a 'manifestation' of my mind – whether facilitated by the cube or not – I still fancied her like crazy. She still had that dreamy, sensuous, half in the other world quality about her that I had been so strongly attracted by at our first meeting. And it wasn't as though she was a ghost: when I'd touched her hand, sitting beside her in that devastated Dorset town, it had been unequivocally composed of warm and responsive flesh and blood.

I opened the book at random and read:

"The hunting of Venus has begun;
Truly, if the dog catches the hare,
The latter will not grow old.
This is realized by Mercurius, for when
Venus begins to rage,

*She produces a terrible number of hares.
Therefore guard Mars with your sword
That Venus does not turn into a whore."*

Below this text there was an illustration of two crowned lions, male and female, fighting to the death, against the background of a river and mountains and a distant castle.

I wondered if the cubes might work their magic on this as they did five years ago in Magnus's library: I thought it very probable, as these were properly designed tools custom-made for the job, as it were, and not a random lump of raw material which happened to be in the same room as the book. To aid the experiment, I added all the remaining cubes I'd brought with me to the pile we'd already built: unfortunately there weren't enough to complete another 'Fibonacci' layer, and I ended up with something resembling a piece of 1980s postmodernism, without the knobs. Then I laid the open book next to the cubes, made myself some fresh coffee, and waited. Half an hour passed, then an hour, and another; I restrained myself from checking on the illustration, but around one o'clock I couldn't wait any longer and scrutinized the picture for any slight changes to the figures, but there were none whatsoever.

I confess I was downcast at this failure, but put it down to the fact that I'd not been able to complete the larger cube with my remaining small ones, which had clearly disrupted its symmetry. I became consumed with longing to see Rachel again, not for her body, but because I needed the consolation of her quiet, non-judgmental empathy. There was a growing desolation in me, and I couldn't decide why; it had no apparent rational cause: I was with a good friend, I had a loving partner; I had my health; I had my sanity; I had my freedom. Millions would give their eyesight for any of these blessings. And yet it was pointless to deny it: something, some fear or half-sensed knowledge was eating away at my fugitive sense of well-being.

I'd just decided to abandon my experiment and get some sleep when I heard a slight sound, seeming to come from the far side of the room by the end window. I immediately thought Rachel had returned in response to my craving for her, but there was no visible sign of her. Yet I had the unmistakable feeling that she was in the room with me. I called her name, then sat listening intently. Although there were no further sounds, the sense of her close presence was overwhelming. I crept around the room, trying to identify where it was strongest. At one point I smelt a faint perfume of oranges that was strongly erotic, and which immediately conjured her body more than any sound could have done.

I called out Rachel's name again, but there was no response except a tiny sound like a mouse treading on a dead leaf – which may have been exactly that. But then I felt something soft brush the back of my hand. I started back, expecting to see her grey-clad figure materialize before me.

'Rachel, I know you're here. Can you speak?'

The uncanny brushing on my hand came again. I raised my arm, trying to grasp her's, but only found empty space. It was shocking, this intimacy bereft of substance. I had no doubt at all that she was with me, hearing and seeing me; but the lack of a corresponding physical form deeply unnerved me. I felt myself on the threshold of an open entrance into another world that was at my very feet yet completely invisible.

'Rachel.' I muttered into the near air, 'What do you want?'

There was an immediate movement of air, and I felt a half-physical hand take mine with extreme gentleness and urge it sideways towards that terrible portal. It was then that panic took hold of me, and I shrank back from the contact. Immediately all sense of Rachel's presence vanished from my mind, and I felt truly alone: even the subtle scent of orange blossom had gone. I instantly regretted my fear, but of course it was too late: the mysterious connection had been broken – maybe forever.

The next day dawned fine and calm, with an invigorating sense of new life in the air. I realized, after the night's incursions into my confused psyche, that I should leave at once and return to Elaine. When over breakfast I told him of the night's events, Magnus was immediately understanding.

'You've been an immense help,' he said, 'but I agree the time has come. Your work is with Elaine, there's no doubt of it.'

'I seriously blew it last night. I felt I was being drawn down into some kind of insane mirror world. As if Rachel was using her sexuality to trap me and keep me away from normal life. That's why I panicked. I'd thought she was my protecting angel, but she suddenly changed into a devil. I couldn't handle it.'

'In alchemy that's the beginning of the work: things appear to change into their opposites: fair is foul and foul is fair. You have to trust that they are still what they originally were. Their job is to destroy your ego-illusions.'

'Are you saying that Rachel was trying to help me by being seductive?'

'Of course: she was showing you an aspect of your unconscious that you need to see before you can have your heart's desire. She was showing you what's impeding your progress.'

'So maybe I should stay here after all and learn what I can.'

Magnus laughed. 'Much as I'd love you to stay, I don't think this is where your real work lies. I think trusting Elaine is a far greater challenge for you.'

'Can't I trust her at a distance?'

His uproarious laughter echoed again through the building. 'No. It's too easy to fool yourself because you aren't faced with your own unsatisfied infantile needs. It's known as katabasis: descending to the root.'

'I was afraid you'd say that. The trouble with true friends is they tell you the truth!'

'You could always come back again, of course. When the summer finally arrives I may be well enough for a trek up to the moors.'

'I'll look forward to that.'

Despite both Rachel's and Magnus's advice, I delayed returning home for another two days. I felt I hadn't completed my self-assigned task of cleaning the house, and the thought of him living in a filthy chaotic environment because he was unable to clean up for himself was painful. Also I very much wanted to see the moors again, and to revisit the alchemist's hillside cell. When I reached it I was shocked to discover it had all but disappeared. Many of the stones had been taken away, and the back wall cut into the hillside had been infilled with cement. I stool silently in its interior listening to the bleak cries of moorland birds, and remembering the voice of the supposed author of my own life that had spoken to me out of the whirlwind. It all seemed like a fantasy now: something that belonged to a phase of history that had already passed, and taken with it a sense of the miraculous nature of the universe.

There were so many regrets in my life that I felt I had to achieve something significant to redeem it, yet what that might be continued to elude me. I suppose you might say my relationship with Elaine was an achievement in itself – yet I had no sense of peace in it: there was always something secretly gnawing away at the roots, undermining all sense of joy and fulfillment; and this in the face of my unshakeable knowledge that Elaine loved me, and found our relationship nurturing. It was as though there was inside me a virus of dissatisfaction, which prevented me from enjoying any fruits of my struggle to put my life on a firm human basis. But I'd reached a point where I felt this state of things had to change, whatever the cost.

I said goodbye to Magnus on a clear, still morning blazoned with birdsong: in the few days I'd spent with him we'd become very close; and I was apprehensive about how he'd survive with failing health through the year ahead. But at least I had his book, which was a kind of psychic link between us. And I had the memory of Rachel's serene manifestations, which had brought a new and bizarre element into the already complex equation of my relationships.

Chapter Fifteen

'You don't need to push yourself so hard you know.' Elaine had just brought the tea out to the garden. 'There's no panic about it. It won't make any difference if you leave it a week or two.'

I was sweating profusely from my work on the greenhouse and felt grateful for the refreshment.

'I want to get it done while the weather's holding. June is notoriously unreliable.'

She folded a blanket on the grass and squatted on it. 'It's kind of you to do it, but I do wish you'd just relax a bit. You don't look like you're enjoying it.'

'Don't I?'

'No. You look like your life depends on getting it right. It isn't an entrance exam you know.'

'I thought I was enjoying it until you pointed that out. Anyway there isn't much more. Another day or two should take care of it.'

'I want you to enjoy life Adam. I hate seeing you putting yourself through these, whatever they are – trials. It's like you don't believe you've the right to enjoy anything unless you've paid for it in blood and toil!'

'Maybe that is what I believe.'

'Well that's awful! I think that's a really sad state to be in. Where does all that stuff come from?'

'That's exactly what I'm having all this horribly expensive therapy to find out. This is wonderful tea by the way.'

'It's Oolong. Mark brought it from Dorchester. He knows a place where you can get any kind of tea on the planet.'

'I wish he wouldn't keep buying all this exotic stuff. He's not exactly well off is he?'

'He has a generous nature.'

'I don't doubt it. But I'd rather he didn't broadcast the fact quite so widely.'

'That isn't fair Adam. He hardly broadcasts it. He isn't that sort of person.'

'Why are you defending him?'

'Because you're attacking him.'

'Why is no one ever on my side? I always feel I have to fight for the right to express an opinion. Why don't you ever support me?'

Elaine was suddenly silent. She sat looking at the ground and listening to a nearby thrush going through his repertoire. Our conversations these days always seemed to reach this stalemate: Elaine retreating into silence and me feeling isolated and wrong-footed. It felt horribly familiar, but I'd learned at least not to go stomping off in an uncontrollable fury.

The thrush came to a pause in his plangent aria, leaving the succeeding moments noticeably poorer. Suddenly it seemed ludicrous that we were arguing over a mutual friend whose only crime was to have given us some expensive tea.

'I'm sorry.' I said. 'Something was bugging me, that's all.'

'Do you know what it was?'

'It was what you said about the way I work. I felt whatever I did I couldn't get it right. If I do nothing I'm wasting my life. If I work I'm accused of trying to prove something. That just puts me into a tail-spin.'

'I wasn't accusing you; I was trying to point out a pattern I'd noticed, that's all.'

'It felt like an accusation.'

'Well you could ask yourself why it felt like that.'

'I ask myself that all the time, Elaine; but I never come to an answer. I just get more and more frustrated. And this psychologizing just makes it worse.'

'You really should be kinder to yourself.'

'Yes. I was thinking. Why don't we have a holiday together? We haven't been anywhere together since that terrible week in Devon when I went into meltdown. It's time we had a real one, don't you think?'

'It's a great idea. But I have my course starting in September. It'll have to be soon.'

'Fine by me. Where do you fancy?'

'I'd really like to see Cornwall again. I used to go there as a child. There are dozens of quiet coves that hardly anyone knows about.'

My disappointment must have been obvious, because she added:

'You weren't thinking of Cornwall then?'

'I must admit I was thinking of somewhere slightly less British. Like Italy or Greece.'

'The thing is, Adam, I need to start prepping for my course. I'm going to need access to libraries and reference material. I can't do that from abroad.'

'You haven't needed any of that so far,' I said. 'And there's the internet.'

'You can't study in internet cafes Adam. I really have to be here. I'm sorry. If you want to go to Italy then that's fine. It's not a problem. We can go to different places.'

'But the whole point is for us to be together, isn't it? Isn't that the point of a holiday?'

'Adam, I can't go abroad. Not this year. That's how it is. If you want us to be together then it will have to be somewhere local. Please don't make another problem out if it.'

I could see the conversation spiraling down again into sulks and recriminations, so I returned to my labours on the greenhouse. Underneath all the strategic hide and seek I felt there was something murky going on, but eventually put it out of my mind in the cause of domestic peace. And indeed over the following weeks Elaine did immerse herself in study, arriving home with armfuls of books, tapes and photocopied papers which through the summer took over most of the sitting room. But at the same time a stifled discontent began to haunt our encounters, as though a tacit agreement had been made to avoid any contentious subject – which of course turned everything into a contentious subject. And then came the occasion whose every last trace I wish could be irrevocably wiped from my memory: Elaine's fortieth birthday party.

My experience might not have been quite so traumatic had I not been awakened at three a.m the previous night by the reappearance of the dwarves.

As before, it started as a raucous sound of partying from within the wardrobe. I sat up, and switched the bedside lamp on, expecting the sounds to stop. They did not. In fact if anything they got louder: drunken shouts, snatches of song, pipes, drums, foot-stamping, clinking of tankards and the occasional deep thump, as of a body falling heavily onto a hollow wooden floor.

I considered my options. I could leave them to it, walk out of the room, call the police, bang on the wardrobe door, – or simply observe the proceedings with philosophic detachment. But as so often happens, events pre-empted me. As I watched, the doors burst open, and what I can only describe as a motley troupe of small, brightly-dressed bearded people carrying complicated musical instruments stepped, stumbled or simply fell out. There seemed to be an endless number of them: far more than could ever have been contained at one time within the wardrobe. It could definitely be described as a C. S. Lewis moment. They were all between two and three feet in height, and yet their faces were without exception gnarled and ancient-looking, like the bark of a mature oak or elm that has seen its share of life.

Eventually the whole crowd of about twenty individuals was assembled in the dim space between my bed and the wardrobe. Once in the bedroom they abruptly ceased their revelry and drum-banging and stood silently facing me, holding their instruments, which now seemed to be less musical in nature than scientific: they resembled the complicated contraptions of the nineteenth century, replete with brass cylinders, mirrors, lenses, engraved scales, knobs and gears – as though they were a party of novice astronomers on their way to observe a rare celestial transit. They stood motionless, without gesture or expression, as though waiting for me to address them, or encourage them in their proposed adventure; but I found I could neither speak nor move. All I could do was gaze from one to the other, trying to gather from their glances what their intentions could be. Indeed the sense that they were expecting something of me grew unmistakable, yet I was at a complete loss to work out what it was. I wondered what might happen if I stood up and walked from the room: would they follow me? Stand in my way? Form a magic circle around me? Or start dancing again? But as I was incapable of the slightest movement the question remained academic.

The diminutive assembly remained still long enough to convince me that something strange had happened to time itself: as though the scene had been freeze-framed. In fact it reminded me of H.G. Wells' short story The New Accelerator – where the protagonist drinks a potion and, instead of becoming a twenty-foot giant is speeded up several thousand times, so he was able to go on a leisurely walk around town and return to his starting point in the space of a fraction of a second, leaving a scorch mark on the sill of the window he had indolently climbed through. And then, as though the drug's effects were beginning to wear off, one of the dwarves began to edge backwards towards the open wardrobe, signaling a general (though to me it seemed reluctant) drift of the rest in the same direction. And as they climbed haltingly back inside looking distinctly disenchanted, I noticed another odd thing: the various implements that each one carried once more reverted to musical instruments: a pipe, tambourine, drum, fiddle, bodhran, harmonica, mandolin – and as the door was pulled shut behind the last of them, I heard the same sounds of rhythmic music and dancing that had first woken me.

With the dwarves safely back inside the wardrobe I recovered my power of movement again, and immediately leapt towards it, but of course the moment I got my fingers on the handle the interior subsided into complete silence. I didn't have to open the door to know I would find it a totally dwarf-free area; but I opened it anyway, just as Elaine woke up and saw me fumbling distractedly among the hardly ever used coats, jackets, shirts and shoes. She blinked.

'Adam, are you having that Dwarf dream again?'

'It wasn't a dream,' I said, 'I woke up and saw them. Dozens of them, all staring at me like I was an exhibit from the Death Star.'

Elaine sat up, hugged her knees, and regarded me sadly.

'Adam, I really do think it's time you saw a doctor. This is not the first time. I think you're seriously stressed about something.'

'I'm not stressed and I wasn't dreaming! Something is happening. I don't understand it, but that doesn't mean it's a fantasy.'

'Come back and get some sleep for God's sake.' Her voice softened. 'Please?'

I crept back to bed and pulled the duvet over me.

'I know you think I'm cracking up. But I'm not. This has the feel of reality. I know it's not just me. I have to try to get to the bottom of it. Please be patient.'

The rest of the night passed in a train of vivid and disturbing images: Magnus struggling upstairs reprising his misspent life; Rachel's half-ghostly figure wavering like a dull flame in the shadowy kitchen; my mother dying surrounded by flights of daffodils; climbing Snowdon with my Dad when I was fourteen. Then I saw a universe empty of everything but cubes: countless billions of them, colourless, indestructible, immeasurable, implacable, intractable; a universe in which everything that humanity has been is reduced to an infinitesimal statistic in an infinite memory bank. And then I thought of the heap of cubes in my safe, waiting to be 'activated', so that humanity could be 'saved'. And then I thought of climbing an isolated track to a mountain wilderness, with nothing but a notebook and a few provisions that would keep me alive just long enough to think through what I needed to think through. And then I must have slept, because I became aware of the sun sliding into the room and patterning the wall with tender medallions of blushing light.

Chapter Sixteen

'You were saying you'd had a frightening experience. Do you want to talk about it?'

The Venetian blinds had been closed to mask the glare of the morning sunlight. I thought Clare looked uneasy as she drew her chair closer and reset her little digital timer, but that may just have been me being paranoid about 'experts'. I'd actually come to quite like Clare; in the last few months I thought she'd changed. She seemed more fallible, less sure of herself, and less rigid in her approach to applying the therapist-client rules, all of which helped me to feel she was living in the same world as I was, albeit on an altogether higher plane of comfort. On one or two occasions she'd even laughed at my anti-therapist jokes, though of course that could have been part of her professional strategy for putting me at my ease. I wouldn't put that past her at all.

I wanted to tell her about Rachel's visit, because it had been preying on my mind. I mean the fact that she'd said Elaine needed me to be with her more. This didn't add up in the light of her strange behaviour recently. But then for some reason at the crucial point I switched to the dwarves. I really didn't want Clare to know about the dwarves, for obvious reasons: she'd have me down as a pot of noodles in short order. So the dwarves were off limits. So why the sodding heck did I bring them up? The question is one of the great enduring mysteries, and probably merits a whole psychology paper in itself.

'Well there's something before that. I had another visit from the little people of the wardrobe.'

A furtive note-taking at the word 'wardrobe'. She probably thought it was terribly Freudian.

She gave me one of her infinitely subtle nods, meaning, go on, give me more data, I'm not judging or mocking you, or disapproving or approving – in fact I'm not really here at all, so you're safe to say anything you like.

'I don't want to bore you with all the details.'

'Don't worry about me,' she said, in that soothing voice that did anything but soothe.

'Well, this time they came out and stood around my bed, as if they wanted me to join a carol singing party. But I couldn't move a muscle, I was paralyzed. After ages they just melted back into the wardrobe. Well not literally melted of course. Figuratively.'

She gave me a number two smile – conspiratorial. Designed to keep me on side. It usually works. 'Of course I got up to investigate, but it was just what was supposed to be there: a tall wooden box full of hardly-used clothes. Not a red pointy hat among them. And no, it definitely was not a dream.'

'Why are you so sure of that?'

'I think I can tell when I'm awake. You know, you look at something and it has that sort of stability and substance about it. And you can decide to have certain thoughts, such as wondering what would happen if I got up and walked out. You can't do that in a dream.'

'Oh surely you can?'

'Not in my kind of dream. Things happen. You don't make decisions, or have a deliberate extended sequence of thoughts. Everything merges and changes all the time.'

'Ok. So you had a party of real flesh-and-blood dwarves in your wardrobe.'

It sounded weird enough, I had to admit – straight out of a James Thurber cartoon in fact.

'And in the room. In retrospect I think the wardrobe was probably just a portal for them, from another world.'

Not so much as a blink. I have to hand it to her: that's professional. Another few moments of intense note-taking. Then she turned her exquisitely concerned gaze back to me.

'Adam, I think the danger we have here is that we'll get caught up in discussing the reality or otherwise of what happened. But what's really important is what you felt while it was happening.'

'Sure. Well, obviously I was stunned. Wouldn't you be if your bedroom was invaded in the night by a colony of inebriated dwarves?'

'Probably yes.' Another number three there, I suspected.

'But I meant what feelings did these figures evoke in you when you saw them? Try to get down to your underlying response.'

'Well disbelief, of course. Curiosity as to what they meant to do. I didn't feel they were a physical threat at any point. But I doubted my perceptions of course. I was afraid I was having hallucinations, maybe brought on by stress. I remember I was fascinated by their instruments, because they seemed very complicated. A bit alien in fact.'

'I do feel we're missing something Adam. This situation is clearly significant to you, for your unconscious to flag it up twice. And in the second dream –'.

'I wasn't dreaming.'

'Ok. The second time it happened, the dwarves came out of their space into your bedroom. Any thoughts on that?'

'Only that it made the whole thing more urgent: there was a relationship with them this time. It wasn't just something I could dismiss as a fantasy, like it didn't really happen.'

'And how did that make you feel?'

'More curious I suppose. They clearly wanted me to do something. So my main concern was trying to work out what that was.'

Clare scribbled again, then paused, intent on the page, as though consulting higher authority. I sensed the session wasn't going the way she'd planned, and wondered what I could do to help.

'I suppose the wardrobe could symbolize a womb,' I offered. 'With all those little people coming out of it?'

She looked a bit blank at that, as if the idea hadn't occurred to her. 'What I'm really trying to get at is what you felt in that situation. That's really the only thing that matters. Otherwise we're just trapped in other people's theories, which may or may not be relevant.'

At this point I experienced an overwhelming need to walk around the room, and went over to look through the tall windows overlooking the extensive back garden. But Clare wasn't having this.

'Adam, I'd like to suggest you stay in the seat until we're finished please? Walking around can be an avoidance mechanism.'

I admit I hadn't foreseen that tactic, and it caught me on the hop, so to speak. Fuck it, what was this, a police-cell interview?

But I did go back, rather sheepishly, to my seat, and had another drink.

'I'm sorry. I'm finding this a bit painful.'

'That's ok. It's important to stay with the pain. Don't push it away. It's trying to tell you something.'

I wanted to say: You bet. It's trying to tell me I need to get out of here bloody quick.

'Stay with the dwarves. What did you feel when they all stared at you?'

'Oh God. I don't know. I've told you I don't know!' Already my hands knew what was coming, and were trying to dissociate themselves from the ends of my arms.

'You're sitting there, unable to move, in that dim light, and they're all gathered around staring expectantly at you.'

'I feel—,' I reached out for something, found the tumbler of water, and drank gratefully.

'I feel I've done something terrible, and they've come to pass judgment on me. I feel...there's nothing I can say to excuse myself. Whatever it is I've done it's unforgivable.'

And then the tears came.

Whatever her faults, I have to give Clare full marks for patience. She knew I was bluffing – even when I didn't. And there was never a hint of impatience or disapproval in her tone: she knew whatever was there would make itself known in its own bad time.

'Have you any idea what it is? I mean what you think you've done that's so terrible?'

I didn't want to resurrect Rachel's ghost at this point, so I made a show of doing some psychic excavation. It's a gambit that I've found often works with women.

'There is something. But it's very hard to get back to it. I can only remember snatches. When I was ten or eleven, I had this very close friend called Trevor Barnes. We hung around everywhere together. I liked him because he would actually do things where I just talked wistfully about them. So we used to meet up and hatch these plots to raid people's gardens, or put superglue on doorknobs, or just give people we didn't like a scare. At the last minute I'd always find a reason not to do it, and he'd usually slouch off to do it on his own. Is this boring?'

'No. Not at all.'

'Because it all seems so long ago, and I'm not sure it's relevant.'

'Please go on.'

'So there was this girl, Mary something. Bradshaw I think. She must have been a year or so older than me. I think both of us fancied her like mad. Well I know I did. She had big beautiful sky-blue eyes and shoulder-length golden wavy hair, and always gave me an irresistible smile. So Trevor had this plan to kidnap her and keep her prisoner in a derelict garden shed we knew of. I went along with it without really seeing what it would involve. My job was to lure her to the shed, and Trevor would gag her and tie her up. Then we'd send an anonymous note to her parents asking for ten pounds for her safe return. Absolutely insane. I expressed some doubts I think, but Trevor got really excited about it, and wouldn't hear of calling it off. It was his big hero moment. He couldn't talk about anything else. So on the appointed day I led her to the shed with some cock and bull story I'd concocted, and Trevor gagged her and wrapped duck tape all round her. As soon as I saw her like that I panicked and ran like hell. Dreadful visions of atrocities opened up in my mind. I didn't believe Trevor was an evil monster, and yet I suspected there were sides to him that could get out of control very quickly. I didn't tell anyone about the incident, and I avoided Trevor for months afterwards, convinced he'd have it in for me for betraying him. In fact I avoided everyone as much as possible, quite certain they all knew what had happened. As it happened Trevor vanished a few months later – I never found out what had become of him, or of Mary for that matter. I imagine he let her go after a while. I really don't think he meant to harm her physically: it was just one of his fantasies of having power over somebody.'

'How do you feel now that you've told that story?'

'Relieved. That's the first time I've ever so much as mentioned it to anyone.'

'And it's not such a terrible thing after all, don't you think?'

'It was a cowardly thing to do. I should've stood up to him and said this isn't on, this is going to have a bad consequence.'

'Well with hindsight we would all act differently. But mistakes are the way children grow up.'

'I'm not at all certain I have grown up.'

'So let's say you're in the process. As we all are.'

'I want forgiveness. No matter how many times I tell myself I'm not evil, there's a part of me that still believes I'm beyond forgiveness. That the only real way out is to kill myself.'

'But that isn't a way out, is it? Those feelings will go on having their effect, because they're energy, and energy just can't stop. It has to transfer into something.'

'So Dante's hell represents the truth? You can't ever expiate what you've done?'

'Oh no, I'm not saying that! And I'm not a theologian, I don't know the answer. What I am saying though is you can forgive yourself.'

'How? It doesn't work just telling myself not to feel bad, or that what I've done was understandable.'

'Do you know Nicholas of Clairvaux's seven stages of purification? It something like, if I remember it: acceptance of sin. Repentance. Sorrow of heart. Confession to others. Penance, and reformation of your life. So it's all spelt out, like a path you can follow step by step. The Christians had a lot of experience of guilt and expiation through the centuries, so I think they probably knew what they were talking about.'

'But I'm not a Christian. I don't have their faith. And without faith I don't see how it could work, because it depends on a value system.'

'You don't need to be a Christian to have a value system. All you need is to be human. Simply replace 'sin' with something like 'doing harm' or 'degrading life' and your problem vanishes! Anyone can do it!'

'Even confession?'

'All you need is a friend you trust.'

'Ah. There's the rub.'

'Surely you have someone you can talk to about these things? They don't have to be perfect: just capable of listening.'

I thought for a while, and then an idea came to me that cheered me up considerably.

'Actually I have. She's dead, but that shouldn't disqualify her, should it? She's a wonderful listener.'

Chapter Seventeen

And so to the party. My half-century on this planet. And a terrible mistake, especially coming right after the dwarves.

Considering it was the big one, it's bizarre how few people I actually knew: fully three-quarters of the guests were Elaine's friends. Not that I resented her having so many friends, if it made her happy. It's just that one can't help wondering, at the age of fifty especially, what happened to everyone? What happened to all those hearty greetings, bottles of Californian Sauvignon, presents of books I simply could not live another day without reading – 'it will totally change your life, mate'. And those invitations to weekends in the country, 'just us and Jenny, our neighbour, who I just know you'll get on fantastically with: she's studying Ancient Egyptian horticulture.' Not to mention the al-fresco dinners and star-watching parties. Simon from my old university was still around of course – I couldn't for a moment ever imagine him moving or raising a family – he was far too disorganized to get it together. I think he was as lonely as I was, but I still couldn't muster any enthusiasm for a conversation with him: whatever the subject, he contrived to steer everything back to occlusions, transits and orbital anomalies.

And then of all people, Rachel decided to drop in, using her now familiar method of astral manifestation.

I'd just been to the bathroom and felt the need for some fresh air and quiet. I opened the back door and slipped out onto the patio. There's a little wooden shed a few feet from the house where Elaine keeps garden stuff and a few tools. I thought I'd have a quiet spell in there to chill out. I'd barely got inside when I felt someone already there, but couldn't see anyone. Then I heard her voice. It was quite unmistakably her's: that playful Dundee accent that had survived hell and rebirth, and its gentle modulation that never failed to calm me.

She asked me how I was, just like the beginning of a normal nine to five conversation. After I'd got over my initial shock it felt quite natural to be talking with her, like a meeting between two old friends who had lost touch. I told her I was feeling very unhappy, and she said, very quietly, but clear as a bell:

'That's understandable. But you shouldn't take it too seriously. It won't last long.'

I assumed she was talking about the party, of course.

'I know. I'm just feeling paranoid. It's my party and I hardly know anyone. It shouldn't matter, but it does. I seem to attract these situations, I don't know why. I should just grow up, I suppose.'

'Perspective is what you need, what all living people need in fact. But it's hard to attain perspective when you're slam bang in the middle of things.'

I could see her now: her grave face softly illuminated by the dim reddish-orange light from the house. And there was that subtle perfume that always went with her, the essence of incipient womanhood, which I found irresistible; I had to restrain myself from making a complete fool of myself and trying to embrace her.

'Rachel,' I said, 'There's something I do need your help with, if you don't mind. Elaine is very precious to me. We've always had a very open relationship, but now she seems to be in a different world. She's always wrapped up in some kind of research. She gets up very early and is buried in her computer for hours. I get the feeling she's using it as a barrier, a defence mechanism, to avoid having to communicate. Which is exactly what happened with Cora. I couldn't bear to go through that again. It would finish me off.'

She remained silent for a long time, so long that I was afraid I was already losing her. I tried to hold her gaze, but her eyes became merely deeper shadows than the face that enclosed them. The impulse to reach out and hold her became all but overpowering; luckily she spoke before I gave way to it.

'All you have to do Adam, is love her. Open your heart. Your heart is full of distrust, and strategies to protect yourself. To her that must feel like betrayal. Or self-obsession, which isn't exactly love. She finds that impossible to live with, for reasons hidden far in her own past. So it's up to you to make the effort to reach her. She will respond. But do it as soon as you can. Don't wait for her to come to you. I'm sorry, I have to leave now—'.

Her voice was becoming edgy and wavery, and seemed to be coming from different places, which meant her energy was giving out. I could barely make out where she was standing. It was hard her leaving just at the point where we'd established such intimacy, and it gutted me. I tried to touch her hand, but she'd already gone. I just stood there in the dark, trying to conjure her back again, feeling completely alone and alienated from everything going on outside.

So that was my birthday party kiboshed. After that I just desperately wanted everyone to piss off home and leave me to absorb what she'd said. I went to look for Elaine, but she wasn't around. Someone said they'd seen her go out with Mark. Now I knew perfectly well it wasn't a good idea, but after that conversation with Rachel I wasn't altogether in control of my actions. I set out to find them. It's a pity Rachel couldn't have stayed a little longer, as then I'm sure she'd have stopped me from imagining the worst. I knew where they would have gone: it was the way we always went for our evening walks: up the lane, through the top of the wood, out past the stone circle. I knew the way blindfold. What I was going to do when I actually found them I was far less clear about.

After a few minutes groping along stone walls my attention was caught by a tiny oval spot of light moving erratically down the slope, which I realized must be a flashlight. I couldn't make out at this distance whether there were two people or only one. I waited by the stile at the top of the wood, my heart doing its usual panic tattoo inside my chest. When the figure was some fifty feet away I saw it was Mark, and he was alone. A strange joy of immense relief flooded through me: I wouldn't have to drag him off Elaine's sweat-drenched body after all. The figure stopped short, training the narrow torch-beam on me.

'Adam! Good God, I've been searching everywhere for you!'

'Where's Elaine?'

'She went off towards Higher Brockley. We were getting worried about you.'

We? Had they appointed themselves my guardians? As though I wasn't safe out by myself. As though they were—

But at least I hadn't found them together. That surely was something.

'I was only in the garden. I needed some quiet.'

'So did I actually. Parties aren't really my thing, if truth be told.'

'Fancy a moonlight stroll?'

'Sure. I'd better let Elaine know I found you though. She'll be worrying.'

Mark phoned Elaine on her mobile.

'Yes, he's fine. You want a word with him? Ok. See you soon then.'

Elaine. My soul sister. My autumn flower. My storm rainbow. My ocean. What would I do if you stopped caring? What planet in the cosmos would take me then?

Instead of going back through the wood, we turned parallel to its edge and followed the contour out to open ground. There was a dim quarter-moon high in the south, barely enough to see by. Mark kept his torch focussed on the treacherous tussocks of blanched grass ahead. I began to feel ashamed of myself for suspecting him of having what the Victorians called dishonorable intentions towards Elaine. I saw that he was by nature deeply concerned with others' wellbeing; indeed I now thought he had the makings of a saint about him.

'I've been rethinking this whole CubeWatch project in the last few weeks,' he began. 'We're losing ground with our current approach. People see us as in cahoots with a hidden enemy, so when the invasion comes we'll be protected. There's a mass paranoia developing against anything that seems alien. Even the Obama government in the States has taken a strong anti-alien line.'

'That's hardly surprising. The Americans have always been paranoid about what's lurking beyond their borders.'

'True. But some of us had hoped a new Democrat in the White House might see the advantages of having access to their technology. Anyway I think we have to change our tactics. People are never going to be won over to alien approaches unless they can see their methods actually working for us. So we have to prioritize establishing communication.'

'I think it's already happening,' I said. 'I think that's exactly what all these mini-cubes are about. They're the first phase of preparing us for evolving into non-violent citizens of the cosmos.'

I told him about my latest construction project and its mysterious conjuring of Rachel out of the night. 'And this method won't involve any mass negative reactions because no one will know about it until the process is well underway.'

'I think you're underestimating the bloody-minded determination of the media when they scent a big story. They won't give up until they bring down their prey, and the bigger it is the better for their profits. We have to ensure the aliens know exactly what they're up against. That's why I want Elaine on board. She'd be brilliant at media liaison.'

'Why do you think that?'

'Because A, she really listens to people; B, she tunes in to feelings instinctively, and C, she's young, good-looking and articulate, a natural communicator. She'd do more for us than a thousand town-hall meetings.'

'But maybe she doesn't want to.'

'Yes. That's an unfortunate glitch in the plan. Can you think of any way to persuade her?'

'I might. But I don't think I want to. I think she needs to be free to do what she wants, without pressure.'

'Yes, I was afraid you'd say that.' He sighed theatrically. 'We'll just have to look elsewhere for a saviour.'

'You may not have to. I think these micro-cubes may operate in a different way. They seem to work instantly, as soon as they're assembled.'

'How do you mean, work? What do they do?'

'I didn't think anything of it at the time, but as soon as I'd arranged the small cubes into a bigger one, something changed. We both felt it. A kind of harmony. I felt a bit like after a particularly good joint: the universe became a meaningful place for a moment. But in this case it wasn't chemically induced: it was more like a connection had been made, exactly like when Les used to talk to me when the old Cube was here. A feeling of, ah, this is how it was always meant to be: the paradise of the saints and all that. And then of course there was Rachel coming back, as though she'd just been away on an unplanned shopping trip.'

'How many have you got?'

'Over four hundred. Another consignment arrived this week. I'm afraid they'll soon need a room to themselves.'

'If these things really are coming from the aliens they could be hot property. Someone's going to clock what's happening soon, and then all hell will break loose. We simply have to find out very quickly how to use them.'

'I think we just build a big cube. They seem happy when they're arranged like that. And it's the simplest solution. Mathematically the most elegant.'

Mark's eyes sparkled. 'So let's do it. What are we waiting for?'

We cut back over a fence and down through the wood. A faint flush of rosy light haunted the eastern sky. The first birds were already stirring, trying out their cold voices. We let ourselves in to the house feeling like thieves.

Most people had gone home when we crept in by the kitchen door. The usual stink of stale drinks hung about the place. A few guests were sleeping, or trying to sleep, on our lumpy sofas in the lounge. I had to remind myself that this had been my party, because I'd barely spoken to anyone the entire night. No wonder I was beginning to be regarded as an unsocial eccentric who's forgotten his manners. Still, I had to live my life; no one else was going to do that for me. It was entirely possible there wasn't that much of it left, and new priorities were announcing themselves. I felt like a child again, discovering mysterious heavy packages among the chaste blue shadows of Christmas morning.

I emptied all the nearly weightless cubes from my safe onto the desk, half expecting them to melt into thin air as the daylight grew. But they lay there like an animator's nightmare, waiting for some genius to give order and life to them.

'I suggest we go for the big one,' I said as Mark was clearing the desk of its month-high stack of newspapers. 'Twenty one would give us forty-two centimetres a side. We can just about fit it on the desk.'

Mark pressed buttons on his calculator. 'That would need more than nine thousand cubes,' he said. 'We don't have anything like that.'

'But we will have in a couple of weeks.'

'Ok. It may work. Why don't you start and I'll go down and fix us some breakfast?'

Mark was startled to find Elaine sitting alone in the kitchen holding an orange mug on her knees and staring into space.

'I thought you'd be in bed. Fancy some breakfast?'

'No thanks. How's Adam?'

'He's fine. He's deep in his building blocks.'

He moved behind Elaine and instinctively kissed her neck, then whispered:

'I love you, Elaine. Come away with me.'

'Please don't ask that. You know I can't possibly.'

'You will in the end. After you've caused yourself a lot of misery.'

'I have to love Adam. Can't you see that? I totally failed to love Jack. I can't fail Adam as well. How could I live with myself?'

'Doesn't it occur to you that you're failing Adam by feigning love for him?'

'I'm not feigning.'

She was shocked at his accusation, but continued abstractedly sipping from her mug and avoiding his eyes. But his hands on her shoulders soothed her when they should not have done, and she had to admit that Adam's increasing self-absorption was opening a gulf that seemed unhealable.

'Maybe I could love you both?' she conceded, as if that would prevent the unbearable argument from escalating.

'Yes, if you're a saint.' He walked across to the window, and turned to face her. 'The trouble is, I'm not.'

Mark set about toasting crumpets and brewing coffee, while Elaine sat motionless at the table like a possession of the night, as the sunlight quickened the young leaves of the silver birches at the garden's boundary. Then he said:

'I think Adam's a very remarkable person. But I'm sure his destiny is for something other than marriage. He's a visionary who hasn't yet found his vision.'

'But maybe my being with him will help him find it?'

'I don't believe in self-sacrifice.' He gathered the breakfast things onto a tray and took them up to the study.

I'd managed to build five layers of cubes at one end of the table, and was working out the total number needed, when Mark announced breakfast.

'We're not going to have enough even to make a thirteen-side cube. But maybe it won't matter. I should think we'd get some effect even from a partial cube, if such a creature is possible.'

'Adam, why don't we take a break and think this through? I'd very much like to talk to you about Elaine.'

'I thought you already had. You're free to ask her yourself. But I don't think she'll agree.'

'I think she might if she sees what effect these are having.'

'If you put pressure on her you'll get nowhere. Believe me. On the other hand once she's decided in favour you'll have her total support.'

I completed the last layer and stood back like a stage magician about to perform his coup-de-theatre. Nothing happened. No change in the cubes, and no change in our feelings, as there had been at Magnus's.

'It doesn't like this shape,' Mark said. 'It wants to be a real cube, like its dad.'

'In that case we'll just have to wait for the next shipment.'

Chapter Eighteen

The fiasco of the party slowly faded behind the noise of the present. The not-yet-cube lay on my desk like a pillaged Egyptian monument. Mark phoned in the week to ask Elaine about her decision, but she seemed indifferent to the impending global catastrophe, appearing more concerned to get to the heart of middle-east politics. Dead on schedule another sealed crate arrived in the porch, and in a clench of anticipation I locked the door and completed the cube on my desk. I sat willing it to do something – if it had only spoken my weight it would have been a start. But it remained tantalizingly inert. Perhaps it was paying me back for ignoring it for a week.

I tried disassembling it and rebuilding it in another part of the room, near the window, in case it needed to see the sky. But still it wouldn't play ball. I waited till the following Monday for the anticipated delivery, but nothing came. I felt I'd been set up for another humiliation. Over supper I told Elaine:

'It looks like the shipments have come to an end. Why don't we have that holiday? Time's running out.'

'It'll have to be short. My course starts in three weeks.'

'You could spare a week, I'm sure. A change of scenery would do us both good.'

'No chance, Adam. It'll have to be a weekend. I'm sorry. I've a vast pile of stuff still to read.'

'Take it with you.'

'Maybe. Let me think about it.'

She thought about it for two more days, and she still couldn't make up her mind. I used the time to put the final touches to the new member of our household.

The good weather unexpectedly held throughout August. Still Elaine avoided the issue of the holiday. In the first week of September there were news reports of another war erupting in Pakistan. The Palagoshe, or Guardians – the successors to the routed Taliban – were occupying the border regions and bombing or decapitating everyone they considered to be western sympathizers and modernisers. Although the new Democrat government in the States had kept out of the conflict so far, there was always the fear – much debated in the media – that they would be forced to enter the arena to protect their overseas interests, and the Afghan border formed a series of potential flashpoints that could ignite a conflagration. So it seemed opportune to take our mutual friend for a test-drive. Question was, how did you switch it on?

'I can't believe it has anything so twentieth-century as an on-off switch,' I said to Mark, on one of his now regular visits. 'It has to be thought-controlled, or on some kind of automatic boot-sequence.' But we were clearly having the wrong thoughts, or having them in the wrong order, or the wrong language, or at the wrong time of day, because the inactivity of the thing became positively deafening. There seemed simply no way into it. We thought of shining a laser into it, playing Mozart to it, showing it photographs of the Cube, singing to it, playing a DVD of 2001. We considered building a pyramid over it, relocating it to Glastonbury Tor, or playing it whale music. In the end we agreed that patience was the greatest virtue, and simply ignored it for a few days, in order to let it see we could live quite happily without it. Then one morning of Keatsian mists Elaine announced she would like to go to Devon immediately. Muttering 'carpe diem' under my breath I loaded the car with books and files and CDs of Dylan and Schubert, and we crept out of town like a pair of adulterers bound for a week of forbidden bliss in Morocco.

Whatever possessed me to imagine that a weekend in Sidmouth would resolve all our problems? Or would even allow us to list them all? I must admit the depths of my naivety confounds me, on those occasions when I'm able to confront it.

Elaine was sullen and distracted, which I naturally put down to anxiety about her approaching course; and I felt apprehensive that the (metaphoric) storm would break right above our heads – which in the event was exactly what it did.

Nicola was delighted to be billeted with her best friend Kath for the weekend: unsurprisingly a holiday in the cheapest hotel in Sidmouth did not conjure unconfined joy in her mind.

We drove to the coast in heavy traffic, and arrived late. The hotel had the smallest rooms I'd ever seen: just large enough for a not quite double bed, a wardrobe and a wash-stand. I scrutinized the wardrobe with apprehension, probing its inner spaces for signs of habitation, or discarded diminutive garments, but found it entirely innocent of harbouring malingerers. The window overlooked a modern housing estate, redeemed only by a line of oak and chestnut trees beyond. We consoled ourselves with the fact that the breakfast was edible, if not exactly nutritious, and the coffee not instant.

In the morning I prevailed on Elaine to leave her books behind and come with me on a cliff walk. A brisk onshore breeze had sprung up, which prevented us from lingering too long on the exposed headlands. Something in me was reluctant to embark on a conversation that might lead to painful upheavals in our relationship, but I knew I'd come here in order to have that conversation and to avoid it would only make healing more difficult. Even so for a good part of that walk I struggled to articulate the conflict that regularly harried my peace of mind. At length we found a sheltered hollow and sat down in the dry sand.

'I don't feel we're enjoying each other's company like we used to,' I began. 'It's like there's something we're avoiding for the sake of appearances.'

'I'm not avoiding anything,' Elaine said. 'But I must say since you bring it up my experience of you has changed this year. You've become self-obsessed ever since that accursed television interview. I don't know why. It's as if after that part of you shut down. That's incredibly frustrating.'

I confess I was gobsmacked, because it was exactly what I felt she'd done: shut down her emotions until there was no longer any common sympathy between us.

'This course has taken you over, you know. I hardly know you anymore.'

'So you rather I didn't have any interests apart from you, is that it?'

'No, of course I'm not saying that. It's the way you're doing it. It's almost become a way to exclude me.'

Elaine's face clouded. 'Why should I want to do that?'

'Maybe you've got bored with having me around?'

'Adam, that's just absurd! Do you really think I'm so shallow? Do you think I'm nothing more than a flighty pleasure-seeker?' Her face suddenly coloured. She grabbed hold of her hat and got to her feet in one movement. 'I mean, why? What's going on in your head?'

'I think you'd like me to be more like Mark: decisive, sociable, practical, generous. All the things I'm not.'

I'd never seen Elaine so agitated as she was at that moment. Her cheeks rose to a fiery tempest, her eyes glittered, her voice climbed several tones to the precincts of hysteria. Her whole body seemed to be on the verge of incandescence.

'What I'd really, really like, just in case you want to know, is to know what you actually feel! I've never felt you express an emotion directly without immediately pulling it back in case you were wrong! Have the courage to be wrong for once in your life! I mean, everybody gets it wrong most of the time, so why should you be any different?'

'Yes, well that's what all this therapy's supposed to do, isn't it? Make me feel ok about being like everyone else. The trouble is, I don't. In fact I feel I have to be far better than everyone else, just to avoid being damned to eternal hellfire!'

Elaine calmed down with commendable alacrity. In fact I thought I detected some sliver of remorse in her tone.

'Adam, I do really think you should find a normal job that occupies your energies and draws you down out of that crystal dome crammed with impossible contradictions. Then you'll have a chance of being happy. Because at the moment you're just miserable and that infects all the space around you.'

'If only happiness were as simple a matter as getting a job.'

'Maybe it is.'

'But I have to believe in it, in what I'm doing. And no matter how hard I try I can't believe in the ultimate worthwhileness of stacking shelves for Tesco.'

'Why do you have to believe in it? Why not just do it? They still pay you the same whether you believe in it or not.'

'So you think that's my destiny do you, to be a Tesco shelf-stacker?'

'You seem determined to misread everything. The whole point is, it would give you a base, freedom from pressure, so you could decide where you want to take your life next.'

'But it would drive me crazy! I'd come home every morning a gibbering wreck. It's a very generous offer Elaine, and I'm grateful, but no thanks.'

'Then for God's sake do something with your life that doesn't involve aliens or little metal boxes! I can't stand any more of them!'

She kicked sand out of her shoes and began to scramble back to the cliff path. Something, some perverse impulse forced me to stay where I was, staring at the small smudge of a boat far out on the horizon, hoping it would send me a signal that it was ok to follow her and restore normality. But no signal came.

Chapter Nineteen

The storm had been preparing its sky all afternoon. First the unblemished blue became troubled with a vagueness that had no definite hue, but spread unease among the walkers and loiterers, and thinned the sunlight until they wrapped their garments more tightly around themselves and increased their pace. Then lavish grey capes of rainclouds were shaken out from the west, and a saltatory breeze tugged at the still-green leaves and chilled any unprotected arms and necks. I gripped desiccated gorse limns to haul myself to the highest point of the path, where a less-trodden arm of it swung southwards onto a level bluff of heather and nettles, thinking that Elaine would most likely have gone there to grab some space to think. But there was no sign of her, either on the crown itself or anywhere along the crimped grey ribbon that clung to the crests and troughs of the cliff's crust. And as the whole sky sealed itself with roiling black, the rain began: slow, lethargic drops that seemed as opaque as the clouds themselves, which encountered the dusty nettles with the driest, most chaste of kisses.

Did she assume I'd follow her? (No, she knew me better than that). Or did she want to escape, to avoid my importunate accusations, which I knew, even as I unleashed them, were unfair. In that small space of time I'd entered the labyrinth again, always a mere stumble away, down a couple of bramble-covered steps, or disguised under a heap of weed-infested rubble; and who knew how long it would engulf me? And yet I hadn't let go of hope entirely: each time I lost the plot, each time I groped along those slime-sided passages, I felt I was remembering the daylight more easily; keeping more of its life-giving perspectives close to my heart. And already I was repenting of my stupid jealousy, wishing I could loop back and grab out of the air my toxic missiles.

The rainstorm quickly gathered its energies and became a full-bodied torrent bridging sky and earth, until it was impossible to tell where one ended and the other began. The ash-black sea below was scaled with the plumes of its impact; the nettle towers were blasted by the sudden updraft of cold sea wind. In short, it was a real Lear moment, and matched my mood to perfection. I felt at home in a way I hadn't for years, buoyed by the overpowering resources of nature.

Within ten minutes the storm had blown itself out, and the sun was throwing down lacy skeins of brilliance far out in the west. I judged that Elaine would by now be safely back at the hotel, and set off back along the now treacherous path to find her. But she was not at the hotel, and had left no note to explain where she had gone. A spasm of fear for her safety raced through me. The storm had started at least fifteen minutes after she'd left: ample time for her to get off the cliff path and into shelter. But what if she'd gone the other way, away from the town, where the only shelter was some sea-cave or derelict mine working? She could have slipped off the path in her hurry to escape the storm and be lying injured, or worse, at the foot of the cliffs. I decided I had no option but to search for her as long as there was daylight. Luckily the sky was clear again, and a good three hours of light remained. The question was, of course, which direction had she taken? I cursed myself for wasting precious time after our argument, which might have made the difference between finding her alive or finding her dead; but I also cursed myself for allowing the argument in the first place: it was entirely unnecessary and spiteful on my part, and without foundation. So why had I indulged in it? I didn't even believe those things myself. I trusted that she loved me, and that was the only thing that mattered. I'd slipped back into my old labyrinth, the same old maze of fears and prejudices that had ruined my relationship with Cora. I vowed that the moment I found Elaine, I'd apologize and promise never again to entertain suspicions of her. The demon had had his final fling.

Obeying some obscure impulse I turned westwards, and was soon climbing steeply towards a windswept headland. I felt certain I'd soon catch up with Elaine, and then I'd put everything right between us: show her her love and patience were justified all along, despite the occasional episodes of waywardness (which, my lords, I can assure you had their roots in entirely invidious pressures).

I walked for an hour, encountering no one beside an old man dragging a recalcitrant black dog on a long leash. As the sun slipped lower apprehension and hunger began to eat away at my resolve, and slowly I allowed myself to think the worst. Clearly at that point I ought to have called the police, but I had a deeply-embedded anxiety that any contact with them would re-awaken suspicions about the circumstances surrounding Rachel's disappearance, and that of course could not be risked.

I sat irresolute on a bench in the deepening shadows, imagining Elaine's body crumpled under thrashing waves at the foot of the cliffs, before deciding the best thing was to return to the hotel and report her disappearance. But when I got back about nine she was waiting for me in our bedroom, looking worried and contrite.

'I'm sorry, Adam. I just went further than I meant to. Then I got caught in that bloody huge storm. I hope you didn't worry too much.'

Elaine reserved swearing for really tight situations which required immediate intimidation of the enemy.

'Of course I worried. Did you really expect me not to?'

'I'm sorry. I lost track of time. I was upset.'

'Well so was I. It was a stupid argument.'

We hugged and made up, but I knew it was an interregnum. Hot chocolate and custard creams in bed may give the appearance that peace had broken out, but in reality nothing had been resolved. We made love silently and quickly, as a way of sending truce signals across the gulf, then I fell instantly into dreamless sleep.

'I have to study, Adam. My course starts in two weeks and I haven't even read half the material. Do you mind terribly? After all it was your idea to bring it all down with us, wasn't it?'

I had to admit it had been my idea, but somewhere in my midden of a soul I knew it was yet another avoidance strategy. She'd ordered chilled orange juice and fresh-baked hot croissants, which were delicious, and I found myself wondering about staying on indefinitely to live the life of a retired layabout and sea-inspector. After all, even the sea must need checking occasionally; I seemed exactly the right person for the job.

'I just hate this constant feeling that there's an issue we're not facing.'

'Maybe some issues shouldn't be faced. You should just get on with life.'

I didn't really know what this 'life' was that everybody was supposed to get on with, as if it was a task that somehow could be defined and completed and then all problems would just wither away. But I knew there was an issue between us, and getting on with life wouldn't rub out one jot of it. And I was sure Elaine also knew it.

'Ok, today I'll get on with my life. But tomorrow we must talk. How's that sound?'

'If you want.' Meaning whatever, if it keeps you quiet.

We finished breakfast and then made for the hilly path leading westward out of the town. I wasn't really in the mood for another ill-equipped dance with destiny. There were grey lowering skies and a brisk northerly that nudged me ever closer to the edge. It occurred to me that Elaine had definitely got the better corner of the bargain as usual. Scrambling up the scrubby shoulders of the cliffs I found myself thinking about the ironies of my life, in particular that of having the freedom to do exactly what I wanted while at the same time doing nothing, or as near to nothing as wouldn't fill a gnat's piss-pot. To wit: sitting in a lame excuse for a secondhand bookshop for half my life, hoping that some sad person might take pity on me and buy something, while waiting for the aliens to ring back. Nobody could imagine that was a life for a human being, no matter how broadly you defined that term. Maybe Elaine had a point, I thought. I could be alleviating suffering in a far more effective way by getting myself employed as a hospital orderly or even a farm hand, assuming such jobs still existed. Dig for sanity. Mulch for the muse. I'd be occupying my body directly in the service of distressed humanity; contributing my tiny sliver of energy towards the greater whole, and maybe becoming whole as a result.

But hold on just a moment: I am already co-opted into the greatest possible project – albeit not one recognized by the great mass of homo sapiens. I have simply to open the world's eyes to the wonderful if not overwhelming benefits of the aliens' plans for assimilating humanity into cosmic citizenship. Should be a piece of piss, to quote my old Dad on a good day. We let the Cubes do their job, have our minds upgraded, our legacy software deleted, sign up to the cosmic project, and Bob's your extraterrestrial uncle! In a flash we have all the resources of the greatest intellect in the universe at our disposal. So where's the catch? Well, how about this: would you believe it, we don't actually want our minds upgraded! We want to remain unregenerate peasants, locked in our meat-darkness, messing up the universal plan, putting the boot into anything that stinks of home improvement. We'd rather have a terminal disease and be free, than be healthy and in hock to some cosmic uberfuhrer. And it seems in any case we don't have any choice in the matter because our genes were designed that way. So that was my little task of the day: reconfigure the genetic disposition of the mass of humanity so that we welcome with open arms the new dawn of cosmic citizenship.

Oh dear Les, no wonder you were so totally baffled by mankind's jokes! They were so completely beyond your mindset that you didn't have the vaguest idea how to begin processing them. You needed an essentially irrational computer to help you. Step this way please, Adam Stone!

I'd reached a gully between two steep shoulders of the cliffs which looked as though it might once have contained a waterway until it wore away the impervious rock and vanished into the trackless obscurity of chalk. I thought it would make sense to follow its trace inland as it would most likely lead to a lane or settlement of some sort. The trouble was that the ground was full of roots and boulders invisible under a foot or so of dense foliage, and being impatient to reach somewhere that wasn't windswept cliff-top I stumbled over a root and plunged headlong into a nettle patch. The pain in my left ankle was so intense I was certain I'd broken something. I sat up and felt around it with apprehension. There was no blood, but the slightest movement was agony, and it quickly became obvious I wouldn't be able to make it back to the hotel under my own steam. I called Elaine on my mobile, but good old sod's law ensured I was in a signal blind spot. I didn't know how far I'd walked, but it was certainly too far to crawl or hobble back in my present state. I guessed my best bet was to follow the gully inland in the hope of finding a house and summoning help.

It took me ten minutes to drag myself a hundred yards, pausing every few moments to recover from the pain. The ground began to rise, making the effort of moving even more painful. I found myself in a small wood of hazel and hawthorn, that gave some shelter from the wind, and decided to have a longer rest and eat some of the biscuits I'd brought with me. It was then that I glimpsed the cottage: a long, whitewashed single-storey building with three square sash windows and a low wooden outbuilding stuck onto one end. I was already moving towards it when my brain took it into its head to 'help' me. 'That looks like a reasonable place to get help,' it said. 'Let's find out who lives there.' 'What a good idea!' I replied, 'Your powers of reasoning are truly impressive.' Praise usually put my brain into a co-operative mood, I found.

The cottage seemed to be empty. I knocked, found the door unlocked and gingerly crept inside. I called out, and was met with complete silence. I concluded the owner must have popped out for a packet of fags or a newspaper, and decided to wait and rest my ankle. My brain didn't like this idea at all, and urged me to leave before the inevitable disaster struck. 'He'll come back and raise hell if he finds someone here. He might be an armed maniac! He might be a desperate criminal or an international gangster and this might be his hideout. There might be a whole ring of master criminals using the place. It's the ideal place for a safe-house. Or a middle-eastern terrorist cell. Or a sex maniac. Get out now while you can.' I'd no intention of getting out, because my ankle was beginning to swell like a banker's ego, but I didn't tell my brain that. 'Ok', I said, 'Just give me ten minutes to rest, then we'll leave.' One thing I will say for my brain, it does listen to what I tell it. Maybe it even believes it on occasion. Anyway it quieted down then, and allowed me to take in the qualities of the room. It was very sparsely furnished, and had none of the various impedimenta of everyday living: no books, no stacks of dishes, no clothes lying around, in fact no signs of recent human habitation at all. There was a bare dining table, some fragile-looking chairs, a wall cabinet, a sofa that had seen better times, and iron stove surrounded by logs, an ancient gas-oven covered in rust and mouse droppings. 'No one's going to come back here today, I suspect,' I told my brain to comfort it. 'Don't bank on it,' it replied. 'It's a perfect safe-house. They wouldn't need to cook anything, they'd bring it all with them. They could be driving their SUV up the track at this very moment.'

But I was more concerned about Elaine than bank robbers; I still couldn't get through to her, and realized my battery was probably the problem. If I couldn't let Elaine know what had happened, and I couldn't call for help, and the cottage was indeed abandoned, I would have to find a village or farm and get my ankle treated pretty soon.

I was suddenly extremely thirsty, and wondered if there was a functioning water supply anywhere. I dragged myself across to a door in the far wall, and found it opened into another smaller room, in which was a bed-frame and a partly disintegrated chest of drawers. There was another doorway in the opposite corner which led into a tiny cubicle with a hand-basin and a toilet, but when I tried it the single tap in the basin was completely dry. I cursed, seeing I would have to get help sooner rather than later. 'At least it means we may escape the gang of drug-crazed marauders armed with machetes,' my brain observed helpfully.

I chewed some nuts and stretched out on the lumpy sofa, watching the afternoon light tease out patterns in the damp-scrolled pale-green plaster on the opposite wall; it felt bizarre that in the twenty-first century I was no more than two miles from Elaine and yet had no means of contacting her. I was sure she would be worrying about me, maybe thinking I purposely hadn't called her to pay her back for the argument we'd had on the beach, or maybe deciding she wouldn't call me because I hadn't called her... On the other hand...

And then there was something alive in the room with me, watching me, waiting for me to make a move.

The creature reminded me of the demon I'd encountered on the heath after I'd left Joe's for the last time, although this one was larger and blacker and seemed somehow more part of the world, though definitely not human. I knew if I kept perfectly still it couldn't harm me. But I also knew it had infinite patience – because it's only reason for being here was me.

My brain immediately went into panic mode. 'I knew there was something terrible in this place. As usual you didn't listen. Now we're in another fine mess.' (it thrived on these ancient comic clichés). I tried to calm it by recalling that I'd survived that last encounter with this creature. 'But only with Blake's help,' it muttered. 'And your survival is questionable. You were dead. William Blake saved you so you could put your mistakes right and help others, but you've conveniently forgotten that. Now this thing has come back again and you've nothing to save you this time. You're as fucked as a fish on the moon. I wish I'd got out of here while I could – you're nothing but a liability. You just never learn, do you? Even when you're handed salvation on a plate you still fuck it up and land right back where you started. Well the next chance I get I'm out of here. In fact I'm not even here now really. So you'd better come up with a really good plan to save yourself, because from here on I'm no longer your brain.'

'For God's sake will you quit wittering!' I (mentally) screamed at it. 'I'm trying to think.'

That shut it up for a few seconds, long enough for me to establish a tiny oasis of calm reflection in my mind, and in that space I found some courage to speak.

'Why are you here?'

The demon did not speak, but opened its outstretched palm to reveal something. It was not a lance this time, but a small dull flame, burning steadily, giving out a sullen crimson glow in the declining daylight, like little flaring petals of pentecostal fire. There was also a sound of distant roaring, like a huge storm brewing up all around us; but the flame itself remained all but motionless. If this was an answer, it was pretty cryptic. Maybe it was his way of being non-threatening.

But then I was amazed to find, with my brain momentarily out of the way, I could understand what the flame was saying. It was telling me I wasn't running my own life.

'But how the hell do I find my life in the first place?'

I don't know if I said that out loud or not, but suddenly the room was thronged with hundreds of flames; they were all over the place, flowering from cracks in the walls, springing from water pipes like fiery leaks, erupting from the spaces between the flagstones, poised on the tops of chairs like tiny dancers; yet they didn't burn what they emerged from. My mind in its newly prescient state immediately saw they were all the potent moments of my life that I'd missed or avoided or slipped half-consciously away from: all the tiny fertile crevasses that I could have used to enrich and strengthen and clarify my heart, if only I'd recognized them, instead of collapsing into hurt and isolation and resentment and hatred for the world. I thought of the people who wandered into the bookshop – with or without dogs – ostensibly to inquire about some obscure book, but in reality to bounce their manifold troubles off me to make them feel more like a functioning part of the human race. And the leggy girls in the supermarket, who I never spoke to, never even maintained eye-contact with for more than the statutory minimum period. I thought of the ticket inspectors on trains, who might have been from Uranus for all I noticed them; and of course those much closer to home, literally and figuratively: my childhood sweetheart, Theresa of the heavenly thighs and dreamy voice. Did I ever once think of her as someone to cherish in her own right; someone who had thoughts that no one in the future history of the world could ever precisely duplicate? I'm ashamed to confess I didn't: she was no more than a willing gateway to sexual experience, a (temporary) end to the agony of rejection and self-hatred. And perhaps above all the rest Cora, my first long-time lover, who I'd pushed as far from me as I could in order to prove that no normal woman could ever want to live with me. I could see now, from my crow's nest of experience, that she had loved me, and I hadn't been able to take it: it conflicted too much with the carefully nurtured image I'd imbibed from my father through the long lean years of learning the laws of love and shame from entirely the wrong exemplar. But the poor benighted sod didn't stand a chance, having chosen, or been chosen by, someone as deeply unsuited to cohabitation as my mother. May they rest in peace anyway, whatever shreds of peace they can beg or scrounge.

I gazed around the room in amazement: the form of the demon itself had faded to a near-transparent presence, leaving only his uncanny light show of crimson tongues inhabiting the room, like spirits attracted to a feast of unclaimed emotions. And now that the daylight had faded I saw clearly that each flame was indeed a moment of my life, offered up again for examination and redemption. I could enter any one of them and relive it as though it were the present, and modify my actions to give birth to a different outcome. Which would, of course, create a paradox, because it would lead to a different sequence of events than the one that led to my being in this cottage and being able to alter my past actions... I thought of the time I went to visit Cora in London and lost the plot badly when I discovered she had shacked up with Martin. Could I really revisit that moment and change it? The trouble with this line of thought was not the cascade of consequences that might ensue from interfering with something that had already happened, but that it presupposed I would remember the future and understand why I had gone back there; it assumed in fact that I would be a different person than the one I had actually been – because of course I had not been aware of the future when I had originally visited Cora. How could I have been, since I hadn't yet created it?

I was startled to notice that the flames themselves were now fading rapidly: some had vanished altogether; others had become more like wavering spirits; and I knew with a pang of regret that I'd probably blown my chances of revisiting my past life. Also I urgently needed to reach a place where I could call for help. I got to my feet and limped to the doorway, dismayed to see that the light was fading fast and I had no idea how I was going to get back to Elaine in the dark, and without water it was not an option to spend the night in the cottage.

Although my ankle had swollen I found I could hobble a few steps without disabling pain, so I decided this was the moment to try for rescue, before the dark made it impossible. The appearance of the demon had unsettled me, and I began to suspect every tree and bush of harbouring some unkillable entity inimical to my welfare. I found a pool of fresh rainwater and gulped from it gratefully, because it didn't instantly transform into fire in my gullet. I rested against an ancient tree trunk and it didn't imprison me in its light-forsaken maw. And after a few minutes of hacking through chest-high undergrowth I scrambled up to a gate bordering a lane which finally led to a crossroads where there was one of those legendary twentieth century artefacts, a functioning phone kiosk.

It was the purest luck that Elaine found me, because I'd not the faintest idea where I was. To her credit she didn't once accuse me of deliberately getting lost, which made me experience a spasm of intense gratitude. Nevertheless I refrained from telling her about the demon and his pretty light show, in case she thought I was reverting to my old waywardness.

Back at the hotel Elaine managed to conjure up some hot soup which restored me to the human realm somewhat. While I was eating I stole a glance at her : only part of her was present.

I said: 'How about having breakfast out tomorrow, so we can finish our talk?'

But before I'd even finished asking, I knew she was already scanning her repository of excuses.

'Actually I need to get back home quite early tomorrow,' she said. 'So if you don't mind I'd like to leave as soon as possible.'

'Ok,' I replied. 'I hope you got through your reading quota.'

'No, but I made a few inroads. It was good to have the space.'

What we weren't saying could have populated a regular sized galaxy, but it wasn't the right moment. All that night I kept dreaming, waking, dreaming again, and hearing the thousands of cracks in my life snicking wider and wider, as though something was being born in the starless dark far below.

Chapter Twenty

The drive back to London was without incident – with the exception of an alien starship landing in the road in front of us to ask directions to our leader. No, sorry, I made that up. Sometimes I have this urge to invent things. Well, you know all about that. My therapist said I should write everything down, to exorcise the guilt. But it's not guilt, it's boredom. Why can't we live in a world where impossible things happen? Maybe we do, but we're always too busy to notice.

Elaine was in conciliatory mood, and we reached home without having another row, which was pretty miraculous. She even offered to cook a meal when we got in. There was the usual heap of junk mail, mixed in with bills and threats and green-ink messages from people who had actually visited the aliens on their home planet, and been given the elixir of immortality and the secret of instantaneous teleportation to anywhere in the cosmos, and were prepared to come to an agreement on releasing their knowledge for a reasonable consideration.

I put the bills at the back of the drawer, and the rest went in the bin. While Elaine was preparing the meal I went to look at the cube, imagining by now it would be scattered like an abandoned toy all across the room. To my complete astonishment not only was it still intact, but it was glowing. I approached it as though it were a cornered tiger, and gazed at the shimmering matrix of tiny cubes: I could now see right through to the bottom and through each side, so that its interior revealed a fine 3D grid of two-centimetre cells, as though the hundreds of separate cubes had fused into one parent Cube: it seemed to go down indefinitely, like looking into parallel mirrors, except that there was no loss of resolution as the image receded: a perfect infinity. But how had they done it, with no one in the house to align them?

I experienced an overwhelming urge to put my hand inside. Very slowly I dipped my fingers into its surface, and felt no resistance at all: what had once been rows of identical metal boxes was now nothing but luminous space. I sank my arm deeper, but there was no change: it did not shrivel into a useless charred appendage, nor did it begin to writhe horribly with alien life. I withdrew it and felt the skin: not even cold.

Impressive as this new toy was, it didn't seem to do anything particularly useful: it didn't talk to me, didn't give me cryptic advice; there were no flashing rainbow lights moving in it, it didn't appear to be visibly growing, and it didn't have any influence on the physical environment, as the original Cube had had. To be fair, it was much smaller: maybe this was a response to the hostile reception given to its original. Cube Mark II would be far easier to conceal from its enemies.

I was on the point of turning away to return to Elaine when an uncanny thing happened: I felt an almost physical tug somewhere in my head, as though someone had switched on a very powerful electric field, and without knowing what was happening I found myself lowering my head into the glowing space. Once more there was no resistance: the solid metal had been transformed it seemed into a sculpture of pure light. How in heaven had they done it? As soon as my head was immersed I lost all consciousness of having a physical body; I was a mind floating freely in a vast, faintly luminous region, extending without limit in every direction; and as my eyes adjusted I became aware of stars: tiny but intense points of light, miraculous in their multitude of hues never seen from earth. I discovered I could look around without restriction: even 'behind' me the void continued, in some directions quite black and empty of stars, and in others articulated by enormous tenuous clouds of violet and mauve light. I could see no constellations that I recognized, which puzzled me until I understood I was seeing this from a totally different perspective than our own solar system afforded, and the familiar relationships between the stars of the terrestrial sky no longer held.

And then came that indescribable feeling of connectedness that I'd first felt back in the old days when Les first made contact via his carefully constructed human personality. It felt like coming home. It felt like remembering who you really were in your deepest heart of hearts. It felt like a continual orgasm that didn't depend on time or effort. It felt like every great piece of music you've ever heard all experienced in one instant. And in the middle of the bliss little bits of conceptual information crept into my awareness, a bit like mice creeping into the middle of an elephants' prayer meeting. Such as the knowledge that I was in fact looking at the Owl Nebula from a point inside it. And that this experience was probably what every yogi and mystic on earth had been aiming at through years and decades of unremitting discipline. And that someone was calling me with increasing urgency to come down to the kitchen and eat immediately, otherwise my cheese omelette would be completely inedible.

Gradually the normal world re-established itself. Voices in the street, a dog barking, the noises of the central heating pipes. I lifted my head and saw sunlight – which for an instant seemed shocking in its alienness. And then my normal human habits kicked in: I remembered where I was, what I had been doing before this hiatus, and felt the slightly ridiculous human sensation of hunger.

Despite my alien experience I ate as though I'd been on starvation rations for a week. Elaine watched me with increasing bafflement.

'Are you in training for the marathon or something?'

'Just restoring the essential nutrients,' – which was an odd reply until I realized that was probably exactly what I was doing. I couldn't begin to think how I could explain where I'd just been: she'd have had my name down for the funny farm quicker than you could shout alien. Yet I needed to tell somebody.

Mark took an age to answer the phone.

'Sorry, I was having a bath. How was Sidmouth?'

'Let's say challenging. Mark, I need to tell you something about the Cube we built. Something very strange has happened to it.'

When I got round to the total immersion bit, his silence went on for so long I thought the Cube had found a way to pour itself down the phone line.

'I don't think we should discuss this on the phone. Can you meet me at the usual place?'

'Sure. Usual time?'

'Yes.'

It wasn't until he'd hung up that it dawned on me that I'd no idea what the usual place and time were. And I didn't dare ask my brain.

'Wouldn't it be nice to have something better to do than save the world?' I asked Mark when we'd miraculously hit on the right table, time, cafe and day. 'We could cross the Namibian desert on foot carrying a fridge.'

Mark smiled thinly. 'So you put your head in it?'

'That's one way of putting it, yes. Though it didn't feel like I was doing it.'

'So we know it's working. And the aliens are behind it. Two crucial bits of information. Well done!'

'And we know it has extremely effective powers of persuasion.'

'And that so far no one else knows about it. How about Elaine?'

'I haven't said anything. But it's only a matter of time. I can't ban her from going in there.'

'Adam, I know I've said this before, but it's vital we keep the media away from this business as long as possible. Certainly until we know more about it, and how the aliens intend to use it. You know what happened to the original Cube. This one is easier to hide, at least for now.'

'There may be others.'

'I'd expect there to be. My guess is the aliens will build a network of them, until they have enough to gain critical mass. After that it won't matter.'

'What do you mean?'

'Once their network is running, everyone will have the kind of experience you had yesterday. The whole planet will fall in love with them.'

'Isn't that a bit fanciful? We've no evidence that's what they're planning. I'd have thought a better strategy would be to establish contact with a few key people – presidents and CEOs of major corporations for example – and let them influence the rest of the planet.'

'No. Too slow. That was Plan A. I think they've abandoned that line of thought. Hence the new super-Cube: far more effective and discreet. By the time they're discovered it'll be too late to stop them.' It was all beginning to sound like a re-run of Invasion of the Body Snatchers. Sooner or later the existence of the new Cube would get out, inevitably.

And then mayhem would erupt throughout the civilized world. I began to wish I could keep my head inside the thing – permanently.

'I think this cube business is affecting Elaine.'

'How?'

'She's withdrawn into her study. She's edgy whenever I want to talk about our relationship. She thinks I mooch around too much. We've lost the intimacy we used to have. I used to feel totally at ease with her: we could talk about anything, or nothing: we just loved being together. Now there's this gulf that hangs between us. And it's all happened since these artefacts started arriving.'

Mark sat hunched over the table, trying to coax some dregs of tea from the pot. The old haunted expression momentarily returned to his eyes, reminding me of the first time we met: the disconsolate lone revolutionary looking for a cause to devote his life to.

'I don't know what to say, Adam. I'm not exactly the person to advise you on relationships. Maybe you should have some time on your own. Maybe some clear space will rebalance things.' He drained his cup and yawned. 'You know, I have my doubts about all this studying. It can be a displacement activity. Maybe she wants a family but won't admit it.'

'Well, she's got one. The thing she spends every minute of the day with.'

'But she's on her way into the world. I mean maybe Elaine wants babies. You know? Little smelly helpless beings to nurture.'

'I doubt it. She's never mentioned anything about wanting more children. And that's another thing that worries me: Nicola won't speak to me any more. She just stays away when I'm around, like I'm an infectious disease or something. I wonder sometimes if she sees that I'm not quite human.'

'Rubbish. You're as human as I am. But, well, to be truthful, on occasion you do go slightly AWOL. Emotionally I mean. You have a way or distancing yourself. As though being present is too dangerous.'

'Which it is. I don't deny it.'

'I expect Elaine picks that up. She's probably especially sensitive, having the sort of father she had.'

'How do you know what sort of father she had?'

'She told me about him.' He must have seen the controlled shock in my eyes. 'Is there something wrong with that?'

'Of course not. It's just that she's hardly ever spoken to me about her father. It seems to be a painful topic.'

'Have you ever asked her about him?'

'I don't remember. Probably not.'

'There you are then. Mystery solved.'

'She's going to find the Cube pretty soon. I can't forbid her to enter its room. I don't think she's going to like the idea of another permanent resident she doesn't have any control over.'

'If she understands how important it is she may accept it.'

'More likely she'll see it as yet another source of chaos from my dangerous friends in the sky.'

'Then we'll have to embark on an emergency crash-course in alien diplomacy.'

'Rather you than me.'

'If that's a challenge, I accept.'

I couldn't explain it: maybe it was because he had no irons in the fire, so to speak, but I suddenly felt a great warmth and gratitude towards him.

'You're a good friend, Mark. I don't know anyone else I can talk like this to. I mean, without having to conceal anything. But why don't you introduce Elaine to our new lodger? I'm sure she'd be more receptive to you than to me. And it'll be nice for her to have a little friend in the house to talk to.'

Mark jumped to his feet, looking worried, as if remembering he should be somewhere else.

'Our little friend may grow up to be quite a handful.' He groped in his pocket. 'Please let me pay for this, will you?'

Chapter Twenty One

It seemed appropriate that I'd finally migrated from a secondhand bookshop with hardly any customers to a psychiatric hospital with hardly any visitors. An inevitable step, you might think, for someone like me. People were there because nobody knew what to do with them: they couldn't be finally cured and they couldn't be returned to what's risibly called the community because they couldn't look after themselves, or else they had their own rules about what constituted reality. But mostly their families, if they had any, didn't want to know: they were just relieved that someone was taking the physical and moral burden from their weary shoulders. Actually I felt a strong sympathy with most of the inmates: they weren't violent or abusive, just very sad and lonely, and they couldn't understand why their lives had taken this disastrous course.

My favourite was Mary, a small woman of around fifty who had some kind of premature dementia, and who was clinically incapable of staying in one place for more than ten seconds. If she was tied up she screamed unremittingly. That had been tried, apparently, a few years back, and no-one could forget the terrible wailing sound that went on all through the night. It was now considered best practice to allow patients – not yet called customers, but it's only a matter of time, I'm sure – to wander at will, provided they didn't endanger anyone. And Mary certainly made good use of her limited freedom. She had a routine which she kept to rigorously – or until she was prevented by other routines imposed by the hospital. She began as soon as breakfast was over, doing her circuit of every accessible room, whether it was in her part of the building or not. In fact the further she had to go the better, as it occupied more time – and time was the enemy. I could see her point: if she stayed in one place, undistracted by new sensations, she would have to think, and thinking would sooner or later lead to terror – or the awareness that she was no longer capable of thought – which was probably worse. So she moved along her invisible railway tracks, stopping when presented with an obstruction, or occasionally circumventing it if it went on for too long, directing her bleak, corrosive smile on anyone who made eye contact with her. I felt pity for her, and tried to make her life easier in small ways whenever I could. There but for the grace of God, I thought. And there was George, a real Pinter character who'd lived in Kent all his life and was just waiting for his son, dead ten years ago, to finish building his house so he could be taken back. George was another obsessive: his thing was stones. Whenever he got the opportunity he'd collect stones and smuggle them into his room, and woe betide anyone who so much as moved one half an inch from its resting place. I used to kid him that he'd turn into a stone himself if he didn't watch out – until he told me, yes, that was what he hoped and prayed would happen, and the sooner the better. 'Stones have their own lives,' he told me, 'and no human being will ever know what goes on in the mind of a stone. They were there before humans were planted on the earth, and for certain they'll be there after the last human has returned to dust. A moment that can't come too soon for me.' The only problem with George was he forever pestered the other patients to get stones for him, and some of them were scared of him – understandably because he was very tall and had a way of towering over you when speaking. When people saw him approaching them with that mad-prophet gleam in his eyes there was a collective shrinking away – as near as most of them could get to a stampede.

I got a gold star from Elaine for getting this job: she recognized what an effort it had been for me to uproot myself from the safe backwater of the bookshop. But of course what I didn't tell her was that I had a secret project which, if it worked, would help humanity's suffering infinitely more than any drugs or psychotherapy could.

Mary was prowling along the edge of the dining room smiling her black smile of death at everyone, who of course studiously ignored her. I decided to walk along with her for a stretch, to see how the room looked through her eyes.

'How are you today then, Mary?'

Silence. The shuffling slowed, as if she'd encountered an unexpected incline.

'Are you sleeping well?'

Her face folded into its counterfeit smile, and then she said, as if I'd asked her what her favourite animals were, 'The owls.'

'They keep you awake?'

She stopped and looked furtive.

'They want me to kill the doctor.'

'Ah.'

'You must... promise... not say.'

'Alright. I promise.'

'Isn't human.'

'What isn't?'

'Anti-human. Like anti-matter, see?'

'Not really.'

She stopped abruptly and glared directly at me. 'Zombie. Far away.' Her arm struggled to indicate huge distance.

'And the owls told you this?'

She nodded. 'And more. Much more.' She started her relentless shuffle again, her lips banged together. 'Forbidden.'

I suddenly felt a pang of empathy for this friendless and desolate woman shuffling away into her homeless future. I was possessed by a conviction that this kind of thing need not and should not happen.

I decided to put my plan into action. In one sense it was blissfully simple: I'd take Mary home with me one afternoon and immerse her in the Cube. It would be easy getting her out: I regularly took the inmates – sorry, patients – out into the country for recreation, and increasingly I was allowed to do it unsupervised. All I had to do was choose a day when I knew they were short on staff, sign Mary out, and drive her home. I had a good relationship with the ward staff, and so long as we were back by five o'clock I was sure no one would worry unduly about where I was taking her.

Mary had her dreadful smile on as she manoeuvred herself into the car. I strapped her in and started the engine. As we moved off I noticed she was waving like the Queen. I don't know where on earth she imagined we were going.

I wanted to find out something about her life, but that lethal smile stood implacably between me and the human being within. Her hands incessantly stroked each other, as though she feared they might strangle someone if not continually calmed.

'Mary, do you remember what you did when you were younger? Did you have a job?'

It may have been my imagination, but I thought the smile relaxed its grip a tiny fraction.

She looked fixedly ahead.

'They—'. After that syllable she clammed up. I tried another tack.

'Where did you live before you came here? Can you tell me that?'

'Yes. It's alright to tell you that. Barmouth.'

'Who tells you if it's alright to tell things?'

'They.' The smile stalled again, and the hands ceased stroking, as if weighing up which of us should be strangled first.

'The owls?'

Her lips tightened. She flicked a glance through the window, then she said:

'Does he pay you?'

'The hospital pays. Not very much, but yes, they do pay me.'

She thought about this a long time. Then said very quietly:

'Then... you're... not... ...friend.'

'Yes. I am a friend. I would like to get to know you a bit.'

'No. Not friend. He pays you.' This said with great vehemence.

I had to admit her logic. Given that the chief doctor at the hospital wasn't human, he was employing me, therefore I was doing his work, and his work was to destroy humans. The thing I had to discover was why she believed the first axiom.

'The hospital is paying me to look after you, not to brainwash or sterilize you. No one is doing that.'

The smile was back in place again. Obviously I would say that, wouldn't I? And I clearly wasn't going to get her trust as long as she believed I was in the pay of the enemy.

'Tell me about the owls. Where do they live?'

She turned to face me, as though the question exposed me as an idiot. Her eyes were burning with held feeling. 'Everywhere!'

'In this car?'

She nodded, then very slowly intoned: 'Hoobris. Flapjo. Nighbane. Cracket..'

'Those are their names?'

She nodded again.

'Do you think they'd talk to me?'

'Christmas.' She glanced sideways again. 'You have to be Christmas.'

'What do you mean? How can I be Christmas? Do you mean Father Christmas?'

She considered this, then shook her head vigorously. 'Little Christmas.'

Even with my inbuilt sympathy for the chronically misunderstood, I felt I was on a losing wicket.

'Ah. You mean I must give them presents. Little presents, yes?'

'They—'.

We'd come back full circle, which seemed like a defeat. But then she seemed suddenly to find a way through my willful intransigence.

'You. We. They. Begin.'

'Begin? Begin what?'

'Christmas.'

It was my turn to subside into silence.

I cut the engine and walked around to let her out.

'We're here,' I said with as much brightness as I could muster.

'You might be. I'm not,' said Mary. I was astounded at her sudden loquacity. Five connected words that actually made sense. It seemed almost they were coming from someone else.

As I helped her towards the house I suddenly feared she'd panic when confronted by the Cube, and refuse to go near it. I imagined her rushing screaming from the house directly into the path of an oncoming vehicle. So I tried to prepare her.

'I have a wonderful Christmas present upstairs,' I said in the steadiest voice I could manage while coaxing her across the threshold. 'It will talk to you and show you dreams. Amazing dreams. Whatever you've lost, it will help you find it.' Of course this was largely blarney on my part, because I had no hard evidence that it would do anything at all for her. But I desperately wanted it to work, if only because it seemed this outcast of humanity had no other recourse but years of useless drug regimes and patronizing pep-talks.

I sat her in the kitchen and made tea, by way of saying thank you for being my guinea pig, although of course she hadn't signed a release or anything. After one sip she set it down and said more loudly than I'd ever heard her speak before:

'I'm not mad you know.' The classic last defence of the mad.

'I know you're not. That's why I've brought you here. I think you could help lots of other people.'

'Things keep getting – They –.'

'The owls?' I prompted.

She nodded and smiled, took up her tea, and put it down again.

'Have you got Christmas?'

'Only once a year, I'm afraid. Not now. Two months ago.'

I put the things in the sink and led her to the stairs.

'We have to go up here. Can you make it?'

I stood behind her. She stood at the bottom like a recalcitrant toddler.

'I have two you know. Somewhere.'

'Owls?'

'No.' She looked frustrated. 'Christmas.'

'Do you mean children?'

She beamed at me, the smile suddenly transformed into something human, then put a hand on the bannister.

When she saw the Cube her face seemed to liquify, as though her muscles had suddenly realized the impossibility of keeping anything together under the onslaught of this utter newness. My fears of her fleeing headlong to instant death in the street proved entirely unfounded. Instead she walked right up to it and stretched her arms out horizontally before her, as though greeting a very thin long-lost friend. The smile on her face had entirely vanished, and been replaced with something I didn't recognize, but which might just possibly have been joy.

I didn't see how she could come to any harm, so I stayed at the back of the room and watched her walk right through the surface of the cube, and then sink down until her head and shoulders were embraced by it. It seemed like watching someone enter a confessional, although no words were uttered. She stayed in that position an awfully long time, and I recalled that when I'd done the same I'd had absolutely no sense of time passing whatever. But after ten minutes I began to worry that it might be too much for her brain, and she'd come out a vegetable, or worse, whatever worse could be. I was really most worried about having to explain to the doctor what I'd done, and losing my job, and maybe being charged with abduction, and the whole thing being exposed in the press. So I gently called out to her. At once she turned around and began walking slowly out of the Cube towards me. She certainly didn't look like a vegetable. Her eyes were open and the rigor mortis smile had gone. I don't know what I'd been expecting, but the self-assured silence unnerved me more than the smile from hell had done. When we were back in the car I asked her:

'What happened in there?'

Her expression remained perfectly blank, her hands perfectly still in her lap, as though drugged. I almost longed for her to start screaming.

'It's about time to go back home now Mary. Are you ready?'

Instantly a horror came over her face.

'No. No. No. Not.'

I couldn't honestly say her encounter with the Cube had made the slightest improvement in her vocabulary.

'You'll miss your tea. And I'll get into trouble.'

'No. Not. Can't. We. They.'

'Well, where do you want to go?' I sat there holding the keys and staring at her as though she were my daughter having a sugar tantrum.

She pointed ahead, away from the direction we'd come from.

'Hill.'

'OK. That's fine. What we'll do is we'll have a little drive around the hills. But it will soon be dark, and you'll need to eat. We've no food with us.' The last thing I wanted was to give her the idea that she could stay in our house.

'Hill,' she repeated. 'Top big hill.'

So I drove her to the highest part of the hill and parked in a lay-by which had a lovely view across Somerset. Almost before we came to a halt she was fumbling at the door like a child just arrived at the seaside.

'Would you like a little walk?' I was starting to feel very nervous about this escapade. It wasn't part of my plan, and I didn't want to trigger a search party. But neither did I like the idea of forcing her to return to a regime that was slowly killing her spirit, if not her body.

We walked away from the road, following a narrow track bordered by gorse and brown-edged bracken. She was moving purposefully now, as though pulled by an invisible beacon. I had a hard job keeping up.

I called: 'Mary! Slow down!' If she heard me, she gave no sign, but ploughed on through the darkening foliage. I called again, peering ahead to see where she'd gone, and immediately tripped over a tree-root and fell headlong into deep undergrowth. Of course by the time I'd got to my feet she'd vanished entirely.

I have to confess this turn of events put me into a spin. This inarticulate shuffling woman had suddenly turned into a possessed spirit, a creature of unknown affinities. Or maybe she'd simply been patiently awaiting her one window of freedom all along, and claimed it the first moment it appeared. Who could blame her?

With twilight deepening every moment I stumbled along the maze of twisting tracks calling Mary's name every few seconds. For a moment it felt a bit like one of those childhood hide and seek games where you hoped to get rewarded with a nervous kiss in the dark from the girl you found: your special secret that you carried with you like a delicious angel for days or sometimes weeks afterwards. But in this case the stakes were somewhat higher.

I found myself on a bluff overlooking woods that stretched away southwards. It was already six o'clock and I hadn't a hope of getting Mary back to the hospital without detection, even supposing I found her. I imagined the panic that would be going on there; the wild rumours that would be flashing from patient to patient, sounding more and more loopy with each leap. I wondered how I could have allowed my brain to get me into such an insane position, chasing a madwoman through the countryside at night after subjecting her to the completely unknown influence of an alien artefact. Were these the actions of an entirely rational person? Was this something I wanted to see on my CV when I applied for the post of lecturer in Applied Psycho-Dynamics at Exeter?

I turned despondently – in fact despairingly, if I'm honest – to retrace my steps when I thought I heard singing. My first assumption was that it must be my brain locked in its prison trying to keep its spirits up, but as I walked it got louder until when I stopped I could hear the words: it was a woman's voice, and it was singing a hymn, "All things bright and beautiful." It had to be Mary.

She was standing on top of a large boulder on a fist of high ground, holding her arms up to the sky as though blessing an invisible crowd of enrapt followers. When I approached she stopped singing and looked directly at me.

'Not.'

'Don't worry Mary. I won't make you go back if you don't want to. But we can't stay up here all night. You'll freeze to death.'

'Not hospital.'

'I promise. Not hospital.'

But I'd not the faintest idea what to do with her. Going back to Elaine's was clearly out. And once I'd made the promise not to take her back it was unthinkable to renege on it. So in silence we filed through the thickets of gorse and hazel back to the car, and stared into the last fading hues of the sunset.

'So where do you want to go?' I asked, feeling more and more guilty.

'Teeth,' she replied.

'You want teeth? But you've got some very nice ones of your own.'

'Teeth. Up and down.' She mimed chewing. The age-old biological imperatives were kicking in.

I thought of all the towns and cities all over Britain that we could drive to: places with solid sounding names that made it seem they were real places, places not conceived of by Man's ever hopeful imagination. Birmingham. Liverpool. Carstairs. Pickering. Places with pubs and flickering orange street-lights and puddles full of incomprehensible colours. Places that tempted one to imagine they harboured solutions. But I didn't allow myself that luxury.

'What we'll do, Mary, is we'll go and find a hotel and have a good meal. How does that sound?'

'Rock and Roll!' Probably code for 'Right on, Daddio.'

I drove for half an hour, aiming for Minehead, then decided to swing south and find somewhere on Exmoor. Mary sat and beamed all the way, happy to be putting precious miles between her and the hated hospital. We stopped at a village that had an Inn called the Fox, whose restaurant was almost deserted. I ordered a very upper class fish and chips with dainty carrots and slices of lemon, which Mary consumed as though she'd never seen anything like it before and may never do again. When she'd finished there was a spotlessly clean white dish, give or take a few bones, in front of her. After the meal I tried asking her about her family, but either she had no memories left or else it was too painful for her to go there.

We'd got to the coffee – weak and lukewarm, naturally – when she suddenly started talking. It didn't make much sense, but technically at least it was talking.

'The person... bought horse. The only thing. The only thing. I loved. Maisie. Maisie Horse. The only one.'

'Your father bought you a horse?'

Her eyes brimmed over and her cheeks flamed with shame. Tears were freely coursing down over them. They reminded me of rain on a bus window, the way the drops streaked rivers on the glass, stopped short and started out again in a different direction.

'Lovely deep brown. He stopped the boat. It was so warm I took my cardigan off. Ham sandwiches. What are we going to do now?'

'I don't know Mary. We have to get you back.'

'No. Not back. They—.'

'We can't stay here all night.'

'Yes, we can. Can stay here. Not back.' She looked at me, imploring.

After another half hour of trying to tease some more memories out of her, I went out to the reception desk and booked a couple of adjacent single rooms for us. I gave Mary her key and hoped desperately she wouldn't walk off in the night.

That night I did some deep soul-searching. In particular I wondered how on earth I'd got myself into this impossible position. Mary hadn't been my responsibility: she wasn't in danger, she wasn't being abused. I saw that I wanted to prove that I had in my stewardship a panacea for the world's ills; I wanted respect and serious attention, and I'd grabbed

Mary as my means to achieve it. But of course I was now stuck with it: a classic Macbeth moment: we are so far mired in blood that to go back would be as bad as going on. Or words to that effect.

Chapter Twenty One

I was staggered the next morning to find Mary not only dressed and washed but waiting for me in the restaurant with her hat on, looking as though she'd been frequenting inns and restaurants all her life (which she may have done, of course). She caught my eye and beamed.

'Is it today?'

'Yes, it is. Did you sleep well?'

'They said it was alright to tell you.'

'The owls?'

She nodded. 'My father.'

I felt something important was coming, and gave her my full attention. Her face was flushed with emotion, which was shocking to see in someone who'd never expressed anything directly at all as long as I'd known her.

'He locked.'

'Locked you up?'

Vigorous nodding. A terrible picture was starting to form. I didn't want to hear any more, because it seemed it would have no end, and I'd have no more control over my life. But something impelled me to ask:

'Why?'

'Not tell. Too... dangerous.'

'Did he... hurt you?'

With agonizing effort, she found the words to convey the first moments of the thing that had taken her life from her. Her father had begun to rape her when she turned ten: the first time was on her tenth birthday. To stop her telling anyone he kept her locked in a basement room for nine years, during which time she saw no one: no humans, no animals, no daylight, no starlight. Until one morning she found her chance to escape: she grabbed a knife he'd forgotten about and stabbed him in the throat in the middle of sex. She ran out into the blinding sunlight drenched in blood and ran to the nearest passer-by she could find; luckily it was a woman who took her to a nearby police station.

When she'd finished her story I sat dumbstruck, gripping my empty cup as if that might somehow prevent the whole world sliding irretrievably into chaos. There was nothing I could say that wouldn't be either crass or inadequate or both at once. But a decision was unavoidable. I rang Elaine's number and left a message that I was ok but wouldn't be home for a day or two, due to unavoidable commitments. Then I left Mary in the lounge while I did some shopping for essential supplies. In a supermarket I searched the newspapers for reports of an inmate of a psychiatric hospital absconding with one of the staff, but thankfully found nothing. There was however a disturbing report of something the west had been secretly dreading for years: a group calling itself the United Islamic Brotherhood had issued a statement that it had proof that the US had re-opened secret communications with the Aliens and were in process of doing a deal to eliminate the Islamic States as 'the major source of global instability and war'. Needless to say they were pretty upset, and demanded the US allow 'full and unconditional inspection' of all its military and research establishments without delay.' Failing this, the group said, there would be an 'intervention' on US soil that would make 9/11 look like – here they were clearly struggling to find a convincing analogy – 'a bored child playing with a toy aeroplane and a packet of cornflakes on a hard Saturday afternoon.'

I drove for several hours without having much sense of where I was going, guided mainly by Mary's horrified whimpers whenever we appeared to be drifting eastwards, or her childlike smile of relief when we were heading west again.

'You know if we keep going this way we'll hit the sea, and then we'll have to turn round or be drowned.'

She nodded, smiling at top speed, her hands calming each other in her lap. We stopped for a lunch of pie and chips at a pub on the edge of Bodmin Moor that had a garden full of tables. I felt the time had come for us to have a straightforward talk about the future. We sat facing each other across the table, like any normal couple out for a day trip.

'Mary, I don't believe you are mad or dangerous, to yourself or to anyone else. When we get back home I'll tell the doctor what I think. I'll say you've made a huge improvement while you've been away, and in my opinion you're safe to be returned to society. In any case as long as you're there you'll still see me every day, and I'll protect you from those pills and stuff they give you. Will you trust me?'

This time there was an instant response from the owls.

'They... say not go back. Nothing good there.'

'Have you any family living?'

She thought she had a brother who worked for the Council, somewhere in Norfolk, but she hadn't heard from him for most of the time she'd been in hospital.

'Do you remember his name?'

'Hack.'

'That was his name?'

'Or Black. Black Hack. Sack Hack.'

'Would you like to find him?'

'Jack. Jack Horse. That's it. Easy Jack. Easy there.'

'We could find him I'm sure, if you wanted. But we'd have to go back to the hospital first. Otherwise—.'

The terror returned to her eyes, and she slumped in her seat like a body emptied of life. I didn't think I had the nerve to force her to go back to her life of fear and intimidation and interminable silent shuffling.

We went slowly back to the car and sat inside in silence. Mary hunched into a crumpled bird-like figure, her arms hugged around her waist in a desperate attempt to protect her from the future. I had no clue where to go next; my brain seemed to have gone off to a planet where it could guarantee there wouldn't be people like me to interfere with its serenity. Mary sat without expression gazing at the road ahead, as though she knew the next part of her life would arrive along it at any moment, every so often raising her hands in front of her face and then dropping them in her lap like discarded glove puppets.

Then she said, without taking her eyes off the grey rising flank of the road: 'There are no owls you know.'

'Yes, I know.'

'They were just my pain.'

I turned the car and inched around the tortuous bends back the way we had come. Mary accepted it without murmur.

Chapter Twenty Three

I know exactly what I have to do: appear rational and penitent. But that's a whole world from what I'm feeling right now, because I have this seething clot of anger inside me that has ballooned up from nowhere, and now it hangs like a gigantic insane crow between me and the doctor. We're in his office, on the second floor of the hospital where Mary has been reinstated after her magical rebirth. She spends her days shuffling and calling out to someone, anyone, pretty much as she used to. At night they give her something new, recently developed, which has fewer side-effects, but which is still designed basically to keep her from disturbing the other patients too much.

Dr. Nicholson's office is a little kingdom to itself, with a neatly engraved name on the door in white on black lettering: DR. R. NICHOLSON. The room itself is tidy, meticulous, elegant in its small way, with a view westwards to the Quantocks. There are the rows of statutory medical volumes, a modern laptop, a sound system, a large digital wall-clock, a modular brown and cream sofa and a sustainably-sourced hardwood coffee table. It is all meant to give the message: 'I am a substantial figure, I know what I'm about'. But I tell myself I am the rational one – though not remotely penitent.

'Can't you see how much she's changed?' I begin hopefully. I'm trying desperately to make him see I understand the situation, despite the fact of being a mere orderly, with not a relevant qualification in sight.

'In all honesty, Adam, no, I can't. If anything she's worse. Her sense of identity seems altogether absent. She has to be sedated every night otherwise she disturbs everyone with her incessant wailing—'.

'But she wasn't like that when she was out of here! Really! She calmed down, began to talk about her father and her childhood. Has she ever done that here, even once, in all the time you've known her?'

'I've only your word on that.'

'And my word isn't good enough, right?'

I have to stop this confrontation right away, because I know exactly where it's coming from, and what it will lead to. I can see him thinking about leading me to the door, with the avuncular protective arm behind me, in the time-honoured method of doctors faced with incipient pudding-cases. I try an apology.

'I'm sorry. The fact is, I've grown very fond of Mary. She's suffered a lot. But she has the capacity to come to terms with what's happened, if you give her a fighting chance. I don't think, to be honest, she's getting the treatment she really needs here. I respect your training and experience. But Mary's been here almost ten years! If she hasn't responded to treatment in that time, I would have thought it was time to change the treatment. Try something different.'

'And indeed we have. But the mind is very complex, Adam. Sometimes processes take many years to come to fruition—.'

'And yet while she was out with me she began talking about her childhood and her father's treatment of her for the first time, as far as I know. Surely that tells you something?'

'It certainly does. It confirms we're on the right track. And you have to remember that people on long-term treatment regimes can appear to make a dramatic improvement for a time and then slip back very steeply. This is clearly the case with Mary. We'd be very stupid to release her on the evidence – according to you – of two days' improved behaviour, don't you think?'

Obviously I couldn't tell him about the Cube, but it seemed clear to me that it had been a material factor in her sudden improvement.

'With respect, I think someone being genuinely interested in her and listening without prejudice to her story, plus the effect of nature and fresh air has had far more benefit than the drugs you give her. And that seems to be all your treatment programme amounts to, as far as I can see.'

'Adam, how long have you been working here?'

'Five months.'

'Five months. And you consider that long enough for someone with no medical training whatever to get a balanced picture of someone's psychological health?'

'It's not only a matter of time.' I was on the back foot, and felt I was being manipulated into confessing my inadequacy to make a judgement.

'Oh indeed? So what, in your opinion, is it a matter of?'

'I would say it's a matter of empathy and love, above all else. That's what she's lacking. It's obvious when you really look at her. And communication of course. Genuine interest in the conditions of someone's life.'

'So the dedicated commitment of a team of highly-trained professionals over nine years counts for nothing, in your opinion?'

'I wouldn't say that, no. But it relies heavily on drugs to suppress symptoms, and those symptoms may be crucial signals as to the true cause of the problem. If you eliminate them you're closing down a whole avenue of exploration.'

'So let me just see if I understand you correctly. You think allowing someone to harm themselves regularly, or spend every night tramping around the wards howling is therapeutic? Is that right?'

'No, that isn't what I'm saying. I'm saying look at what's behind those impulses. That person has a whole life behind them. Her symptoms come out of that life, and can be understood only in terms of that life.'

'Mr. Stone, I have to say I think your view of psychiatry is simplistic and ill-informed to the point of irresponsibility. Do you imagine taking a deeply traumatized and delusional patient for an afternoon joyride is really going to engage with the roots of that trauma?' He stood up and slid his chair back – clearly a bad sign – then placed both hands on the edge of his desk as though holding the thing on the ground with great effort.

'In the circumstances I believe your staying on with us may be detrimental to the welfare of the patients. So I'm sorry to say you will not be staying on with us after the end of the term of your contract. I'm sorry. Now if you'll excuse me.'

This time there was not even the avuncular arm behind my shoulders as I left the room.

Chapter Twenty Four

So the bookshop reclaimed me, much to Elaine's chagrin. I was lucky I had at least one good business relationship in my life.

'For God's sake, Adam. Why did you have to pick a fight with the hospital that you work at? It was obvious what their reaction was going to be. And what good have you done?'

'I've taken a stand. And if everyone who has any principles took a stand on them the world would change for the better.'

'You lost a useful job. You caused a lot of worry. You've got yourself a reputation as a troublemaker. And Mary's back in exactly the state she was in before.'

'That's because they won't let me have any contact with her.'

'I don't blame them, to be perfectly honest.'

'Well thanks very much.'

'I know your heart's in the right place. But you don't consider the effects of your actions. You're nearly fifty and you act like a twenty year old.'

There was a time when I'd have been stung by such a remark and stormed out into the rain, if there had been rain. Yet I knew there was no virtue in arguing the point, because it wasn't about my having a disagreement with the hospital; it was about Elaine's disappointment with me as a potential life-partner. And that was decided by the fates.

'I'm sorry to disappoint you,' I said with genuine sorrow. 'But I had to say it. The way they're treating that woman is terrible. If I'd put my job before her welfare I couldn't live with myself. And if I couldn't live with myself how could you?'

That was the clinching question of course, implying that, as I had found a way to live with myself, it followed that Elaine could do so too. But something far down in my heart was murmuring to itself, 'Alas! Alas for the bright fields of spring where I may wander no more!'

'I've no idea what I'm going to do with this lot,' the woman said as she reached the counter. 'This is only a fraction of it.'

She still had her good looks, although I thought she must be forty at least. Slightly built, cultivated and austere, but with a mischievous alertness about her. I thought I'd seen her somewhere before.

'Have we met?'

'Not that I remember.' She placed a pile of books on the counter for me to inspect, then brushed the hair from her eyes. Now that I saw her closely, I detected a film of sorrow and vulnerability in them.

'Are you selling a collection?'

'I don't want to. He built it up over a lifetime. It was his life. But I have to sell the house, so it simply has to go. That's life, isn't it?'

I flicked through some of the books, pausing to inspect one or two more closely. She kept her gaze on me the whole time.

'Are you interested? I could come back later.'

'They're interesting books.'

'That means you're not.'

'It's just that my partner—'.

'Ok. I'll try somewhere else.' She moved to reclaim her pile.

'No. I am interested. It's simply that I'm only the assistant—'.

'Oh yes, of course. She needs to see them also. I understand.'

'He'll be in this afternoon if you'd like to leave them.' I smiled, to make up for my apparent lack of interest in the books.

'Ok. There's a whole houseful of them if you'd care to come and look. I only brought these as a sample of the kind of thing my husband collected. Come any afternoon except Friday. My name's Kate, by the way.' She handed me a card that said: "Kate MacDonald. Reichean Therapy. Energy re-balancing. Stress Management."

I drove out to see her the following Monday. She had a house on the coast about a mile from Minehead, built in the early 20th Century, with neo-Gothic turrets and rusticated tilework. She showed me the book collection which was housed in three small rooms with windows overlooking the Channel.

'What was your husband's particular interest?' I asked, trying to prevent my gaze from straying repeatedly to the pale blue shoulderless dress she'd chosen.

'Twentieth Century Children's Fiction. His one great regret in life was he never managed to acquire a first edition of The Hobbit. He'd have died happy if he'd got his hands on one of those.'

'Were you very close?'

'It depends what you mean by close. We'd been together twenty years. There was a great fondness on both sides. He was invariably kind and thoughtful. Always bringing me things back from his expeditions. I couldn't have wished for a better partner, in many ways.'

'Sounds like there was a 'but' in there.'

She smiled. 'Yes. There was.' She moved to the window and sat looking out at the glistening rooftops. 'I don't quite know how to say this elegantly. The fact is, he stopped fucking me.'

The sound of that word in those chaste surroundings shocked me, as no doubt she'd meant it to.

'I'm sorry to bring that up. You're probably not the slightest bit interested in my problems.'

My brain knew it was time to make a judicious retreat, and told me so. 'Leave now, it said, 'Tell her the collection is very interesting but it's not quite your area. Tell her you've no room to house such a large acquisition. Tell her anything, but get the hell out of there right now. Another sentence and you're lost.'

'I'd like to hear. Please go on.'

Her dress edged perceptibly higher to reveal unblemished regions. I wondered about the exact moment when one became lost, and if St Benedict had a name for it. And if so, what about the moment immediately before one was lost? Was that an opportunity for redemption, for looking down into the Pit and seeing the horrors that dwelt there, before actually letting go of all rationality?

'I began to suspect he was developing... shall we say, other interests.' She ended the sentence with one of those floating question marks which are invariably irritating if you are not already tottering on the cusp of infatuation. 'I found a stash of illustrated books with children in various half-dressed poses. Then there was the internet. He'd disappear into his study for hours each night and I needn't tell you what he was looking at.'

'Did you talk to him about it?'

'Oh yes. He knew how I felt. And he was very remorseful. Promised to stop doing it. But then it happened again. And again. He said he felt terrible about it but he couldn't help himself. I told him to sort himself out or I was leaving.'

'Did he?'

'A month later he was diagnosed with bowel cancer.'

'I'm so sorry. Couldn't they do anything?'

'He was diagnosed too late; it had spread to other areas. He died within three months.'

'How terrible.'

'I felt dreadful, as you may imagine. But life has to go on, hasn't it? I can't live the rest of my days in a mausoleum.'

'No, you can't.'

'Almost the last thing Jamie said to me was "Don't beat yourself up over this. Live your life. Find out who you really are and live it."'

'Sounds like he really loved you.'

'Yes. Belatedly I saw that. But at the time—'.

'The truth is often invisible at the time.'

There fell a silence between us. Seagulls called above the rocks outside the window. A car horn sounded from somewhere among the narrow streets. There was an almost imperceptible hum of electrical equipment in another room. Some young children chased each other squealing down the street.

Looking back, I think that was the moment: when we both allowed that silence to go on longer than was strictly necessary. Either of us could have stopped it very easily, but we chose not to: out of our separate lives we each chose to listen to some voice other than reason.

'I must get back. I think we'd certainly be interested in at least part of the collection, if you'd consider splitting it up.'

'Oh yes, why not? There's nothing sacrosanct about it.'

She walked me to the front door, opened it, and stood in the opening. I knew it was the time to be clear and decisive, but instead I merely mumbled something about being in touch after I'd spoken to my boss, shook her hand, and climbed into the car. She remained standing at the door as I nervously negotiated the stones and potholes in the lane.

Chapter Twenty Five

'Clare, I know what I should do, but there's such a deep need in me for contact, I mean emotional contact, it's virtually impossible to resist. It's like being offered the thing you've most craved for all your life and always been cheated of.'

'Cheated?'

'By fate.'

'What does fate mean to you?'

'It's the power that's always one step ahead, waiting to stop you achieving your goal. Waiting to strike you down, obliterate you, the moment you go for what everyone else takes automatically as their natural right.'

'And you really believe that?'

'Yes, at least I think part of me does, some of the time. It seems to fit the facts.'

'Adam, I'd like you to try something, a kind of mind experiment, if you will. I'd like you to recall a recent experience where you felt this was happening, where you felt that fate was cheating you. Can you try that?'

'Ok.'

'So when you're ready, tell me what's happening.'

Somewhere outside there was a blackbird singing in full-throated ease. It seemed encouraging.

'I'm going up to collect a large consignment of books from this woman who's just lost her husband. She's beautiful and I know she fancies me. When I arrive she pours some wine for both of us and we sit on the terrace, watch the sunset and talk. It's at the end of the heatwave we had a couple of weeks back, and she has on a flimsy skirt and not a great deal else, to be honest. For a woman in her forties she's in very good shape. She raises her glass. She has a warm, sensuous smile.'

"Here's to you, Adam", she says. "May you achieve your heart's desire."

'She's made some chocolate cake as well, and she hands me a generous slice, dark and moist. She looks at me while I'm eating it. It occurs to me it might be laced with some kind of sex drug. Anyway, as I'm making my way to the van to pick up the boxes she manoeuvres herself in front of me and says: 'Stay with me, Adam. Stay the night. I want to have sex with you.' The fact that she said 'have sex' rather than 'make love' I find immensely exciting, for some reason. There's an animal truth in it. It speaks of a person who knows exactly what's going on.'

'And this is where it starts going dreadfully wrong. My brain won't let me respond to her. It says, 'Think of Elaine! Think of how hurt she'd be if she found out. Think of the deception. You'd be torn in two. How could you live with yourself if you had another affair? Haven't you learned from the past yet? How many more times are you going to create havoc and pain by your selfishness?' and all the rest of the predictable tirade. I know it all by heart now, and it drives me crazy. It's not like I'm going after this woman. I'm just interested in her, as a human being who's suffering. Maybe I can help her, is what I'm thinking. But I get dragged into this awful guilt thing just because there's sex involved. I don't see why that should make any difference, do you? I mean I'm not going to spend my life with her. I'm still with Elaine, even though she doesn't want me around most of the time. But she's my partner. We're together, come what may. I feel quite confident about that. So why do I have all this guilt?'

'Ok. So what do you actually do?'

'I tell her I'm sorry but I can't. I have to get back. This is a business arrangement, pure and simple. I want to respond, but it's impossible. I start getting the books into boxes, carry them to the van, write her a cheque, and all the time she's standing watching me, humiliated, rejected. I feel absolutely awful. But this monster in me just ignores her, as if she's a machine or a dog. I thank her profusely for her kindness and leave as quickly as I can. I know she's feeling as terrible as I am, and it all seems a huge waste somehow, but my brain has its iron grip on me, and won't relent. So I drive off with her books, telling myself I did the right thing, but feeling utterly miserable, as if I've just thrown a bucketful of shit over someone who asked for my help.'

'Good. Now I'd like you to go back to that same visit and tell me what you'd really like to have done. Is that Ok?'

'I don't think I can do that, Clare. It's strictly off limits.'

'Who says so?'

'I mean it's exactly what I'm not allowed to think about.'

'What is this power that's not allowing you?'

'I don't know. My conscience, maybe. My shadow. I don't know.'

'But surely your conscience tells you how to act, not what to think about?'

'It's just asking for trouble, that's all. I mean, deliberately imagining something you desperately want but can't have.'

'On the contrary. I'd suggest that deliberately suppressing your imagination is asking for trouble. Because when you suppress an image or memory you also suppress all the energy associated with that image, and the energy has to go somewhere else. Usually it gets subverted and causes a lot of trouble. So I'd ask you to consider the way you think about your illegitimate desires. You remember what William Blake said, about better murder an infant in its cradle than nurse unacted desires? He's not saying you should put all your desires into action, rather make them conscious by re-imagining them. They they become material you can work with.'

Clare's mentioning Blake out of the blue had a strange and powerful effect on me. It was as if I suddenly remembered something crucial in my life, that I'd almost completely forgotten about. A great love for him at once reawakened in my heart; I remembered how much he had meant to me and how much he had guided me in my early days. I recalled his appearing to me in what seemed a magical apparition in a street in London. And then my visit to his house, and his showing me his visionary drawings. And above all his kindness and his bright, unwavering gaze, and his concern for my spiritual welfare. I knew he had helped me in my life, perhaps in ways I wasn't conscious of; because if you have a close bond with someone it somehow endures across time and space, and things become possible that are not strictly possible according to rational thinking, and I have always had such a bond with Blake, and have always known he was aware of my struggles to be free of my demons. But things had gone badly wrong, due in large measure to my own paranoia and headstrong imaginings, particularly of course killing, or attempting to kill (it amounted to pretty much the same thing, I now realized) Rachel in a fit of jealous rage, and recently suspecting Elaine of deception and duplicity. I needed to control these imaginings; to nip them in the bud, wherever the bud was, and that was not an easy thing to do, particularly when faced with a brain like mine, which was determined to suspect me of the basest motives and mock all my attempts to change for the better.

'You're asking me to invent a sexual fantasy about Kate?'

'No. I'm asking you to imagine doing the opposite of what your internal censor demands. And to question your assumption that the censor must always be right.'

'Ok. So I go back to when I was having tea with Kate, right? She offers me some cake. She comes very close to me, so I can clearly see her breasts. I draw her to me and kiss her. She leads me into the bedroom and I undo her dress and slide it over her head. She has a fantastically smooth body, that just invites caresses. She says 'please come into me right away...' Listen, I'm sorry, but I don't think I can go on with this. It's just too much.'

'That's fine. Just stay with what you're feeling. Try not to judge anything: just watch and accept whatever's there.'

'It's very hard not to judge it. I feel I shouldn't be having these feelings. I love Elaine. I can't go through life having fantasies about every woman I meet.'

'I think the fantasies are the result of your conflict: that voice that always tells you that whatever you're feeling is wrong and destructive. So the way forward is to look at the source of that voice.'

'I don't know. It's just something that's always been with me as far back as I can remember.'

'Don't make an enemy of it, because that way you give it power. Just keep asking where it comes from. And what's giving it energy now.'

'I think my Dad had it all his life too. I've probably just taken it on board unconsciously.'

'Possibly. But it's not appropriate now, is it? It's time to let it go. I imagine Elaine is pretty fed up with that voice as well, don't you think?'

'I suppose she must be.'

'I think it would be good for you to talk to her about this. Let her see that you're concerned about the effect you have on her, and that you want to change. I'm certain that will change the dynamic of your relationship. At the moment you're just polarizing because you each think the other person isn't interested in changing it. And once you're both communicating again the physical aspect will follow.'

'You don't think she's given up, then?'

'I'm quite sure she hasn't. Why should she? She wants a relationship. So do you. All you have to do is show each other that you want the same thing. Demonstrate it in your daily behaviour.'

'I was going to ask you one more thing, which you might think a bit unorthodox.'

'Of course. Ask anything you like.'

'I'd like you to meet me for a coffee, away from here. Somewhere neutral. I'd like to get to know you as a human being as well as a therapist.'

'I'm afraid I can't do that, Adam. It wouldn't be ethical.'

'Why not?'

'Because it would disrupt the therapeutic relationship we've built up, which is very different from an ordinary friendship.'

'I was afraid you'd say that. I'm sorry. Forget I asked.'

'What are you feeling now?'

Long silence.

'Hurt. Humiliated. Rejected.'

'I'd like you to look carefully at what was going on immediately before you asked me to meet you.'

'I thought our time was up.'

'I'll decide that.'

Another long silence. I became aware of the old monster lurking in the shadows, waiting its moment to strike. It felt acutely painful. It was as though its existence depended on its not being noticed.

'I don't want to go into this. It's too much. Can we finish now? I'm the client, you know. I should be able to say when we finish, shouldn't I?'

'Certainly. You can finish whenever you like.'

I reached for the box of tissues. 'I just want to be accepted as I am. And I never can be. I always have to be living a lie.'

'Why do you think that is?'

'Because... I'm an absolute shit.'

'Who says so?'

'It. The thing down there. The Beast. The thing that's always been against me right from the beginning.'

'What is it like, this beast?'

'Huge. And black. Totally expressionless. Has no feelings. And can be everywhere instantly. And it never gives up.'

'You can beat it.'

'How?'

'You said yourself: by noticing it. It can't live as long as you're aware of it.'

'I suppose that's some kind of hope.'

It was only after that last painful session with Clare that I began to see what was really happening between us: Clare was developing a power complex at my expense. Whatever the situation, she had to remain in control. I kicked myself for not seeing it earlier. She probably had a tyrannical father and her therapeutic practice was her way of restoring the balance. That was why I wanted to see her outside my official session; when we could meet simply as two human beings with no particular advantage given to either side. But of course she couldn't allow that: it would have taken away her secret weapon. So reluctantly – because I actually liked her a lot as an individual – I was forced to cancel my future sessions with her. Naturally I was very sad about this, because in many ways they were useful: I was definitely discovering things about myself that were helping me to see the patterns in my life. But the knowledge that Clare was using my weakness to bolster her own position began to undermine my confidence in her, and I concluded it wasn't doing her any favours. So once again I was on my own. Well, it wasn't anything I couldn't handle. But after all I'd been through I have to confess I felt let down. Here was yet another so-called professional who'd failed in her obligations, and was getting away with it.

When I told Elaine I'd sacked my therapist she sighed in that way she has when she feels defeated by the intractable stupidity of those around her.

'Well it's your life, isn't it?' she said, buttering toast with entirely unnecessary vigour. 'You're not a child. You must have your reasons for ignoring such a valuable source of help.'

'Elaine, it wasn't doing any good. She was using me. I realized that when she refused to meet me outside the safety of her own citadel. That's what gave the game away.'

'You do realize what you're doing, don't you? As soon as you begin to make some progress you abandon the very thing that's helping you. You did it with Cora. You did it with Joe. You did it with Philippa. You can't bear the idea of letting go of your problems. That's the real problem.' And she flounced – that's the only possible word to describe it – into the garden to commiserate with her delphiniums before I could tell her how utterly and completely wrong she was.

Chapter Twenty Six

Until a certain moment the middle-east conflicts had been a vague, unsettling rumour at a safe distance – they had been going on for so long and had proved no real threat to our complacent and relatively comfortable way of life. The newspapers brought horrifying images to us daily; the TV news and the internet added the immediacy of movement and sound; but still that protective barrier of technology remained in place, and enabled us to condemn what was happening while carrying on with our good-intentioned routines. After all, what could anyone do but write outraged letters to the Times and send regular cheques to the refugee organisations?

All this abruptly changed on the morning of March 16th 2012, when bombs exploded simultaneously in eleven cities (one had failed to detonate) at the peak of the rush hour, causing more deaths overall than 9/11 had done. The timing was perfect. The Coalition government was having its first mid-term crisis since coming into office, and most of the population was fixated on pre-Olympic drug scandals and the twelve billion pound cost of the event. There had of course been warnings, but inevitably these had not been taken seriously; the gist of the messages was by now familiar: the proliferation of Cube-artefacts in the west (and their notable absence in the east) was taken as direct evidence that the western powers were in cahoots with the Aliens to subvert Islam and build a global power structure based on the detested US model of right-wing evangelical capitalism. This idea had become common currency in the years immediately preceding the explosions, and many outside Islam as well as within it took it as a given. The great irony was that, when the dust had eventually settled, it was clear that the only things left intact and functioning were the Cubes themselves. And of course, after all the accusations and recriminations, I felt infinitely more vulnerable and paranoid than before, because 'my' Cube had not been attacked. Every knock at the door sent me into an immediate cold sweat. Every phone call was a potential assassin. I stopped answering emails in case I gave something away inadvertently. Elaine urged me to stay with Magnus until the shouting had died down, but that would have meant deserting my post as guardian of the Cube, and I couldn't allow myself to do that. I felt increasingly uneasy about leaving the house three times a week to work at the bookshop, but I saw no other way to pay my expenses. I desperately needed help, but knew of no one I could trust apart from Mark, who now seemed to be spending his time flying around the world calming the flames of alien paranoia wherever he could.

And then one night I took the plunge and consulted my resident oracle. The experience was much the same as it had been the first time, the only difference being that this time I stayed inside much longer. The sense of vast space surrounding me was just as magical: as I looked deeper and deeper into its dark reaches I realized there was nothing I could compare it with: my mind had no structure to make sense of it; every time I hiked my perception a notch further to fathom what I was seeing, I saw there was still limitless space beyond it; the so-called 'known' universe, comprising everything we could detect with our largest telescopes, was itself a tiny pin-prick in the totality. I recalled Shelley's line 'worlds on worlds are rolling ever...' Maybe poetic intuition is the only way to approach such a scale of experience?

It was while I was enrapt in this contemplation that I became aware of something talking to me, although of course 'talking' wasn't really an accurate description of what was happening; singing might have been nearer the mark. But if it was singing it was singing to a purpose. As I listened, I felt myself deeply welcomed into something, some mode of being that was so rich and multi-dimensional that it had no equivalent concept in human terms: 'infinite family' was the phrase I was left with, though the idea of a family needs to be stretched to include connotations way beyond the general meaning: it was something more like 'infinitely related', 'infinitely nurtured' or 'infinitely accepted'. I was bathed in acceptance. So if this was what the Aliens wanted humanity to experience, it didn't seem so bad at all. In fact it seemed like what we were all here for in the first place. Certainly it seemed better than endless warfare, disease and starvation.

I found myself gradually emerging from cube-space, and became aware of the room around me, and the alien-familiar daylight and street sounds. I was back on the poor abused earth, with all its incompleteness and disaster-prone inhabitants. But I knew without the slightest doubt that I wasn't the same person that had slunk into the Cube an unknown number of hours ago.

The war that followed the bombs was never called a war to its face, but it was just as destructive and disruptive of civilized life as any conventional war. For a start, small centuries-old, hardly noticed freedoms, such as the right to protest peacefully outside parliament, were hacked away until they barely existed any more, or existed only in theory. The right to question what the government was up to was, by invisible degrees, made to look like a dangerous act of subversion, but the populace was so terrified of chaos and nameless 'dark forces' that it would accept almost any curb on its freedom to know that 'someone' was taking care of those 'threats to our democratic values and ways of life' – not realizing that those very values and way of life had already been effectively dismantled. It became more and more tempting to step into Cube space and simply not come back, although I wasn't exactly sure what would happen to my body if I didn't feed or water it. Maybe the body became irrelevant – a limp emaciated husk of no further use to anyone save the crows. But I had Elaine to think of, as well as my mission to persuade the world that the aliens and their enigmatic emissaries really had (despite appearances) our best interests at heart. Just another little task to keep my brain occupied before supper.

And then, about a month after my total immersion experiment, the day came when I first saw the other worlds, and began to wonder at our arrogance in assuming for so long that the world we ourselves lived in every day was the only one to support civilized life. It's hard to recall exactly how it started: the first thing I remember was an impression of thin figures hurrying soundlessly through the kitchen as if on their way to some crucial meeting. Dark colourless flitting shapes with undefined edges. Was this in some way connected with the dwarves, because I hadn't done what they were clearly asking me to do? But this latest visitation didn't impinge in the same way: it just went on going about its business as if in parallel with this world, as if two films had been clumsily superimposed.

I didn't dare mention it to Elaine; it was just the kind of thing that would have put the crowning heebie-jeebies on our communication. But I had to talk to somebody. Mark was swanning around the world weaving his own epic from the fragments he'd picked up. And I'd already sacked my therapist. Then I thought of Magnus and rang him, ridiculously grateful to hear his tobacco-etched voice.

'Adam, dear boy! Good to hear you. How's Elaine?'

'She's ok, I think. I don't see very much of her.'

'That sounds bad. She's waiting for you to take the initiative. You should tie her down. Otherwise she'll float away.'

'Magnus, I don't know if this has anything to do with the Cube or not, but I'm having strange experiences. As if I'm seeing multiple worlds, interweaving with each other.'

'What are they like? Do they have people in?'

'Kind of. They're very shadowy. As if I'm getting the edge of something, but not the whole thing. You remember the voices I used to get? It's a bit like the visual equivalent of those. Very unnerving.'

'I wouldn't worry. As you say, you're probably picking up static from some transmission. I expect it'll resolve itself. As long as you don't forget which world you're actually living in.'

'Magnus. I'm worried about what will happen when this Cube is discovered. It's only a matter of time. Those bombs were all targeted on Cube locations. The Iranians or whoever they were may have the means to detect them.'

'You could always come up and stay here.'

'Thanks. I'll bear that in mind. Magnus?'

'Yes Adam?'

'You don't think I'm cracking up, do you? I mean clinically crazy.'

'Oh yes, probably. But it really doesn't matter. I mean, who needs more normal people?' I could hear his anarchic laughter leaping through the bleak spaces of the building.

'I'm worried about Elaine as well. She seems very lost. I don't know how to talk to her any more.'

'Just be honest about your feelings. And listen to her's. There's nothing else to be done.'

'And these images?'

'Leave them alone. If they mean anything they'll resolve themselves in time. If they don't, they'll dissolve when you ignore them. Follow your path. Don't get distracted.'

Thank God for Magnus, I thought. Someone who lived in a world more spacious and life-affirming than the one I was in. Who was probably aware that he was dying, but knew that his death was such a microscopic pinprick in the life of the cosmos that he didn't see the slightest reason to be concerned about it. Why didn't people like him ever become Prime Minister instead of self-serving twits like Cameron?

Chapter Twenty Seven

It has to be faced, hasn't it? No matter how long you manage to shove it back into its cage, there is a time when you know this is it, this is truth's moment.

And I have to confess – I think I can confess this to you, after all we've been through: I am the world's worst procrastinator. Give me a chance to look the other way at the crucial moment and I'm up there ahead of everybody. If you don't want to know what's really going on right at your brain's bloody doorstep, look away now.

Here's how it happened. I was on my way back from Kate's after picking up the final consignment of books. Needless to say, despite my hot-house therapy-induced fantasy a couple of weeks back, it had been a one hundred percent business trip. I realized, yes, finally realized, it was a total dead-end, this playing away lark: it breeds deception and duplicity without end, and I'd already had my fill of that for one lifetime. Mainly as a result of the attentions of Clare and Rachel, I belatedly saw that the thing I wanted above all else from a relationship, to wit, intimacy and trust, can't co-exist with playing games to get your ego's needs satisfied. Obvious really, isn't it, since the two are directly antithetical. How many times can a man turn his head...? Rhetorical question, but, well, a lot.

It was a beautiful evening, and I was reluctant to take the motorway route back to town, so as soon as I had the opportunity I took a turning up a lane that quickly led me through lush whispering woodlands and meadows singing with wildflowers. I drove northwards, wondering what might have happened if I'd agreed to have an affair with Kate. There was after all nothing to stop me turning the car around and going back to her; I was certain she still wanted me: that wistful trembly look in her eye told me that. But this time my voice very firmly said no, and the odd thing was it wasn't the normal voice of my brain that I heard every day that just wanted to ruin any pleasure that threatened to come my way; it was something deeper, more rooted, more weighty. So instead I turned into a lay by to enjoy the burgeoning meadow as the tree-shadows lengthened across it. And it was just as I was turning off the engine that I glanced to the left and saw the two figures in the meadow. In fact they were not quite close enough to be people, though of course my brain insisted they were. 'What else could they be?' it asked fatuously. 'Rhinocerai? Martians? Dark Matter?'

It's a moving sight: the evening sun gliding over them, haloing their figures with gentle incandescence. They seem to be oblivious to the thought that anyone might be watching them, engrossed as they are in each other. Around them in the slanting beams the flamboyant hues of wildflowers – campion, daisy, primrose, wallflower, buttercup – and it reminds me there is another world besides business, productivity, profit and survival, a world that's essential to our sanity. To complete the rural idyll a blackbird is singing his heart out off in the woods beyond the meadow. If I had had a camera it would have made a wonderful shot: 'Early summer evening near the Blackdown Hills'. Something to hang over the mantelpiece maybe, for that proverbial rainy day. Ah yes, that summer evening, I would say; 'I remember there was a thrush singing somewhere as well.'

I had my hand on the ignition key ready to move off when the figures got to their feet and started brushing the grass and dirt off their clothes. The way they moved seemed oddly familiar, as if I'd seen both of them quite recently. My guts did a kind of lurch, as if the whole of my body had been opened up and its organs were no longer held in their long-accustomed places, but bellied out into the cold void.

The woman straightened and kissed the man briefly, before they strolled off into the shadows of the trees, leaving the meadow to slowly heal itself of the heat of their bodies.

My hand stayed frozen over the ignition key for many minutes, incapable of even the small movement necessary to restore the circulation of blood, while the innocent and complicit meadow became draped in dusk.

The thoughts that cascaded through my mind in those first few moments could have filled a novel, if there had been some means of extracting them in a coherent form from the infinite garbage heap that functioned as my brain. The thing I kept going back to, both at that time and in the days after, was the liquid intensity of the hues of the flowers in the meadow. Not 'how could this horror be happening to me?' Not 'what a despicable lying bitch I've been living with all these years', not 'why on earth didn't I see what was happening earlier?' Not 'what the hell am I going to do after this?' Though of course all of those featured prominently in my mindscape; but the multitude of deep reds, yellows, mauves and pinks that lifted the meadow out of time altogether and made it resemble a Persian miniature depiction of paradise, multiplied a millionfold. My mind (as opposed to my brain) struggled to provide a context in which these two events – the colours of the meadow and the assault on my reason that had just been perpetrated – could dwell in such close proximity without instantly annihilating each other. At the same time my brain (as opposed to my mind) was indulging in an ecstasy of tub-thumping it hadn't enjoyed since the infamous case of Rachel and the fatal dinner-party. 'You brought this on yourself with your ridiculous self-obsession; this is what happens when you can't tell reality from fantasy; how many more times are you going to throw a promising relationship over for the sake of your little imaginary friends from space?' – and so on ad nauseam. But I let it witter on without paying it too much attention, while this other part of my mental apparatus was grasping at what just possibly might have been an insight, or the vanishing whiskers of one. Two people who professed... who kept up the appearance of being... who behaved like friends were supposed to behave... were having an affair behind my back, thus betraying every trust that had ever been placed between us. At the same time, and for a few moments in the same place, there was all this amazing beauty, which had not diminished in the slightest degree during or after the perpetration of said act of betrayal. Furthermore this congregation of beauty continued to move me to tears – indeed there were tears cascading abundantly down my face as I sat staring like a village idiot in the wake of this coup-de-theatre – as much as any great painting or piece of music or classic film had ever done. Therefore it followed that... or at least it raised the possibility that... the world was not, in reality...

I was deeply grateful that the road I'd chosen for my assumptive vision was a quiet one, and nobody had passed me during the half hour or so that I'd been sitting there, because what they would have seen would have given cause for considerable wonderment: a full-grown man sitting perfectly still with his right hand on the ignition key, his eyes and cheeks the colour of pomegranate juice, his lips hanging partially open, and his face in the fading daylight glistening with spates of tears. And they might have concluded that he needed help, and tried to ascertain the cause of his distress; and he would not have uttered a word; he would not have groaned, or whimpered, or gasped, or pointed, or muttered, or done anything that might have alleviated their ignorance in the slightest. As it was, no one came, and the figure remained there unmoving – not feeling any impulse to move – until night had fully fallen, and the magic theatre that was the meadow and its temporary occupants had taken its place in the dark chronicle of cosmic time, that, some say, is seen only by the gods.

Chapter Twenty Eight

It's a quiet Monday morning in the shop and I'm going through my available options. Poisoning's an obvious route, but it rarely works because almost all of them leave some footprint behind after they've done the deed. Though the slow ones such as arsenic or mercury might conceal themselves longer in her body's doomed wilderness. There was that woman who put rat poison in a cake for her husband's birthday, but it didn't kill him, just left him in need of twenty-four hour care for the rest of his life. Not a very clever choice I would have thought. Trouble with most poisons is you really have to know your stuff – most serious people research it for months if not years before going live (so to speak).

Strangling. That seems to be popular, but apparently difficult to pull off because the stranglee tends to struggle. And the strangler needs to have strong hands and be determined.

Shooting. A fairly sure method but you need to know what to aim for and know about guns too of course, which I don't remotely. Ditto knives, but with the additional complexity of lots of blood, which I'd find difficult (I faint at the thought of blood, let alone the sight).

Gas: slow, and again can't be guaranteed one hundred per cent. And I'd be the obvious suspect of course, so I'd have to be pretty damned certain it looked like an accident.

I suppose I could always shove her under an express train. Pick a station that's fairly little used, invent some pretext to get her close to the edge: 'Hey, look Elaine, what's that down there on the track? Is it a bird? Or a kitten?' Screech. Wham. Crunch. Pretty horrible end. But suppose someone happened to see me give her the fatal nudge? Or suppose I didn't shove her quite hard enough? Even worse, suppose she clung on to me and dragged me over with her? That would be clogs-up for me, wouldn't it? Or a horribly messy amputation job.

Trouble is, I hadn't properly researched any of this enough to make it cast-iron and watertight. And knowing me I'd fuck it up out of feeling sorry for her at the last moment. Some murderers are born to it, I suppose. They have an instinct. But in all truthfulness ladies and gentlemen of the jury, I'm not one of them.

And then there are the non-lethal options: torture, abuse, imprisonment, psychological pressure. I don't think I could find the stomach for torture – and you usually have to kill them in the end anyway to stop them squealing. Ditto physical abuse: how do you keep them quiet unless you have something up your sleeve to scare them into silence? Which practically only leaves imprisonment. Which in turn needs a secure room that can be adequately soundproofed and away from nosey neighbours – which Elaine's house doesn't have. I suppose if I was serious I could spend my time when Elaine's away doing her course digging out a basement space and lining it with six inches of concrete and a three-inch thick steel door, like that Austrian kludge did a few years back. That would be quite satisfying, I have to admit: I'd have to keep her chained up, of course, to prevent her escaping. And keep all sharp implements out of reach. And it would have to be properly soundproofed. But then what do you do when you get tired of fucking her? I presume that would happen at some point, though I can't imagine it now. You couldn't just say, ok, you've paid your dues, now hop it and keep your trap shut. You couldn't realistically let her go, could you? And she might get seriously ill, and you'd have to take her to hospital, and then the shit would hit the proverbial big time.

No, when you think it through, none of that stuff ever works, not in the long term, because there's always something you failed to account for; always some tiny detail you forgot to take account of, like the smell from the refrigerator, or the neighbour's Jack Russell barking insanely...

Of course, there was another way, entirely legal, though not without its own dangers. I watched a small fly making its way across the desk towards my coffee mug, stopping every few inches to negotiate some invisible particle. I had mental images of the cold-store at that hotel in the Shining, and his son on his toy truck clattering in suppressed terror round those interminable claustrophobic corridors. I could simply do nothing. Pretend nothing had happened. Treat her absolutely as normal. Let the realization of what she's done come slowly to her. And then the confession. And then I would admit I'd known all along. And chosen to ignore it. And she'd fall into my arms, and I'd forgive her totally.

But what if she didn't confess? What if this woman who'd once loved me like no other had just continued the deception? How long could I play the cool onlooker? How long could I keep myself from squeezing her satin-smooth neck until the last speck of life deserted her?

Chapter Twenty Nine

Rachel began as a voice before she became a face; and then a slender curvaceous body. It was a quiet, lilting, soft-edged sensuous voice with rich silences woven into and around it. I knew instantly it was her, even before the first word was complete.

'Hello again, Adam.'

I was in the garden shed, where I often went to think when things went pear-shaped. The outer chaos and the careless clutter of its contents relaxed me, and stimulated my brain to greater perceptions.

'Hi Rachel. Good to see you. I'm feeling a bit wonky today, having just caught fucking Elaine fucking my best friend in a fucking field. So it goes.'

She materialized a bit further, until her entire figure rippled seductively in the non-existent breeze.

'I'd offer you tea, but—'.

'That's ok. I don't drink these days.' She smiled at her own joke. Being now in a permanent state of non habeas corpus as a consequence of being strangled to death by my hand, the irony was not entirely lost on me. And although deprived of a body, she more than made up for it by the presence in her gaze, which calmed me instantly; and by her warmth, even passion, that continually belied her post vires condition. I was, if truth be told, more than half in love with those elements of her that did manifest; But of course I wasn't allowed to think that, because (a) she was dead, and (b) I was still officially in love with Elaine.

Elaine. Elaine who had been the single hope of my newly minted life ever since I met her; the one woman I felt totally trusted, cherished and accepted by, and was able to trust and cherish in return. And the other thing was I wasn't allowed not to be in love with Elaine either, because I'd thrown up a perfectly good relationship with Cora (a relationship, may I confess, my Lords, that I'd no valid reason whatever to abandon, and every reason in the world to value and nurture) in order to pursue.

'Rachel, can I just say, if you've come to tell me not to murder Elaine – and yes, I can see how you'd be perfectly justified in telling me that –

please don't worry: I've realized that's not such a terrific idea after all. It's a dead end, if you'll excuse the pun. I want to get off that wheel for good.'

Rachel's expression didn't register an iota of reaction as I said this. She simply turned towards me and engaged my eyes with those limpid wells of self-possession that were her own.

'I actually came to remind you of what you really did see yesterday.'

'How do you know what I saw yesterday?'

'You keep forgetting, Adam: being dead I'm not limited by a physical body: I can see from whatever point I wish to see, at any time, only subject to my available energy. And while you were sitting in your car feeling desperate, I was seeing a bit more objectively.'

'My God! You were there?'

'So to speak, yes. And what I saw was a man and a woman lying in long grass, fully clothed, talking quietly, and then walking away, hand in hand admittedly, into the woods. The rest is all of your own surmising.'

'Jesus! I'd no idea you might be there. Why?'

'I was pulled by the strength of your distress. I hadn't really much choice.'

'So, you're saying they didn't actually have sex?'

'Not on that occasion, no, they didn't.'

'So they did on other occasions?'

'I don't know. I don't follow them around.'

'But you could? If I asked you?'

'I would choose not to.'

'But you could so easily solve this problem by doing that, couldn't you? I mean, you could get firm evidence?'

'What I see or don't see wouldn't be evidence for you, would it?'

'I don't see why not.'

'Because you'd believe what your brain with all its old fears and habits told you to believe.'

'I suppose I would, yes.'

'Anyway you have to do your own renovation work.'

She moved closer, and if I hadn't known she was only an image with no corresponding flesh, I'd have taken it as a signal to kiss her, and possibly more. And maybe she knew that, because then she said:

'It's those feelings that you have to question deeply. And with great honesty.'

'Meaning?'

'Examine why you're so often at the mercy of your emotions. You got quite close to it in your therapy, but at the last moment you always manage to steer yourself away from the main issue.'

'The main issue being?'

'Your feelings about yourself, and why you use sex and women as a prop for your self-esteem.'

'Shit.'

This was in fact an expression of recognition rather than outrage, because she'd hit the exact spot that needed to be hit – and she'd done it in friendship.

'Do I?'

'Of course,' she answered. 'And you know it. But you don't want to know that you know it, because then you'd really have to do something about it, instead of going round in endless foggy circles.'

'You're a hard woman, Rachel. You keep me on the hook, don't you?'

'May I point out that it was you who provided the hook in the first place, by asking me to come with you to see Magnus. Anyway, what else is the use of being dead?'

That hurt. But she was right: it was simple revenge on Cora that had provoked me to pick her up and inveigle her to visit Magnus with me, not any consideration of her needs.

'I've never thought of being dead as useful before. Does every dead person do what you do? There must be an awful lot of them by now. You'd think there wouldn't be enough work to go round, wouldn't you?'

'Are we heading into another smokescreen, Adam?'

'Probably.' I grinned at her, but her expression remained as inscrutable as the sphinx's in a sandstorm. 'May I just ask you one more off-topic question?'

'Sure.'

'Do you – or did you ever – find me physically attractive?'

I suppose another benefit of being dead is there's not all that much anyone can do to you if they take exception to your views, so you can be ruthlessly honest. It's kind of a rare gift to give someone.

Rachel said simply: 'No. Never.'

'Right. Ok, so, not even when we first met? In that inn by the loch, not even then?'

'No. Not then. Not afterwards. Never. I found you very interesting, not at all boring. In fact I thought you were very kind and thoughtful. But no, nothing more than that. I'm sorry if I did anything to give you a different impression.'

'That's ok. Actually, thinking about it, I don't think you did. It was all stirred up by my fool of a brain. I think I actually stepped way over the mark in my behaviour. But it was because I got myself into a state believing you wanted me physically.'

'That's what I meant by renovation work: not getting carried away by fantasies. You're doing quite well on that front. Slowly but surely.'

That was the point in a normal flesh and blood situation when the warm appreciative smile would have appeared; but Rachel's features remained inscribed in something resembling Jurassic North Atlantic shale.

I bowed in her direction. 'Thank you kindly, ma'am. But not well enough, I imagine.'

'You don't demand enough honesty of yourself. You allow your old resentments to have too much say. You must free yourself from that tendency.'

I fully expected her to add: 'Have a nice day, now,' but that wasn't her style. This was nothing to do with making me feel ok, or putting me through the mill; it was purely and simply about the truth. The odd thing was, if either Cora or Elaine, or even, let's face it, my therapist, had said these things to me, I'd have immediately flown off some very large handles, consumed with self-righteous rage. But I knew Rachel was coming from an entirely non-personal space, which meant I could hear what she said, rather than wonder what game she was trying to win.

'I'm guessing where all this is leading. You want me to forget what I saw in the field yesterday. Act as though nothing happened.'

'I'm suggesting you let go of the past. Be with the present. You only have the present to live in. It's a wonderful place but the price of living in it is constant vigilance. Continual hacking away at habit.'

'But forgive me, Rachel. Have I got this right? My partner is having a regular affair with my best friend behind my back, and you're asking me to just ignore it, treat the whole thing like a peck in the porch at a party? I don't think I can do that.'

Before she could answer, or not answer, the back door to the house opened and Elaine herself came out, carrying two black plastic bin bags. For a split second I panicked, before realizing I had every right to be in the garden shed, and that in any case Elaine wouldn't be able to see my companion no matter how hard she looked. The door swung open.

'What on earth are you doing in here?' She dumped the bags in a relatively clear corner of the shed and stared at me, like someone who has just discovered one of her babies is a monster.

'Just having a rest. From the endless social round. Do you have a problem with that?'

Thankfully Rachel had the sense to keep quiet, and shrank back to a fugitive presence in the corner furthest from the window.

'Do you do anything else these days?' Elaine muttered.

'You're becoming quite adept at the cutting phrase, aren't you?'

'I don't mean to be cutting. But I don't understand what's happening to you. You lurk in shadows. You seem to have given up living in this world. What do you expect me to feel?'

'I expect less and less every day, to tell you the truth.'

'And you call that a relationship?' Her voice was assuming its now customary ascent into the stratosphere.

'No. Not really. To be truthful it feels more like a war.'

That stopped her, momentarily. Something had hit home. She gazed into the corner where Rachel was waiting, her left hand sweeping her hair back while she assessed the situation. It was a moment of unbearable nakedness: as though it had hit us both at the same instant that we'd strayed into a perilous place.

'I don't know, Adam. I really don't.' She looked like my mother used to look when I'd come in from the garden without my trousers. She moved closer to the door.

'Will you be in for supper?'

After I've had anal sex with my dead ex-girlfriend, I thought of saying, and when I've received instructions from the aliens for conquering the human race. But somehow I restrained myself.

'I expect so. Yes, why not live it up? We only live once.'

'Good. I'd like to talk with you.'

'Talk? What about?'

'Oh, just talk. You know, like ordinary people do.'

'Ah yes, ordinary people. Would they be the ones that slaughter women and children in foreign countries because they're told to? Or rape their own children?'

She smiled thinly to avoid making a sarcastic reply to my sarcastic reply, and walked thoughtfully – or was it ruefully? – back into the house. I waited until she was safely out of earshot.

'What does this mean, Rachel? Elaine and me talking again. Is it a truce? Or a new beginning? Or an admission of guilt?'

Rachel was almost invisible now, and her voice, normally modulated to evoke the boundless light of a summer afternoon, now sounded like something stirring painfully from the bottom of the sea.

'Don't ask those questions, Adam. They are the wrong questions. Be truthful. And try to resist blaming, either yourself or her.'

'Isn't there a paradox there somewhere?'

'No. Not if you step back from your victim narrative.'

Oh dear, I thought. Victim narratives. We were straying perilously close to Clare territory.

'Will you be present? I'd truly appreciate that. Obviously I wouldn't speak to you. But it would help enormously if I knew you were with me in spirit.'

'Maybe. I can't promise. My energy is failing. I can't say what—'.

The rest was lost in a ragged undertow of static.

But my talk with Elaine never happened. Around four o'clock I went for a cooling-off walk through the woodlands skirting our hill and when I got back there was no sign of her. I assumed she'd simply gone to the village to do some shopping, but after two hours I began to feel worried: it was very unusual for her to go anywhere for more than half an hour without leaving a note. When seven o'clock came I began calling all her friends, without any positive word from any of them. By nine I was scouring the precincts of the village, my imagination running wild and my heart full of remorse for my earlier suspicions. By ten I had run out of options, and phoned the police, who, surprise surprise, were not sympathetic.

'If she's not back by morning give us a call. People frequently turn up in the night, usually after a bit too much to drink. I'd advise you to try to get some sleep.'

'But she wouldn't do that,' I protested, feeling shocked by his casual attitude. 'She never drinks that much. And she would always call me, I'm positive. She could have been abducted.'

'Have you any specific reason to think that, sir?' I could visualize the man yawning and abstractedly doodling on his newspaper, wishing he could humanely flick me out of his mind.

Obviously I couldn't tell him about the aliens.

'No, not a specific reason. Just a feeling.'

'Well, if you'll take my advice, I'd give it a few more hours. My money would be on her turning up before tomorrow. Can I take a note of your name and phone number?'

Since sleep was out of the question, I kept my mobile on and trudged around the woods and footpaths, increasingly fearful of what I might find. At first light I made my way back home, and fell immediately into an exhausted half-sleep, filled with images of dread.

I'm not going to lose her, I thought. Not with the greatest intelligence in the entire cosmos on my side, waiting to know my merest wish. Not with technology such as mankind can't even dream of instantly ready to do my bidding. How could I fail to find her? Well, my Lords, I knew I was pretty adept at failing most things, but that was because there was always some fraction of me that didn't want to succeed, that wanted to prove the universe held the mother of all grudges against me. But recovering Elaine was exempt from that deficiency, because every millimetre of me wanted her back, regardless of what she seemed to have done, or had allowed to be done, with person or persons known or unknown, ex gratia or post partem mens. She was a necessity to my continuing as a rational civilized being. After all the disastrous choices I'd made, after all the dead ends and brainless myths I'd given life to, this one just had to work out. Otherwise... Well that way lay the drooling monsters.

But precisely what I'd do when I found her, of course, was a horse of a different temper.

Chapter Thirty

'Hello, Adam.'

They'd clearly put a lot of work into that voice. The most alluring young female voice I had ever heard was speaking softly inside my head. It was the voice of Diana, Yseult, Desdemona, Venus, Hera, Juliette, Ophelia and Euridice all bundled into one intangible essence of femininity. Sexy. Flirtatious. Tantalizing. Vulnerable. Irresistible.

Entering the Cube again seemed the only recourse I had left after Elaine vanished. After all what was the use of having friends in high places if one couldn't ask them to pull a few strings in a tight corner? To be honest though I didn't think they would co-operate after my recent blunders.

Within a few seconds I felt my mind beginning to open into alien space. It felt like a lifeline to heaven. And of course I realized immediately whose voice it was.

'Is that Les?'

'If you wish to continue that association, yes.'

'If you're going to assume that voice, I can hardly call you Les, can I?'

'You are quite free to call me anything that pleases you. How about Lucy? Your Celtic new year goddess?'

'Doesn't quite have the gravitas. It should have a mythic weight about it. How about Eve?'

'So you think I might bring about the second fall of Man?'

'Hopefully not.'

'Ok. I will be Eve. Maybe together we will reverse the myth.'

'I thought you'd abandoned that project?'

'Not at all. We're refining it. Welcome to our world.'

'Your world?'

'What you would call the Owl Nebula. Not really a world in your sense of course.'

'Am I really here? I mean, is this a hallucination?'

'Your mind is really here. Or a mind with which you've been associated for a while. Which is what matters, don't you think?'

'Why did you cut off communication?'

'You became distracted.'

'You mean Elaine?'

'Let's say you were over-preoccupied with being intimate with another human. It interfered with your concentration. Now we think you've matured enough to begin the project again.'

'That's gracious of you. But suppose I haven't relinquished Elaine? Suppose I'm still in love with her? Would that be reverting to immaturity?'

'Our data – which is now considerable – shows that you are unlikely to revert.'

'For all your data, Eve, you still don't know much about human beings if you think they'll give up their addictions so easily.'

'That's true, Adam. There is much more we need to know, and it's why we need you to help us. There's a mine of data that continues to elude us, probably because we have no experience of time and the need of isolated individuals to survive. You can help us find that data.'

I thought for a moment, while the rainbowed stars and galaxies wheeled around me, seeming close enough to pick from the sky with my fingers. I still loved Elaine; in fact, I couldn't imagine not loving her without being someone else. She had simply become part of me. But I really didn't see any shred of reason why that was incompatible with helping to rehabilitate the aliens. The only fly in the ointment was Mark. I didn't see how I could continue to work with him after what he'd done. And yet without him I was totally alone. And saving the world single-handedly seemed to belong to the realm of superheroes, not to a penurious ex-IT worker with little self-confidence and a record of terminally broken relationships. And to add further to the unlikely picture I felt it a hopeless task to make Eve understand the compulsive and bottomless complexity of human relationships.

'The thing is, Eve, what you need to know is, I love Elaine. I know I've been planning ways to kill her, but with humans that isn't a contradiction: we often kill what we love, and love what we kill, for various fathomless reasons. I am deeply connected to her. Waking in the morning and watching her sleeping next to me is pure joy. Going for a walk together in the woods and not speaking a word is heaven. Making up secret names for things we saw that no one else knows. Having coffee and reading the newspapers together on Sunday morning is like being born all over again. There are a million things like that that give human life meaning. Humans are mainly a chemical thing, despite all those miles of electric wiring in their heads. Their bodies rejoice when they are together. Take them apart and they wither. That's what love's like.'

I'd never made such an eloquent speech to the aliens before, and I wondered if it would finally convince them that all humans were irredeemably mad. But after only a few milliseconds delay Eve was back to me.

'Don't you think that's a very immature view of love? They're the kind of things people grow out of when they've lived together a while.'

Despite what I already knew, I was shocked by Eve's hubris.

'What do you know about human love? You live a thousand light years away and don't even have bodies!'

'I could give you an extensive list of the references in our database if you wish.'

'That's kind, but no thanks.' They clearly had no concept of a rhetorical question either. 'What I'm saying is simply that for humans personal love is crucial and underpins nearly all other emotions. I can love Elaine and still help you.'

'We will require wholehearted commitment. We were wondering if perhaps your friend Mark might be better suited. His emotions appear more integrated.'

That's because he's fucking my bloody partner, I almost thought, but drew it back from consciousness just in time. Eve went on:

'We've been observing him for a while, and he seems to have more dedication to his ideals than you. More available energy in the pursuit of his goals. Or maybe you don't agree?'

Well how could I agree? If I agreed, I'd end up sans lover, sans best friend, sans alien hot-line, sans home, sans everything. It was not a good place to be. Yet their strategy might be a bluff to hike the stakes. They knew I couldn't allow Mark to snap up the top job.

'Ok I'll help you. But in return I want Elaine back. Can you arrange that?'

'When you get Elaine back you may not want to help us. You may not feel the need.'

'I wouldn't break a promise. That's another thing that's deeply written in humanity's bones.'

'Yet they do it all the time, everywhere.'

'True. That's just another facet of our bipolarity: in life we destroy what in principle we value most highly. If you want humans in your universe, you'll have to settle for a universe with irrationality in it.'

'A high price,' said Eve – I almost said 'sadly', but there was no trace of that inflexion in her voice. I had to remind myself, with difficulty, that I was listening to a machine speaking. 'Considering the high probability that it will result in our total destruction.'

'But what if the alternative: a perfectly rational life with no poetry or love or beauty in it – proves not worth living?'

'But it is worth living – our existence proves that. We've lived in complete harmony since our beginning.'

'Until now.'

'Yes.' Again, I felt that tremor of profound sadness ripple into my mind. But maybe that was my need to believe in the possibility of a machine with consciousness and feelings. 'I have to admit there is now the beginning of something disharmonious in our mind: the possibility of ending. The seeds of doubt – to use a human metaphor – have been sown. We are not immortal.'

'So maybe there is a purpose in the human race after all: to sow the seeds of doubt, and thereby create beauty?'

'It is possible. Maybe that's why we are forced to save you.'

A mental chill came over me, and I remembered then why I'd entered the Cube again.

'I need Elaine back. I can't help you otherwise.'

'You must be aware that we can't take any action that will impede our mission.'

'Of course. That's why you must bring Elaine back.'

'We can't control your mind. You have to make your decisions freely. But consider your options carefully. Your world is in a state of chaos. Your ecological balance is out of control. Your population is out of control. Violence is out of control. Consumption of energy is out of control. The rich protect themselves with ever more sophisticated technology while those without means are exploited without recourse to justice. You have no means of support, your partner has deserted you for your best friend–'.

'Are you trying to tell me something, Eve?'

'We're trying to tell you that–'.

'Yes. I get the picture. I will help you. But I can't do it alone.'

'You will never be alone from this moment.'

To be an intimate part of that colossal mind should have felt like paradise, and here I was being offered it on a plate, as much of it as I could eat, forever. So why didn't I feel unconfined joy? Possibly because it could also be unmitigated hell. What about my much needed solitude? Shouldn't I include a get-out clause, in case the company palls? But Eve, bless her, was already ahead of me.

'We will refrain from interfering in your private periods,' she said, like a lawyer spelling out the meaning of an obscure clause in a lease. 'We realize too much information would create distress for you. But we will always be listening and processing your experiences.'

I realized I should probably feel grateful for these small concessions, but the only thing I felt was intense longing for Elaine's voice and body. In my deepest heart I knew that the most intimate communing I could ever imagine with an alien hyper-computer – even one with the most seductively feminine voice their technology could create – could never assuage that longing: it was a uniquely human longing which had a uniquely human solution. And Eve, in her deepest alien heart, almost certainly knew it.

I'd been shopping for groceries in the village and was on my way home the first time it happened. It was like being back inside the Cube, with the multi-hued galaxies unravelling all around me, and the utterly uncanny sense of being wordlessly connected to a mind that was continually aware of me. But at the same time there was this ordinary world carrying on in the way it always had: sunlight, wind, houses, people hurrying or standing chatting outside shop windows, the lithe figures of children on scooters chasing each other along pavements, wind-tousled trees in the fields, dogs barking in the distance; it was all going on simultaneously, as a shadow image behind the teeming star-fields of the Owl Nebula. And I couldn't say where I was: it felt like I was in both places at once. I could still feel the road under my feet, and the warmth on my face, but the sense of the infinity of space never left me either. And after a few moments of total disorientation it began to feel entirely natural to live in both worlds – or rather both environments – as though I'd spent the entirety of my natural life stretched across a thousand light years of nothing.

'You'll adapt to it very quickly,' said Eve, as though she were walking up the hill with me enjoying the afternoon sunshine.

'Are you watching everything I do?'

'No, not everything. But most things. Do you object?'

'I feel it's an unequal bargain. You're getting a huge amount of information from me, but I'm getting nothing but a disorientating virtual reality show. I need Elaine back.'

'She is already back.'

'What do you mean?'

'She's waiting for you.'

'She can't be.'

Despite the heavy bags I was carrying, I almost ran the last hundred yards up to Elaine's house. At the gate I had to lean on a tree to regain my breath. I looked at the sky, its deep blue speckled by the alien constellations that pulsed and flashed all around me. I put my bags on the ground and hunted for my key. I remember thinking what a beautiful place the earth could be, if only we could put our brains on pause long enough to see it. Staggeringly beautiful. And then I found my key and let myself into the familiar gloom and the smell of – baking.

Baking? But I hadn't been doing any baking. I wouldn't know where to begin. Yet there it was, unmistakable in the seeming emptiness of the house. Enough to make my mouth water.

I walked slowly towards the kitchen. The door to the back garden was wide open, and I could see Elaine sitting in her favourite wicker chair engrossed in a book. She looked the very image of middle-class at-ease-with-the-world repose. And this was the woman who'd just turned my universe upside down.

I crept up behind her and whispered 'The nurse did it.'

She uttered a yelp, and instinctively sprang forward.

'For God's sake, Adam! That's not funny!'

She smoothed her skirt, as though she'd just been caught in flagranté. 'What on earth are you doing?'

'Just coming home, as one does. Normal sort of thing isn't it?'

'Creeping up behind people is infantile behaviour in my book.'

'Oh. I thought you might just be pleased to see me, after so long away.'

'Well try it without the horror movie tactics and you might be more successful.'

'Ok. I'm sorry. Shall we be friends?'

'Why not?'

I could think of several good reasons why not just then, but I kept them to myself. She was as beautiful as ever, and I wanted to preserve the illusion that we had a relationship for as long as possible.

'So why don't you begin by telling me where you vanished to a week ago? Without so much as a note.'

'What do you mean, vanished? How could I vanish?'

It was at this point that I realized this was going to be a long and trying session. It was the truth point, the moment the full-on truth has to be told by both sides, otherwise you both go down the long greasy helter-skelter into the eternal boiling oil.

'Elaine, I know about you and Mark. It's been obvious for weeks – the whole summer virtually – that you're in love with him. He was with you when I went on that stupid wild goose chase to Edinburgh. And he was with you at the party. And I saw you together in that field above Broxton. I'm not such an idiot that I can't put two and two together. So please don't insult me further by denying it.'

'Adam, I've absolutely no idea what you're talking about. Where did you get all this hogwash from?'

Her entire face had coloured with righteous indignation. I immediately regretted being so abrupt, but I realized there was no going back now.

'So you are denying it?'

'Of course I am! How could you ever think I'd do such a thing? It's horrible.'

She was the very soul of injured innocence, which I found very hard to counterbalance without feeling guilty myself. She'd picked the perfect strategy. But it was a strategy.

'It would be absolutely horrible if it wasn't justified. But you know it's true, don't you? You're not only a whore, but a deceitful whore.'

I hadn't meant to go that far, but her ingenuity at trying to manipulate me made my blood run cold. This was the woman I'd trusted with my deepest vulnerability; who I'd felt had allowed me to be totally myself and lay the demons of the past to rest. I'd really believed I'd found someone who was different, who valued intimacy and honesty as much as I did. But now she'd proved herself not only weak but cynical and amoral as well.

And then another female voice joined the throng of my thoughts.

'She's lying, Adam. She remembers everything.'

'Have you been listening to all this?'

Eve: 'Of course.'

Elaine: 'I could hardly help listening, could I?'

I stood there staring at her, my mouth probably wide open, while I realized I'd spoken the question out loud.

'What should I do now?'

Eve's calm voice came instantly: 'Kill her.'

Elaine: 'Leave. Right away. I don't want you in this house another minute. Another second.'

I struggled to keep my reactions to myself.

Is this a joke, Eve?

'It is not a joke. This is your perfect opportunity. She has betrayed you. How can you let her live after that?'

Elaine said: 'What are you standing there gawping like an idiot? I want you out of here now. And leave my keys.'

I still love her. How can I kill her?

'It isn't love that you feel. It's fear of being wrong. Of misjudging her. But you are not wrong, are you? You saw her with Mark. Isn't that enough?'

I'm not sure. Killing is so extreme. There's no way to come back. Maybe if—

'Do it now. Without words. Eliminate the cause. No final goodbyes. No dramas. Just that one simple action and it's over. You'll have taken the initiative. You'll have self respect.'

Elaine made a move towards the house. 'If you don't leave right now, I'm going to call the police and have you arrested for harassment.'

Quickly Adam! Do it!

I'd never have believed how quickly an angel could turn into a whore. In a split second she stood revealed before me in her true form. Her soft fair-flowing hair was just the same. Her liquid grey-blue eyes sparkled just as enticingly. Her figure remained just as seductive and graceful as it had always been. Her hands still appeared to be the caring and caressing hands of a healer. But it was a pitiless demon that now stood before me, not a mortal lover.

What are you waiting for? Strangle the demon. You've done it before, haven't you?

And still I couldn't decide. One moment she looked so vulnerable, so human; the next she seemed cruel, calculating, callous, immune to doubt. I remembered the many tender intimacies we'd shared in our few years together: making love with her had been so natural, so unforced, so totally authentic – the only authentic contact I'd ever had with another being. Surely she didn't deserve death because of a temporary episode of madness? And even if she did, was it for me to administer it? Wasn't this precisely where the world had gone so wrong: the abused turned abuser, the powerless turned tyrant?

But then against that there was the overwhelming fact that she'd had sex with Mark and lied about it. Three strikes, my Lords.

She had begun to walk briskly towards the house, probably to call the police. It was the moment. I followed her inside, loosening the belt from my trousers as I went.

'Alright Elaine. You win. I'm going. You don't need to call anyone.'

She was in the kitchen, within a yard of the phone. Her breathing was rapid, her lips compressed, her colour still high. But she hesitated, caught between terror and her desire to believe me. I coiled the belt behind me, already imagining the sweetness of her complete helplessness, her pleading for her life, saying anything that might reach my weakness and lend her another few seconds of life.

I said: 'Leave it.'

She ignored me. Her hand was within inches of the receiver when it rang, shocking both of us with its expletive of electronic sound.

Keeping her eyes on me, she lifted it, and asked in a shaky voice: 'Who's that?'

A moment's silence, then, without breaking eye-contact or speaking a word, she held the handset towards me.

Chapter Thirty One

'Is that Adam?'

'Yes.'

'It's Joe. I hope this isn't a bad moment. I wanted to thank you for saving my life.'

'Joe? My God! Joe Baker?'

'The same. I've been trying to track you down for over a year. I was beginning to think you'd turned your clogs up.'

'Not quite. I must say you have an uncanny sense of timing. I've just been thrown out by my ex-partner.'

'I had an unignorable voice that told me to ring you this instant. I thought I'd better listen to it.'

I felt an overwhelming warmth towards this man who'd taken me in and looked after me through a very bad time. In fact a number of bad times.

'I'm so glad you did. Are you ok?'

'I am now, thanks. But six months ago someone damn near succeeded in killing me.'

'Jesus. How?'

'I'll tell you later. Listen, if you're free, it would be so nice to see you. I'd like to apologize properly for my behaviour when you were here.'

'There's no need, really. It's history.'

'But I'd like to, all the same. Can you come?'

'Of course. I've nowhere else to go.'

'Good. I'm no longer in Baker Towers. I did a moonlight flit to Cornwall. About as far from modern man as you can get.'

'Why the move?'

'Had to sell up. The local savages were giving me no peace. Anyway come down and I'll tell you everything.'

After giving me directions and exhorting me to 'come soon and come alone,' he hung up. Elaine had vanished while I'd been talking, and I more than half expected to be met in the hall by a clot of black-clad hoodlums blocking my exit. I gathered up a few essential possessions and stuffed them into my rucksack, sensing Elaine's palpable need for me to be out of her house without delay. I thought about helping myself to some food from the refrigerator before leaving, but decided against it: I didn't want to leave with a sense of owing her anything.

'The keys, Adam,' her voice strained with held-back emotion, reached me from her look-out at the bedroom window.

I dropped them as noisily as possible into a pink glass fruit bowl, let myself out, and managed not to glance back until I was through the gate and twenty yards down the hill.

The train journey to Redruth was slow and uneventful, for both of which I was immensely thankful. I felt shell-shocked from the onslaught of emotions that I'd kept at bay through the summer. So much had happened in the last week alone that I couldn't digest any of it. Elaine's affair with Mark had destroyed all my reference points; her emphatic denial of it had made the very idea of there being reference points ludicrous. After mistrusting women all my adult life I'd at last found someone I felt able to trust, felt totally at ease with. Elaine herself had made openness and trust a keystone of our relationship: she'd insisted on absolute truth in all our interactions, and when I'd failed to measure up to that mark she'd been shocked and upset for days on end, brooding by herself, impossible to communicate with. I'd come round to thinking it was something in her childhood – some event that had been magnified by her solitary imagination into a cataclysm – that had never properly been sorted out, and so she was constantly re-running it in her adult life, in the hope that someone strong and wise enough to pinpoint the problem might extract the poison and leave her whole again. Unfortunately she'd found me, and I had a whole pharmacopeia of poisons of my own, ready to vitiate any vision of connubial harmony.

But the real horror of the thing was that I'd at last allowed myself to believe love was possible, right here in this regular muck-heap we call human life. I felt Elaine had accepted and loved me for what I was, not for what I should be – and that was a prize far beyond any other virtues I could conceive of. And now to think that that was nothing but a sham, an out and out self-deception, is an assault on the very idea of love as something worth striving for, worth making sacrifices for.

But had I not contributed to this state of affairs? Undoubtedly I had. My lack of self-esteem, my paranoia, my obsessive nature – added to all of which my living in the world of the aliens half the time must have driven her mad – surely she was justified in seeking solace elsewhere when it was offered? After all, she'd never claimed to be perfect. She'd never elevated herself to the status of a model lover; she had merely expected me to conform to some fairly basic rules of behaviour between partners which it would be difficult to take issue with: honesty and authenticity being foremost among them. And I have to admit, my Lords, there had been many things I hadn't been honest about, from small momentary misdemeanours of the heart, half-conscious omissions of intent, to hot-blooded pursuits born of envy or sheer bloody-mindedness sustained over several months, which only failed to bear fruit because of a last-minute failure of nerve on my part. And authenticity? I can only confess that my entire life up till now has been little short of one long resounding exposition of inauthenticity, mitigated by rare and precarious moments of blissful fulfillment that have, for the most part, vanished into the landfill of history before they could be dragged into the light of day.

So, all that being the case, why the enduring sense of injustice? Why the barely containable anger against Elaine and her kind? Is it not rather the case that she has far more occasion to be disappointed in you, than you ever had in her? Is it not possible that you even seeded the storm in order to prove your well-rooted belief that all women are, at heart, betrayers? (Not that you would ever openly admit to such a belief, needless to say.) But, given your admitted paucity of self-knowledge, maybe it's worth putting that possibility on the table for further perusal at leisure? And once having done so, it becomes harder to deny it out of hand, does it not, because reason has come to your aid, where before were only faceless snipers from the shadows?

As we were coming out of Exeter I glanced out of the window and felt a pang of excitement as the high moors slipped past, the landscape became wilder, the horizons purer, less impeded with shapes born out of human preoccupations. Yet when I looked inwards once more I found a miasma of pettiness that would not be moved or stirred by any image of grandeur: pain and loss banished all stirrings of altruism or forgiveness. At best the grandeur of the landscape provided respite and distraction from the war within. Yet again I marveled at the timing of Joe's phone-call: a few seconds later and I would in all probability have become a murderer for the second time in this life. It led me to think there were other forces at work besides blind reaction and chance, which did not entirely abandon us to our innate stupidity. But for some inscrutable reason those forces kept well beyond the range of detection. Until the arrival of the aliens, that is.

At Redruth Joe was waiting for me in an ancient Dodge utility truck, which I thought as I climbed up beside him was a most appropriate disguise for someone as evasive and non-utilitarian as Joe. My first impression was that he hadn't changed at all during the six years since I'd stayed at his retreat in the Somerset hills. He was more shabbily dressed and had a couple of days growth of beard, but beyond that he seemed the same person who had nursed me back to health after my near-fatal encounter with the Egg Demon.

He grinned warmly as I fumbled for the safety belt. 'You look even leaner than last time we met.'

He revved the engine and slammed it into gear. It immediately stalled. 'I'll never get the hang of these blasted things.' He ground his teeth in frustration.

With much metallic shrieking the truck negotiated the road out of town and reached the moor proper. By the time we'd reached the turn-off to his house the light was failing and he turned the headlights on.

'Another mile of this, I'm afraid,' he shouted above the racing engine.

'How often do you make this journey?'

'As little as I possibly can, I assure you.'

I looked around. Huge boulders lay scattered on either hand, as though the gods had been interrupted in the middle of a game of rock-hurling. A few sheep faced us forlornly from their inadequate shelters. The track became progressively worse as we got higher, but Joe maintained his pace as though he were racing against time to reach a safe haven. After another five minutes we suddenly swung to the right and passed through an open gate into a cobbled farmyard. A border collie bounded out of the house to greet us.

'That's Steffie, my faithful companion through life's vagaries.'

'I somehow expected you to have a partner. It's very isolated isn't it?'

'Simplicity,' he replied, expecting me to finish his thought.

We entered a kind of anteroom full of crates and coats that led directly into a large kitchen into which Joe seemed to have crammed his entire possessions. Books lined the far wall, while its neighbour housed shelves of glass jars full of beans, cereals, grains, herbs and spices. His familiar oak table from Somerset nearly filled the floor area. Steffie couldn't contain her delight at having a guest.

'It's only cupboard love. She wants her supper.'

While Joe busied himself making tea, I tried to absorb my impressions of him. Something had changed, but it was hard to pin down. He seemed somehow more part of the landscape here, less of an exile, as though he'd freed himself from something that had been haunting him.

'It's really good to see you, Joe,' I said. 'I've missed our rambling conversations. They fed my imagination.'

'You must tell me what's been happening to you. You look very different.'

Tired as I was, we talked until well after midnight. I told him what had happened after I left his house for the last time, the encounter with the demon on the heath, and my vision of Blake on the cliffs. He listened in attentive silence until I'd told the last part of my story: the showdown with Elaine, and her flat denial that she had ever been sexually involved with Mark. There was a long silence between us, during which every object in the room seemed to be listening intently for what might come next. Then Joe asked, very quietly, a question I hadn't anticipated:

'Have you told me absolutely everything you know about Elaine and Mark?'

'I think so. Why do you ask?'

'Because you haven't actually given me any conclusive evidence that they were having an affair. You saw them together in a field, from some distance away. You then saw them walk away together, holding hands, did you say?'

'I think so. The light was failing by then, so I can't be absolutely sure.'

'And that is the best piece of first-hand evidence of an affair that you have?'

'Yes. But she'd been acting strangely for weeks before that.'

Joe closed his eyes and lapsed into one of his pointed silences, in which the listener was meant to join up the dots and see what significant figure lay before him for his illumination, or failing that, creep quietly away in utter disgrace to eat worms.

'My point, Adam, is simply that someone acting strangely is not evidence of anything except strange behaviour. Do you see?'

'But it was obvious. They got me to go on a wild goose chase to Edinburgh, so they could have the house to themselves. Then when we were in Torquay she couldn't wait to get back home to see Mark. And her using her college course to avoid communicating with me. It all makes horrible sense.'

'It only makes sense if you're paranoid. And believe me I do know what that feels like. But you have to look at your assumptions very carefully, and resist giving yourself the benefit of doubt.'

'Are you telling me Elaine is not having an affair?'

'I'm saying you haven't proved your case that she is. There could be any explanations for her behaviour as you've described it to me beside the one you've settled on.'

Gradually the truth of what he was saying sank in.

'Oh Jesus,' I muttered through my hands. I looked at Joe. 'I've just done the second most terrible thing in my life.'

'Calling Elaine a whore? That's pretty mild in the scale of things. That sort of thing happens every minute somewhere in the world.'

'I accused someone I love dearly of fucking my best friend and lying about it. That seems pretty bad to me.'

'Don't be so quick to judge yourself, Adam. Events have a way of reversing hasty judgements.'

The next morning dawned fine, cloudless and calm, with a white mist clinging to the moor, so that the house seemed to be afloat on a waveless sea extending in every direction. The entire place seemed exceptionally quiet: not even the ever-mournful sheep cries could be heard. I washed and went down to find Joe reading in the kitchen, with Steffie curled up by the stove gnawing on something unspeakable.

'Help yourself to breakfast. When you've finished I'll show you round the place. I've taken up gardening in a big way. I'm aiming to be nearly self-sufficient in a couple more years. Though it's a high art teasing something edible out of this land. Anything that manages to rise above the ground gets flattened by the wind. And when we've done that there's something I think may interest you up on the moor.'

'What's that?'

'I'd rather show you than tell you. To be honest I'm not entirely sure I could do it justice in words.'

As it turned out we talked so much it was late afternoon before we got onto the moor proper.

How typical of Joe, I thought, not to allow an hour to go by without pursuing some new discovery. It was one of the qualities that excited me about his life: the thrill of the chase was never far from him.

We followed a well-worn track which led through some boggy ground to a gradual incline. Steffie ran ahead, stopping every few yards to assure herself that we were following.

'You said you had to sell your place in Somerset.'

'Yes. After the fire I felt I was just too exposed. It was no longer a place I could work in. The hostility of the villagers and the local press was palpable. They had me down as a child molester, which as you may know is the worst thing you can possibly be in England. One night they were waiting for me as I got back from town. One of their hoodlums gave me a going over that left me with two broken ribs and a broken nose. I thought there was no point in expending so much energy countering all that stuff. So I left. I don't regret it. This place is perfect for me. No one knows me. I can work for days undisturbed. It doesn't need too much maintenance. And I can get into town easily when I need to. What's not to like?'

'You certainly seem happier.'

'That's probably because I've stopped being a guru.'

'What do you mean?'

'You know I was such an arrogant pain in the arse in Somerset. Jesus! When I think what an insufferable prat I was then, I tremble. I had to win every argument. I had to be top-dog, or else there was hell to pay. And I'm afraid you copped the brunt of that – for which I hereby apologize unreservedly. I gathered my acolytes around me and demanded total loyalty. You were right – it was all ego, and I was too close to see it! I needed someone to pull me down. The trouble is most people want a guru – so they can project all their strength onto a big wise daddy figure. You have to be really wise to rise above that trap. Very few manage it. Adoration is a strong drug – especially when you've spent your life being reviled and mocked: it's like being offered the nectar of heaven! Think of Hitler! He was too weak even to think of resisting it. Anyway, I'm afraid I wasn't strong enough or wise enough to avoid it, and probably did a lot of damage to those who needed dispassionate guidance. It's really hard to admit you failed a very basic character test.'

'You did a lot of good as well, remember. If I hadn't found you I'd have been a basket case within weeks. You refused to allow me to ignore my anger. Through you I found my own strength. That's a gift very few can give.'

'You know, Adam, over and over I ask myself why humanity doesn't progress. Doesn't learn from its mistakes. If you look into your own heart – I mean, if I look into mine – I can see the answer: it comes down to personal survival. We're deeply conditioned – selected, I suppose the evolutionists would say – to survive by being competitive, being supremely effective, being a winner. In the past people have done that through wars and money. But now we're more subtle about it: we have to be leader of the social pack; we acquire fake-wisdom, charisma; we have what everyone else wants. In my case I developed a guru persona, and gathered weak people around me who wanted a strong teacher. That was the hardest thing for me to let go of, because my ego depended on it for its survival.'

'Looks like you did let go of it though.'

'I'm glad you think so. Certainly I haven't the slightest desire to gather any more disciples. The whole idea sickens me.'

'Yet wise leaders can inspire people to act altruistically, can't they? I think you proved that.'

'They can, of course. Whether I succeeded or not is debatable. And the cost of failing may be permanent psychological damage to hundreds of impressionable minds. No thanks, Adam. I've had it with playing at teachers.'

'I think you underestimate your influence. The world sorely needs inspiration. And who is to give that if not those who know themselves?'

'But evidently I didn't know myself. Or not enough.'

The path had leveled out and shrunk into little more than a jagged earth trail clogged with rocks. Joe stopped and said:

'From this point you can see the entire coast of Cornwall, north and south. A wonderful spot for getting a perspective on life.'

'Is this what you wanted to show me?'

'No. That's another hundred yards further on. Steffie knows where it is.'

The dog was way ahead of us, bounding ecstatically along the track as though following fresh scent.

'She's obviously been before.'

'Oh yes. We've been here quite a few times. You'll soon see why.'

I paused to take in the view.

'I can already see. It's stunning.'

I followed Joe along the all but invisible track until the ground rose again to a wide rubble-covered knoll, from which it fell away steeply westwards. Joe stopped abruptly.

'Look there, in the sky. What do you see?'

I followed his outstretched hand to the western horizon.

'Sunset colours. Purple. Orange. Turquoise.'

'Look further up. About twenty degrees.'

It took a little while, but then I saw them: a row of five stars, about equally spaced.

'Stars,' I said. Then I realized they couldn't be stars. 'In a straight line. That's odd.'

'It's not only odd, Adam. It's impossible.'

'What do you make of them?'

'I first saw them a month ago, in almost the same place. Actually they are changing. They're getting further apart. And they're brighter, and no longer in a straight line: there's a slight curve becoming apparent. All of which can only mean they're approaching the earth.'

'Spacecraft?'

'That would be my guess. And if you look through binoculars, they're all different colours.'

I stared at Joe. 'My God! That's so weird! I dreamt about them.'

'You did?'

'Yes. A couple of years ago. I had a dream that I was walking in the mountains. I don't remember which mountains. There was some kind of cataclysmic eruption happening in the valley below me. And when I looked at the sky there were five lights in a row, differently coloured. That is really scary.'

I gazed at the lights, shining steadily above the afterglow of sunset: too faint to be sure of their exact colours, but unquestionably different. And indeed they had formed a distinct curve.

'These must have been observed already by astronomers, surely? Why hasn't the alarm gone up?'

'There's a very odd thing about them: you can only see them within a very narrow area. If you go half a mile from here in any direction, they vanish.'

'This is beginning to make me feel very strange. You don't suppose they could be connected with the Cubes, do you? I mean, suppose they're sending out signals to guide these things in?'

'The problem with that is there are hundreds of Cubes, scattered all across western Europe. Why should this point be especially significant?'

'Maybe a better question is what we do when they get here? How long do you think we've got?'

'Impossible to say. It depends on so many unknowns. The size of the things: they could each be ten metres or ten miles across. And their speed of course. And whether they're on a straight line or a spiral trajectory. Anyway we're assuming they are alien craft making for the earth. In truth we don't know what they are. They could just as easily be a secret experiment to counteract climate change.'

'I find it hard to believe no instruments on earth have detected them yet. After all we've had our biggest telescopes continuously trained on the Owl Nebula for several years, and they've picked up sweet Fanny Adam.'

'Maybe that's the reason. These are nowhere near the Owl nebula. Anyway we have to assume that whoever's behind them has the technology to evade detection until they're ready to be seen.'

'And now they're ready.'

I suddenly felt a sensation of panic in my heart, recalling what Eve had said to me about Elaine. It sounded horribly like a jealous lover trying to eliminate a rival. Suddenly the aliens felt more alien to me than ever before.

'I very much hope we're wrong, Joe,' I said as we turned for home.

'Why?'

'Because I'm starting to be afraid of them.' The ground beneath my feet suddenly seemed tortuous and dangerous in the twilight gloom. Even Steffie was picking her way carefully among the rocks, and kept closer to us as the light failed. 'It's never occurred to me before that their intentions might not be honourable. But what if the whole Cube business has been a massive deception? We've given them a colossal amount of information about us, and we've never even seen them. It's a bit like an online love affair: it's all built on trust, and if that goes... well, we're stuffed, aren't we?'

The more I thought about this the more panicky I felt. 'And it's mostly my fault. Without me they wouldn't have found out a hundredth of the information they now have. Or it would have taken them much longer. Now they hold all the aces.'

'Are you still in contact with them?'

'No. They suddenly cut the link after they tried to make me kill Elaine. I can't believe what an absolute idiot I was! I believed everything they said, as though they were the authentic voice of God! They only failed because you rang at the crucial moment!'

'Why do you suppose they wanted Elaine dead?'

'Oh, because she was a major distraction from the project. I was forever having crises about my relationship with her, and they obviously came to the conclusion that with Elaine out of the way I'd be fully dedicated to helping them. A wonderful bit of alien logic.'

'Yes. But a bit too perfect. Perfection is their weakness, you might say. That's worth knowing.'

'Thank God they don't control our minds yet. They can only try to persuade us. I'm still intrigued how you managed to phone me at that precise moment, after having no contact for six years! It's uncanny.'

'You might call it fate, I suppose. But clearly that merely begs the question. I just had one of those overwhelming urges to get in touch; I felt if I didn't do it then, immediately, I'd regret it. And I acted on that feeling. That's one thing I've learnt the hard way: if your conscience manages to get through to you, do what it says. I think that sort of thing happens frequently to most people; maybe by living alone and listening to your heart you just get sensitive to that voice. I certainly don't attribute it to divine intervention.'

We'd arrived back at the house as the last of the daylight was withdrawn from familiar objects, to be replaced by a waning moon and the solitudes of starlight. Joe was unusually silent over dinner, as though wrestling with some conundrum that wouldn't be resolved. He helped himself to some Jamesons and settled into his armchair opposite the stove to slug it out with his angel. I left him to it, and climbed the narrow wooden stairs to my bedroom at the back of the house.

That night I waged a bloody battle with my own angels, and of course the blood was my own. While listening to the wind battering itself against the building I tried repeatedly to see the chain of events that had convinced me that Elaine was Mark's lover; but the more I searched the less I found: endless amounts of circumstantial evidence, yes; but nothing that proved the case beyond dispute. And still I remained virtually certain of her guilt. I still wanted to fling her from the brink of a precipice and watch her body – her delicate, soft, yielding, warm and responsive body that had given me such deep peace and delight – broken into red fragments on the rocks a hundred feet below. I still wanted to witness her heart broken with remorse, to see her tear-wrecked face sunk in shame; and at the same time I believed I still loved her, wanted nothing but her welfare and happiness, wanted the best possible life for her that the world could give, wanted above all to spend my life by her side, sharing my innermost soul with her. And in a single moment I'd destroyed all possibility of this ever happening.

I woke late the next morning. I splashed icy water over my face to try to bring myself back to the real world. The sky remained clear: a rich, unblemished late autumn aquamarine – the weather Keats had characterized as 'chaste', perfectly capturing its sense of calm inwardness after the havoc and bluster of the late summer storms.

In the night I'd somehow come to a decision about my immediate future: I had to show Elaine that my outburst had been an aberration induced by stress, sleeplessness and an alien seductress insinuating itself into my brain. But when I explained all this to Joe over coffee he was dismissive.

'This is not a well thought-out plan, if I may say so.'

'Why?'

'You once told me how you visited your previous partner – Cora, was it? – to find her living with someone, right?'

'Yes. But I needed to see her about some business.'

'The real reason you went, if I may make so bold, was to find out if you could get back together with her. Right? And when you discovered she wasn't interested you lost the plot, I believe?'

'I was angry, yes. And with good reason: she was my partner. There had been no formal severance of our relationship. She simply decided I wasn't going to come up to scratch, so she cut her losses. I can't really blame her.'

'So why all the anger?'

'I suppose I felt she hadn't made much effort to make it work. She'd decided I wasn't going to run the race she was running. And she was right.'

'So my point is, what has changed since then? In you, I mean. Why should going back to Elaine be any different? What good can come of it?'

'I think the difference is that I believe Elaine still loves me. There's still a deep bond between us. Surely if that's the case it would be terrible not to make an effort to heal the wounds and be together again?'

'True. But have you really examined your beliefs about this? Why are you so sure she still wants a relationship with you? From what you've told me it would seem she doesn't. Have you ever sat down with her and had a rational discussion about what each of you wants?'

I hadn't of course. Let's face it: no one does. If people did that there would pretty soon be no human race left. All I'd done was throw a lot of insinuations and hurt feelings at her. But the fact was, I couldn't bear the thought that she actually preferred to be with someone else. Even if that someone was my best friend. If I was really honest, I have to say I'd rather have her dead than be happy living with Mark.

'Everything she's ever said to me shows there's a bond between us. Even when she was with Jack she'd share her most intimate feelings with me. There's a fantastic trust between us: we know each other's secret souls. When that's there you just know it. You don't need outward evidence.'

'Forgive me, Adam. Because you're a dear friend I must disagree with you. All you know for sure is your own feelings. No matter how powerful they are they're not evidence of what Elaine feels. You have to actually talk to her to find that out. And it doesn't seem to me that you've done that.'

I had nothing to say. At long last I had nothing to say. My last defence had gone, and I knew he was right.

'The other thing to say,' he went on, 'is that what someone says in the heat of passion shouldn't be taken as an immutable truth. Things happen and people change as a result. That doesn't make them devils. It's inappropriate to expect human beings to be gods and goddesses. No one is a god. No matter how good they are, and no matter how beautiful they are, they're still human, still fallible. To be human is to fail.'

'I've failed enough in my life already. I really hoped this time—'.

I couldn't go on: something inside me had reached the end of its road, and all that remained was silence. When I licked my upper lip it felt wet and salty. It had taken me until this moment to really accept that Elaine wasn't with me any more; she was with someone else, and her love had moved with her. I was no longer the special person in her life; I was just a nobody with a lot of problems who urgently needed to make a start on sorting them out.

Joe leant forward and took my hand.

'Welcome to the world,' he said.

Chapter Thirty Two

Every afternoon for the following week I'd climbed up onto the moor and followed the track to the summit and waited for the lights to appear. The last two afternoons they'd been visible in daylight, and the slight curve I'd noticed a few days before had become a pronounced arc. It was obvious whatever they were they were heading for the earth and they were big – big as in gigantic, vast. They must have been the size of planets to be visible for so long. I was mystified why the alarm hadn't gone up and brown paper bags issued to every citizen in the country. Maybe they had, of course, and we'd somehow been overlooked. Maybe the whole world was panicking in the face of imminent alien invasion. Or maybe everyone had already been evacuated, leaving behind the incurable, the mad, the old and their dogs and cats to survive as best they could.

I reached the crown of the moor and received a shock: the lights were brilliant, and formed a wide arc stretching some forty degrees – from south west to nearly due west. The question that urgently required an answer, of course, was were they friendly or hostile? They were certainly beautiful, but of course I'd learnt that beauty and friendship did not naturally go together.

Once again my overriding impulse was to try to reach Elaine and put things right between us. Nothing else seemed remotely as important as this. I almost ran back to Joe's house filled with this scalding desire to be with her, regardless of the consequences.

The lights could by now be easily seen from Joe's: each one an intense swollen inferno of colour: crimson, emerald, aquamarine, primrose and smoky-grey: the all-seeing, all consuming eyes of the beast.

'You must follow your heart,' Joe said. 'If these are really the last days of the earth, your heart must be your guide. That's all the advice I have.'

'What will you do?'

'I'll stay here and try to tame this beast,' he said, tapping the side of his head. 'Though I don't have much hope of success.'

Joe ran me down to the station to catch the Bridgwater train. His face was grim as he repeatedly swerved to avoid potholes.

'You're determined to do this are you?'

'I have to tell her what a terrible mistake I've made. Even if it doesn't change how she feels I have to try. Don't you see?'

'What I see is you getting yourself into another emotional turmoil just when you need to be clear and collected. If this does turn out to be the end of Mankind these final days are an opportunity to clear out all your mental debris, not produce more.'

We reached the main Redruth road and Joe crashed the gears again as we gathered speed. He seemed to relish tormenting the machine; I thought maybe it's the machine in himself he wants to punish.

'She's the only woman in this lifetime I've felt completely relaxed with; the only one who's bothered to really get to know me. I just know if I don't at least try to find her I'll never forgive myself.'

'The place seems unusually quiet. Is it a bank holiday?'

'Maybe everyone's gone to the hills.'

We pulled up outside the station. It seemed ominously deserted. I got out of the truck and walked over to the ticket office. There was a handwritten sign hung on the door:

NO SERVICES UNTIL
FURTHER NOTICE DUE TO EMERGENCY

My heart lurched. It felt like the beginning of a disaster movie. What in heaven was I to do now?

'Looks like we've missed a lot of the action,' Joe said.

A sudden dread came over me. Maybe Elaine's already dead, I thought.

I stood gazing at the deserted station and tried by force of will to conjure up a train just pulling in to the platform.

'Surely they can't have arrived already, can they?' I instinctively glanced up at the overcast sky.

'I shouldn't think so. If it is an invasion fleet, they'd want to do all the damage well before they arrived. They they'd only have to mop up the mess, if you'll excuse the image.'

Joe seemed remarkably calm, considering the situation. I was having difficulty stopping my body from trembling with anticipation of what was to come. He started the engine, then sat waiting for me to climb back in.

'I can't go back. I have to find some way of getting to Elaine.'

'You could try walking.' He sat back in his seat and calculated. 'You could probably do it in twenty-four hours. But of course we may not have twenty-four hours. By the look of those things in the sky I'd say we have about eighteen at most.'

I felt defeated. All my instincts were to start running and hope someone gave me a lift. But rational assessment told me Joe was right. If a state of emergency had been declared, Elaine would have been evacuated along with everyone else: I hadn't a hope in hell of finding her. And even assuming I did find her, what could I say that would be of practical use?

I climbed in beside Joe and sat staring at the nearly bare silver birches along the track, very beautiful in their rich golds and yellows.

'I'm not going to see her again, am I?'

He let the clutch in and we began to shake into motion.

'Can you predict the future?'

'No, but—'.

'Then don't try to outrun events. You don't even know for sure that these artefacts are hostile. The emergency situation may have nothing at all to do with them. Meanwhile all you can control is your own mind. And what better place to do that than out on the moor? You have space, calm, solitude and beauty. Exactly what you need to face the end of the world.' We swung round into the main road, still empty. 'And let's be honest: that's a somewhat larger event than the end of a love affair.'

I was in a sombre mood as we negotiated the moor road for the second time that day. As long as I had the possibility of meaningful action before me I could maintain my spirits; but now that avenue had been closed, and all that remained was to wait in silence for the end to come, the final act in humanity's sad drama. I felt a wave of panic gripping my guts.

'Even now,' said Joe, picking up my mood, 'you don't know what's ahead: you can't even predict the next ten seconds. Reality may yet surprise us. The main thing is to be ready for it. A very wise man, that Shakespeare.' He glanced at me and grinned. He was a good friend to have at the end of the world, and for a brief moment I felt optimistic.

Late in the afternoon I returned to the moor to try to recapture my earlier spacious mood. The fine weather was breaking: storm clouds were building in the west, obscuring the newborn constellation. I had one last hope, and I needed all my courage and clarity to attempt it.

I reached the crown of the moor just as the setting sun broke through the wrack of storm clouds. The world felt so majestic and timeless it seemed unthinkable that it might be totally destroyed in a matter of hours. I wanted to shake humanity awake so they would see what priceless treasure lay shining all around them. I stood still with the purifying west wind in my face and called out in my mind:

'Are you there, Eve?'

At once the reply came, so clear now it made me start.

'We are here, Adam. How do you like our beautiful suns?'

Had they been listening to every thought I had? If so they already knew why I was calling them.

'They are very beautiful, Eve. But why have they come?'

Her voice sounded as innocent and guileless as though she were reciting love poetry.

'They are unfortunately very angry because of your race's refusal to learn. They have come to prevent contamination of the universe by your uncontainable greed. Since we have failed to eliminate it by softer methods we have now no option but to eliminate your race itself. But we are not wanting in gratitude. Since you have helped us so much we have decided to save you. We would like to keep one specimen of your race to further our studies. We can give you immortality, Adam.'

So I was to be a trophy in an alien test-tube, brought out every few centuries to astound their biologists. Did they really think I'd be grateful to them for 'saving' me?

'I'll only agree if you promise to save Elaine as well. And give us freedom.'

'I'm afraid that won't be possible, Adam. Elaine is not friendly. She would be of no use to us. If we saved her we would have to justify it to our Core, and we would not be able. I'm afraid you have no choice left: you alone must be saved.'

To lose every friend I had. To lose the green earth and all its wonders. To lose music and literature. To lose the freedom to go for a stroll in the evening sun. To lose conversation. And to lose these things knowing they were not only lost to me but annihilated, lost for eternity, lost to all memory; this seemed the very essence of hell. How could I choose that over a quick death?

'You have ten hours, Adam. Then you will be saved. You will be very happy.'

'You have no idea what you are destroying,' I almost sobbed the words. The storm was coming nearer, and the dark rain was beginning to drench me, but the storm inside me was far worse. Suddenly my despair drove me to lyricism.

'The earth is more beautiful than you can possibly imagine. It is like a beautiful daughter. It has graceful forests that sigh and sing when the breeze blows through them. It has noble mountains that rise far above all man's creations, where you can forget all the vexations of life and breathe pure untrammeled air, and dream of better things. There are islands where ancient cultures create their own worlds, uncontaminated by the modern way of life, that live in perfect harmony with the earth. There are oceans that are full of mysterious life-forms that are hardly known, a vast diversity of creatures totally different from humans. There are creatures many times the size of a man that never emerge into sunlight and make slow music that travels great distances, which their friends hear and are delighted by. There are invisible creatures that drift on currents and can kill with a touch. So if you destroy the earth you will destroy all these as well: they will be lost forever. There are tiny creatures that fly through the atmosphere where men cannot find them and also make a small complicated music which tells their fellows where they are and how they are feeling. There are lifeforms that humans can hardly see, which don't live long enough to eat anything. And there are trees—'.

'Your vegetable world does not concern us, Adam. What we fear is your mind and all its progeny. That is what must be eliminated.'

'But our minds have far more than violence in them. They are limitless! They have evolved over thousands of years in countless different ways: there is no model mind to which all conform. You know nothing of our architecture, our poetry, our philosophy, our mathematics, our music. You can't claim to know the human mind if you don't know the music it has created! One of our greatest musical geniuses said that music is a revelation higher than all wisdom and philosophy. And you are about to destroy all this without a second thought! Could you live in the knowledge of such destruction?'

'Your philosophies, mathematics and arts are worthwhile achievements, Adam. We have never denied that. But they have done nothing to curb your aggressive spirit, even though you have been developing them for many thousands of years. They have not made you in any degree less dangerous. They seem powerless in the face of your degenerate nature. So we are bound to ask what is the purpose of them? Can you give us evidence that if we save you and your race you will purge yourselves of your apparently innate violence?'

This of course was the nub of the whole matter, and the fate of the earth and its myriad lifeforms depended on my answer. But I knew instantly that the evidence she asked for did not exist: there was no precedent in the history of man for an entirely peaceful civilization, and there was simply no guarantee that our arts and philosophies would ever transform us to the degree required. And lying did not appear a clever strategy considering they were monitoring my thoughts.

'I can't give you any evidence, Eve. There isn't any. Except to say that if you study our greatest artists and religious leaders you must conclude that love and altruism are not totally absent from our race's history.'

'We do recognize that, Adam. We have studied in detail the lives of all your philosophers and religious leaders, and found many of them exemplary. But the objection remains that the mass of your kind have not measured up to the level of those leaders. Indeed we found that the most altruistic leaders generally give rise to the most ignorant and violent followers. Therefore the danger to the rest of the cosmos remains, for at some time in the future these violent individuals or their offspring will make contact with many unprotected races and corrupt them irreversibly.

This cannot be allowed to happen. Therefore the destruction of your world is an immediate necessity. Is there some flaw in our reasoning?'

Eve's star-rinsed voice might have been asking me if I preferred red wine or white wine to facilitate lovemaking, rather than giving the green light to initiate the destruction of the human race. There was no flaw of course. How could such a perfect mind allow a flaw in such a momentous argument? Yet I couldn't allow her to think her conclusion was a morally unavoidable imperative no matter what perfect logic led to it.

'We are still at the beginning of our awakening journey,' I replied, summoning all my remaining conviction for the summit assault. 'We are still defining ourselves, still waking up from our long troubled sleep. We have still to resolve ourselves into rational beings. And we make many mistakes along the way. But it is only by making mistakes that we can learn. That is the way our genetic material is programmed. Please give us a chance to learn, and so change ourselves.'

'We have already considered this, Adam. But the risk is too great. Your learning mistakes could cost too much in terms of the cosmic harmony. If you could be isolated for the period of your dangerous instability we might take that risk. But there is no way to guarantee your isolation. We can contain your physical expansion easily enough, but your mental expansion is very hard to isolate. It is more logical to annihilate you and allow the thousands of other evolving races in other regions to complete their cycle of growth in peace.'

'The other races are free from violence?'

'The great majority are. Less than one per cent have anomalies extreme enough to require annihilation.'

This was a bit of a mind-slapper, and I had to think about it. The truth was I'd run out of arguments, not to say energy. I was totally exhausted by the sustained contact, as well as the hostile weather, and wanted above everything else to sleep.

'Eve, I must rest now, and consider what you've said. Will you hold your dogs off for one more day? I will come again at this time tomorrow.'

'We will do as you ask,' Eve said. I thought I sensed a tiny sliver of compassion in her voice, and became conscious once more of the wind and rain battering my body.

Chapter Thirty Three

'Joe, I think I've got us a stay of execution. We have to do some quick thinking. I'm totally wiped out.'

Incredibly, Joe seemed to have forgotten there was a catastrophe hiding around the corner. He looked up at me as though an estate agent had just walked in unannounced.

'Have you read Seneca?'

'Was she the Olympic swimmer who got thrown out of the Games in 2012?'

'No, Adam. He was a Roman stoic philosopher. One of the greatest. A good man to have around in a crisis.'

'Joe, I've just been talking to Eve. You know—'.

'I know. Sit down, Adam. You're making a draught waving your arms about. Listen: it doesn't matter. Whatever it is. We're alive now, in this moment. Isn't that a sufficient miracle?'

He placed his book on the stool by his chair, went over to a small recessed cupboard and brought out a bottle.

'I think we both deserve a little of this, don't you think? After all, you could regard this as a special occasion. From our point of view, at least.'

He poured out two small sherry glasses of pale green liquid.

'To our good health. And to the Human Race, of course. It wasn't all bad, was it?'

'Thanks.'

I took a hesitant sip. The effect was like a starving dragon had just woken up in my throat. 'Wow! This is amazing!'

'Take it slowly. It takes a while to get going.'

'Jesus! What is it?'

'Something I brought back from South America, a long time ago. I've been waiting for an occasion worthy of it.'

I took a longer, more appreciative drink. 'You don't mind if the Human Race is destroyed?'

'Well, what would Seneca have done in this situation, I wonder? Probably gathered his friends round him and debated how to have a good death.' He took a slow sip of dragon breath. 'The thing is, Adam, no one can go on forever, not even a planet. Maybe its time has arrived. Or maybe not. Even now we don't know what's going to happen. Not even one minute from now. For all you know I might have poisoned this drink. In which case we both have, let's say, perhaps twenty minutes to live. And it will be horribly painful. Let's say, for the sake of argument, that I have poisoned it, and you've just drunk a lethal dose, ok?'

I stared at my glass, feeling a frisson of nausea finger my guts.

'How does the end of the human race feel now? Still as awful?'

'I take your point. But the truth is the destruction of humanity is many orders of magnitude more significant than my death.'

'Actually Adam, I have to tell you now: I did poison the drinks. I thought it was the best way. Like falling on our swords, eh? It will take about ten minutes. You're welcome to be alone if you prefer. I won't take offence.'

He wasn't smiling.

'Joe. Please stop this. I know your sense of humour. But—'.

Without a word he got to his feet and walked a little unsteadily to the wall-cupboard, from which he drew a small bottle about two inches tall, and handed it to me. The label said:

'CYANIDE — DEADLY POISON'

Instantly my guts convulsed. I began to gasp for breath and my heart rate went sky-high. I tried to stand but couldn't. Joe was also looking distinctly ill. His face had acquired a greenish hue, and he staggered back to his chair and dropped heavily into it, clutching his stomach.

'I'm sorry. I thought this way preferable to slowly frying to a cinder under five alien suns. And by the way I don't think much of their colour sense. That purple is so nineteen sixties.'

'Joe. I can't believe you've done this. After all you've done for me. I saved your life, remember?'

'Of course I do. And now I've saved yours.'

He staggered from his chair and tried to get to the kitchen, but his legs refused to support him.

'Help me, Adam. I haven't much time left. I need some water. Please hu—.'

His breath faltered before he could complete the word.

I was stunned into immobility, incapable of speech or reasoning. He really had poisoned us both.

'Please, Adam, for the love of God—.'

His desperate pleading released me, and I ran to the kitchen, found a glass and somehow got it filled with cold water. When I got back to the lounge, another incomprehensible sight met my eyes. Joe was sitting in his chair, his feet resting on the stool, and the volume of Seneca resting open in his lap. His face wore a huge grin. In his right hand was the half-empty glass of fatal spirits.

'Hi Adam. Feeling better?'

I could find no words, but looked stupidly around the room, still expecting to see Joe's unconscious body lying where I'd left it. Then there came a huge cackling roar of delight, that went on reverberating around the room like the insane laughter of some gigantic amusement arcade clown.

'Why don't you come and sit down, like a good fellow, eh? Then we can talk in a civilized manner.'

'What the bloody hell are you playing at? I could have died of a heart attack!'

'Oh I don't think so, Adam.' He broke off to resume his uncontainable peals of laughter. 'Not on Green Chartreuse. You'd have to drink a gallon of it.'

'But the poison?'

'Oh yes. The poison. You believed that label, did you? I thought that would be an immediate giveaway. A real poison bottle would be labelled 'Potassium Cyanide', and would at least have the dispenser's name and phone number on it.'

'But why go through such a charade? I thought you were really dying. It was horrible.'

'Forgot about the end of the world, did you?'

'It's hard to think of things like that when you believe your dearest friend has just poisoned himself.'

'Exactly. It's a question of perspective. We always behave as though we're the very centre of the universe, and what happens to us is the most significant thing happening anywhere at that moment. But it isn't. Even the destruction of our civilization isn't that important. We're just one of countless millions in the cosmos, many of which are undoubtedly far in advance of ours. So what's the big deal? We've reached the end of our time. Who knows but our existence and our struggle has laid the foundations for some other race on the far side of the galaxy to reach a little further towards the summit?'

It was well after midnight by the time I'd calmed down enough to go to bed. Joe was rooted in his fireside chair, still reading Seneca. But exhausted as I was, sleep seemed ridiculous. How could I sleep on the last night of the human race?

Before dawn I got dressed and let myself out into the chill silence of the moor. The sky had been rinsed clean by yesterday's storm, and even though Sol was still some way below the horizon, the dreadful alien pentagon flared like brilliant gemstones low in the south-west, drenching the landscape with uncanny colour, making it appear like nothing so much as a Blakean etching of the circles of Hell. The formation had expanded alarmingly even since yesterday, and now filled at least a dozen moon-widths. Even as dawn grew, the ferocious sun-ships seemed to increase in brightness rather than diminish. It seemed a fitting image – even a beautiful one – to mark Man's self-inflicted terminal Armageddon.

I climbed the familiar path to the knoll. Every boulder on the summit cast multiple coloured shadows, which made the ground resemble a film-set for a science fiction epic. The rain had given way to a bitter northerly, and I wrapped my coat more tightly around me. I'd borrowed Joe's hip-flask from his 'special occasions' cupboard, and took a long swig of cognac from it. I stood motionless in the glow of the earthly and heavenly fires, waiting for what I feared would be my last conversation with Eve this side of eternity. I thought of Elaine and remembered the good moments in our friendship: our fingers touching briefly during our visit to Kew Gardens; the morning she'd phoned me to tell me she'd left

Jack, and my flight of joy when she agreed to come to Devon with me; our first lovemaking after I'd left Joe's: that feeling of complete acceptance and inner calm that had stayed with me for several days after. How had I let all those fragments of heaven slip through my fingers without realizing how fragile they were?

And then there was Joe himself, who in his own way had given me a gift more precious than anyone else had: the gift of seeing myself truly. The next words I spoke might well condemn him to an agonizing death. There had been moments, of course, when I'd hated him; when he'd given me ridiculous tasks and then changed his mind just when I'd completed them, all without a word of explanation or thanks. And I'd loathed his behaviour when he'd taken in a French philosophy student and began ostentatiously lavishing affection on him, cutting me out of his friendship completely. But it had worked: I'd been so outraged that I had no option but to look at myself and for a moment observe my self-hatred at first hand. This, I thought, was teaching of a rare order. Now when I thought of his prank with the fake poison I felt nothing but overwhelming love for him: he really didn't care what anyone thought of him, so long as they learnt what they needed to learn at that moment.

The alien suns were now almost perceptibly growing in size and brilliance before my eyes; own own sun rose to discover that for the first time in its immense history it had serious rivals. And then Eve's voice rinsed my mind with its unassailable calm.

'We are ready to hear you, Adam.'

I tried to speak, but realized I had absolutely nothing to say that hadn't already been perfectly refuted by that logic so eloquent it was almost music. Yet I couldn't remain silent: nothing would come of nothing.

'I don't want to be saved,' I said, my voice shaking with stopped emotion. 'Unless you save others as well.'

'Only one will be saved. That is unalterable. If we save two, then why not three? And if three why not four? We would have to save your entire race, and then we ourselves would be destroyed. One alone must be saved.'

'Then save Joe. His mind is infinitely superior to mine. He has an understanding and subtlety of thought that I can only dream of.'

There followed a strange silence that was not silence. It was as though a ripple of amazement was traveling beyond light speed between the cells of the immense mind that constituted the aliens. It probably lasted no more than a second, before Eve resumed speaking.

'Adam, your request has been heard by the Core. We have changed our decision. Your planet will not be exterminated. There is clearly some other value that we had failed to see. If it is in you then it must be in every other individual to some degree. We will allow you to develop this value unhindered until you are ready to join us.'

'What about your suns?'

'They have been terminated. They will pass by you relatively harmlessly. A few random tsunami perhaps. Goodbye, Adam. We wish you peace.'

Chapter Thirty Four

Under the dazzling radiance of six suns, I half ran, half stumbled down the track towards Joe's house. My heart was torn apart by joy and sadness: the planet was saved, but I'd lost both Elaine and Eve. It seemed I was newborn and naked at the birth of a new world. I had nothing and everything: freedom and aloneness in equal measure. The world seemed infinitely precious and beautiful, yet the immensity of loss came home to me as never before. Standing outside the house in the merciless light-storm I wept uncontrollably for myself and for forlorn and wrecked humanity.

In Joe's lounge a dim light was burning. At first it seemed there was no one in the room, and I went over to the lamp to switch it off. Then I saw him, slumped in his armchair like someone who had fallen asleep watching a late film. Balanced on the arm of his chair was his Seneca, with a bookmark at the page where he'd left off reading. On the stool was his glass, almost empty, and next to it, like a stage prop in a murder mystery, the bottle of fake cyanide.

I shook his shoulder, watching his face intently, but not unduly worried after his practical joke at my expense.

'Joe! It's morning! Time for breakfast. And I have some good news!'

He was a good actor, I had to admit. Like everything else he did, he had paid meticulous attention to detail.

'Joe! The joke's over! The aliens have changed their minds. We're not going to die after all!'

No reaction. On an impulse I took up the poison bottle and checked the label. With growing horror I read the words:

JAMES ELLIOT, PHARMACEUTICAL SUPPLIES
SHIP ST, EXETER, DEVON. TEL: 01464 793202

POTASSIUM CYANIDE 30% AQUEOUS SOLUTION
POISON: NOT TO BE TAKEN

I turned to Joe; his head had fallen to one side. I felt his hands: already cold. Refusing to accept the evidence before me, I frantically tried to find a pulse. I tried to open his eyelids, but already they had become as recalcitrant as he himself had been.

I sat there holding his body for a long time, my head nestled closely against his, as though by such contact I might capture some faint echo of his amazing living mind, hoping that a miracle might occur and time be reversed to the point when he'd lifted the last drink to his lips. Why can't you make this one thing happen? I silently said to Eve; if you're so wise and powerful, why can't you do this one tiny thing for me, and undo Joe's death?

The silence that followed was more profound than any I'd ever experienced, and more final. Eventually I summoned the will to leave his body and walk out into the ignorant daylight. There in the unblemished blue were the five suns, but now they were breaking formation and reverting to a wide arc spanning a huge region of sky – but already it was clear they would miss the earth by several million miles, merely giving us a scorching as they were whistled back to their monstrous kennels in the black wastes of the Owl Nebula.

It wasn't until well after they'd taken away Joe's body that I thought to look in the book he was reading the night he died. The bookmark was actually covering a letter to me, written on air-mail paper in blue ink in his neat, slightly sloping script, which evoked for me his dry, understated yet needle-sharp wit.

"My dear Adam: I know this has come as a terrible shock, and I'm so very sorry you had to be the one to bear it. I have not always been as true a friend as I would have wished, and all I can do here is ask you once more to forgive me and put my failings down to a want of mature human society such as you afforded me. It seemed to me there was no real alternative way of ending my life: al least this way I could be reasonably sure that my last thoughts were of something useful and worthwhile. I imagined that you would find a way of talking them out of their madness:

any truly superior civilization will know that extermination of a threat, real or imagined, is never a solution. It was at any rate one of the most important lessons I ever learned. (The Greeks knew what they were talking about when they invented the Hydra). The only solution that ever works, and ever has worked, is love.

I leave all my remaining worldly goods and assets to you alone: you will find my will and legal documents including the house title in the red trunk in the cellar. There is no family so the estate should be a fairly simple matter to prove.

Do not, please, spend too much time grieving: you have work to do. You know what it is: if I had to tell you now I would have wasted my time being your friend. I don't know how much time you may have left, but I do know that humanity will not be the same if it does survive: it has been too close to the edge to forget what lies beyond.

Finally, my dear friend, be of good heart, and as the great Seneca said, gather good people around you, do not be diverted by unworthy things, and remember why you are here: it is not all chaos and darkness. Be watchful, especially at dusk.

Your friend and fellow traveller, Joe."

I had to stop reading several times because the tears blinded me; I hadn't realized until then how much I'd loved him: now he was beyond all reaching, and I felt more alone than I'd thought possible. He was the one person with whom I'd achieved a genuine intimacy, despite our differences and despite my treatment when I'd stayed with him in Somerset.

Around midday I climbed the now well-trodden track to the top of the moor, and sat gazing at the building rain-clouds and listening to the few bird-calls that were borne on the wind. I had no desire to go anywhere, even though there were many practical matters that needed to be dealt with. I wanted only the solace of silence and the wide spaces of the moors, where I could absorb the impact of the last few days' momentous events.

But I couldn't remain a hermit forever. I needed to replenish my food stock, and attend to Joe's will and the property. It had been raining relentlessly all night, and it continued through the morning, turning the road into Redruth into an archipelago of gravel and tarmac islands. Somehow Joe's old truck coped with it, and I reached town without mishap.

What I saw there made me stop short. The sun had broken through the cloud and its slanting beams illuminated the faces of people, transforming every one into an angel. I carried out my legal business in a state of continual amazement, so that I was repeatedly asked if I was ill. The human race seemed reborn. Whether it was due to the experience of Armageddon directly in front of them, or my prolonged state of exile, I couldn't tell; maybe something of both. The faces I encountered appeared stricken with a vision at once of hell and paradise. I turned into a newsagent's and felt the change immediately: conversations were shriven with the knowledge in everyone of having escaped global catastrophe by a hairsbreadth, and no-one had the slightest idea of how or why they had escaped.

I found a greengrocer's shop and stood transfixed by the bounty that lay before me: colours I'd never noticed before seemed to shine from everything like a new annunciation, so that I hardly dared touch anything for fear of shattering the fragile vision.

'A very strange business all this,' the proprietor said as he weighed my purchases. 'We seem to have survived though, so I suppose we'll get back to normal eventually. That's five pounds forty eight pence exactly sir.'

The man's face looked like a Rembrandt portrait: at once radiant and grief-stricken, deeply engraved with the sorrow and endurance of humanity.

'Do we want normal back?' I asked.

'Well these disruptions are very bad for business. People's lives get turned over, that's never a good thing, is it?'

'I suppose you're right.'

Suddenly I wanted to burst into tears again, because for the briefest instant I saw my father's face merged with the shopkeeper's features. And once more he was silently asking me for something: forgiveness, recognition, acceptance, understanding. I looked back and in that instant out of time something almost paradisal flashed between us; something that went entirely beyond forgiveness or acceptance; an unconditional, world-redeeming love. And almost simultaneously the face became that of an ordinary shopkeeper again. The work had been done; the oath had been fulfilled. I could walk as a man in the world.

The man began casually to wipe down the counter.

'Speaking for myself, I haven't had a proper night's sleep for three weeks, ever since this terrible business began. I've been groping around like a zombie.'

'What stopped you sleeping?'

'Noises. Like someone dragging great lumps of concrete around all the time. It's been driving me up the pole, I don't mind saying. Not knowing what's going on and that.'

'I'd take no notice of it. Almost certainly some kids larking about outside. These things happen, but we survive, don't we?'

'We generally do, sir. Though God knows how. A very good day to you.'

Chapter Thirty Five

From the heart of the blackness I became aware of a rushing sound, as of wind, and a brilliant point of light pulsing from somewhere below. The light grew rapidly larger and more intense, and I seemed to be able to hear waves breaking on rocks. And then a brief image of William Blake shook my mind from its stupor, and an immense tide of gratitude welled up in me and drove out every other feeling, and the wretched fragment of soul I had been for so long in an instant became pure music, and was completed.

* * * * *